Motherwhelmed

ANNIKI SOMMERVILLE

O

OneMoreChapter

One More Chapter an imprint of
HarperCollinsPublishers
1 London Bridge Street
London SE1 9GF

www.harpercollins.co.uk

This paperback edition 2019

First published in Great Britain in ebook format by One More Chapter 2019

A catalogue record for this book is
available from the British Library

ISBN: 978-0-00-835169-4

This novel is entirely a work of fiction.
The names, characters and incidents portrayed in it are
the work of the author's imagination. Any resemblance to
actual persons, living or dead, events or localities is
entirely coincidental.

Typeset in Adobe Caslon by Palimpsest Book Production Ltd, Falkirk, Stirlingshire

Printed and bound in Great Britain by CPI Group (UK) Ltd, Croydon CR0 4YY

MIX
Paper from
responsible sources
FSC
www.fsc.org
FSC™ C007454

This book is produced from independently certified FSC™ paper
to ensure responsible forest management.

For more information visit: www.harpercollins.co.uk/green

For Paul, Rae and Greta

One

SOME SAY A SIGN that you're having a breakdown is when you stop sleeping properly. Or get heart palpitations for no reason. Or overreact to something quite minor. The problem is, all these things were quite commonplace in my life, and had been for some time.

From the outside things looked okay. I had a beautiful child and a great husband (okay, our relationship was hard work, but long-term relationships are no walk in the park). I had a job which paid well. I ate a nice lunch most days. I laughed once a week – sometimes these laughs were tinged with hysteria, but that was okay. I cried often but thought this was possibly related to tiredness or the perimenopause.

Besides, did anyone feel happy these days? If I thought of the people I worked with, I'd have described the majority as 'averagely content'. Others were clearly depressed. It was difficult to gauge. I sensed I wasn't the only one who woke up in the morning with a feeling of dread. It's horrible when you realise that the moment you clamber back into bed will be the best part of your day. It was work stress, yes . . . but it was heavier. A sense of time running out, that I had fewer good years ahead than behind (this wasn't strictly true because I'd not really had many good years in the first place). Time was speeding past and I felt isolated. I'd fallen out of synch with the school friends that I'd seen every month during my twenties and thirties. They'd all had babies in their early thirties, and these kids were now entering secondary school. So when I had Bella they'd all moved beyond that small children stage. They were FREE and wanted to drink and re-invent themselves and PARTY! South London wasn't a million miles away from Acton but it felt like it. It was easier to keep a low-level buzz of connection via social media. I could 'like' the pictures but didn't have to listen to all the chat. They were embarking on new careers, getting divorced, or taking up marathon running. What was it with all the marathon running anyway?

And how exactly had I ended up moving from apathy and tiredness to a heart that thudded every morning when Bella screamed from her room because she needed a wee? Well work had been busy (it never wasn't busy).

Work had become a *slog*, and all slog and no fun makes Rebecca a dull girl. And there was the rub. The moments of pleasure, the tiny positive increments that you needed to experience in life to keep going seemed to have disappeared without me even realizing it. The truth was those old friends had been important. There'd been a sense that we were steadily moving towards some common end point, some positive evolution was happening.

I had Kath. At least I had one true friend but it was weird how much my social circle had shrunk down to nearly nothing. She was my oldest friend and I'd known her since school days – one of the few I'd managed to keep in touch with.

It was weird because in reality, once Bella reached about three, I could feel life was getting easier. Nevertheless, it was as if the fug of the earlier, chaotic days was lifting to reveal a vast, empty terrain. With babies, it's easy to get lost in the sleeplessness, feeding, panic, angst and then discover that there isn't much else going on once the mess has cleared. If it wasn't the thudding in the morning, it was the booming noise in my ears in the middle of the night. The noise of my heart ready to explode. Then the thoughts would start up.

Does Bella's nursery teacher hate me?

Have I filed the right version of the loo roll presentation for Friday morning?

Why hasn't the client replied to my last email?
Where have all my tights disappeared to?
Why do I shout at Bella so much?
What is that lump on the back of the cat's head?
Why have I eaten so many potatoes these past few days?
How does everyone else get through each day without giving up?

The only thing I could do to quiet my brain was watch a couple of episodes of *Keeping Up with the Kardashians*. These beautiful, yet strangely cold, women lived in a universe where life looked busy yet relatively easy (and seemed devoid of emotion, each face rendered immobile by Botox). I am sure someone at Mango-Lab, the market research company I worked for, would offer up a cultural context as to why this reality TV soothed me but I'll just say that after watching an hour, I could usually go back to bed again.

'*I don't want to go to nursery!*' my daughter howled up the hallway from her bedroom. It was a Monday. 5 a.m. Up and down the country, children were shrieking at their parents, and telling them they didn't want to go to whatever childcare was lined up for that particular day. It always made me sad to see the drop offs, the weary stooped shoulders of the parents. The red rimmed eyes of the kids. In reality, nobody wanted to be thrust out of bed at some ungodly hour and sent somewhere they didn't want to be – whether it was a jaunty room full of toys and tissue paper collages or a grey tomb, populated with young people hunched over laptops, the room pumped with freezing cold air.

I reached for my phone and saw there were already fourteen emails in my inbox. The temptation to read them was too much. I tried to ignore Bella's cries for a few seconds longer.

MASSIVE PROPOSAL NEEDS TEAM – said the first. URGENT CLIENT QUOTE! IMMEDIATE ATTENTION REQUIRED – the second. CRAFT BEER CLIENT WANTS GROUPS TOMORROW EVENING IN SCUNTHORPE – the third.

The whole thing made me want to curl up into a ball. It would be a day of trying to bat these unpleasant demands away. It was like a depressing round of ping pong. The problem was there were only so many balls you could avoid. At least one would hit you between the eyes.

Also, since when had EVERYTHING been written in CAPITALS?

It no longer gave a sense of URGENCY to anything because it was used in all company communications these days.

The thing was it was hard to get everything done

– having a successful career, a strong relationship, owning a home (well that was pretty much impossible), and having a family. And then on top of that, for me anyway, work had proven so stressful that it had kicked my reproductive prowess to the kerb for a good while.

The morning was a blur of soggy, uneaten cereal, then an alternative breakfast of boiled egg, which went uneaten. Leggings were put on and taken off.

'*I don't want to wear tights,*' Bella said as I hunched over her tiny frame trying to wiggle her legs in. It was a bit like trying to get an octopus to stay still.

'*It's cold outside darling. You need to stay warm.*'

'*I want bare legs.*'

'*You can't have bare legs. It's cold.*'

She grabbed a fistful of my hair and I felt a sudden rush of anger. Should I let her go to nursery with bare legs? Was this a battle worth having when there were CRAFT BEER GROUPS THAT NEEDED TO HAPPEN IN SCUNTHORPE ASAP? I took a deep breath. It was all about *breathing* this parenting thing. And not smacking (though I had actually smacked Bella once and beaten myself up for weeks afterwards). And trying to be much kinder than you felt in that moment. I breathed in and out whilst she looked up into my face, puzzled as to why my lips were pursed together.

'*How about leggings instead?*' I said.

Bella smiled and wrapped her arms around my head, squeezing so tight that I felt my teeth would come out. This was a moment of happiness. Right there. I was trying to get better at spotting them but the moment you did, they flew off again. How could I bottle this emotion so it lasted the rest of the day?

Then a battle with a toothbrush and the blue toothpaste versus the orange one (one washed off and then the other put on the brush instead.) Then off to nursery and a kiss for Pete (we'd exchanged ten words that morning – chiefly about what we'd take out of the freezer for dinner that night). Then Bella was off on her scooter flying towards imminent death, and I was sprinting with my laptop in a rucksack on my back doing the tell-tale run of a parent, stooped stop-start run, walk, run, walk, shrieking – '*STOP BEFORE YOU GET TO THE ROAD!*' Then alternating this with checking my phone to see if there were any new emails I needed to ping a response to, and – '*STOP BEFORE YOU GET TO THE ROAD!*' And then more emails. Then some crying (Bella and I both).

On the train, I took out a small mirror and noticed with horror that another white hair had popped out on the bottom of my chin. These were becoming more common and soon I would resemble Rip Van Winkle. I licked my finger and tried to encourage the hair to lie flat but it wouldn't play ball. Aside from the beard,

I was okay looking. The thing is strong features do you a service as you age as it gives structure to all that sagging skin. It's like a good scaffold. I also dyed my hair blonde every six weeks because whilst I knew grey was fashionable, I wasn't sure if it really was or whether people were just being PC and were too scared to say it looked terrible.

I checked my inbox and it seemed that many of the emergencies had been resolved aside from the craft beer one, and I had a sinking sense that this would be the ball that would hit me and stick. I arrived at the office, which was eight floors up in a lifeless glass building in Vauxhall, and sat down at the nearest free desk. There was a lot of bustle, and it was obvious that many people had been in for some time. Mango-Lab, had changed a lot since I'd started back in 2003. It had originally been a company of ten, and now employed over four hundred (we had global offices too). I had no clear idea who most of the people were. On bad days, it felt like a factory; people came in, got their laptops out, plugged their headphones in, and you didn't speak to them until they got up to leave (and then it was some trite comment about train delays or TV shows or dinner plans). During the day, you wanted to avoid making tea for everyone as you'd be stuck in the kitchen for thirty minutes sorting out the Lady Grey from the Jasmine Green and the builders with just a dash of milk etc.

I had the sense that people used to talk much more but this was now changing. When someone came up to your desk, the ideal outcome was to get them to shut up and go away. We emailed and texted one another as if none of us were in the same building.

Since returning from maternity leave, I worked three and a half days a week and whilst I'd like to tell you this arrangement worked just fine for me, it didn't. I constantly felt like I hadn't got a clue what was going on. There were new initiatives launched every two weeks. There was Monday Power Lunch (where an older person such as myself had to sit with a younger person and be told what was what). Wednesday Round-The-World Breakfast (self-explanatory – again the onus being on talking to one another and sharing our mutual passions for travel and eating diverse food types). Friday Fun Sessions – possibly the worst of all the initiatives as we were made to stay an hour longer and drink beer, when we (I) really wanted to get home after a long day spent collaborating, team-building and being generally enthusiastic. It takes more than a trolley laden with beer to shake off a week's resentments and bitter rival-ries. These initiatives combined with the heavy work-load made life exhausting. You were either answering emails or being forced to bond with colleagues, which afforded very little time to sit in the toilet crying (though I managed this at least once a week anyway).

Still, the company was doing well. Or it was difficult to tell as one week we were told it was good and then two weeks later that it was dicey. They were hiring more people which felt positive. All of them unfeasibly young and fresh. These new hires contributed to the feeling that I was no longer at the 'cut and thrust' of the market research world. There were only a few of us oldies left now, and the three or four favoured ones had their own offices with proper heating, so you only spotted their grey hair flouncing past atop their haggard faces when they walked to the shared toilets. The thing is marketing is all about youth. Our job was to help clients sell stuff. People aren't convinced if you have a face like Bagpuss and are wearing unfashionable clothes. We sold stuff chiefly through talking to people in group situations and showing them bad ideas. Not all these ideas were bad but the majority were. In my youth, I'd thought I was helping bring good things to the wider population but when I reflected more deeply, it wasn't, of course, true.

Back when I'd started there had been more enthusiasm amongst the respondents who came to the focus groups – there was wine provided, the venues were nice and adverts were still seen as relatively entertaining. Now, all that had changed and people were savvy and resented just about everything about modern life.

Once you got people in a room, it became difficult to manage the conversation without it turning into a giant bun fight. Adverts were boring and manipulative. Products were full of salt and often faulty/dangerous. Marketing was to blame but then of course there were also parking tickets, rubbish collection, immigration, the declining NHS, school application processes, the rising cost of basic foods, pollution, the barren high streets . . . the list went on. One minute you would be discussing a dry packet sauce and the next you'd segue into something far more significant. It made moderating the whole shebang very tiring and you needed your wits. The objective was to steer the conversation, and emerge with something that sounded like a palatable answer for the client.

'I know you hate the new rubbish collection system on your street, but can you remember the idea I showed you ten minutes ago for a new toilet spray that activates itself whenever you lift the seat? How would you describe that idea in three words right now?'

'What's the best thing about this idea?'

'What's your favourite word on this concept?'

'Let's think of all the things we agree with, yes?'

The thing was the respondents were right. The world was full of plastic stuff that people didn't need.

Happiness was not on the increase, in fact quite the opposite.

There had also been a time when I'd thrown myself into the travel that came with the job. I'd been to New York, San Francisco, Paris and Milan. The thing was it was lonely. You arrived at a hotel, checked in, went to a small, dark viewing facility, and listened to someone talking to a bunch of people about an idea that nobody liked.

The typical days back then went something like this:

5.30 a.m. – fly to Munich to research a new mustard sauce proposition

9.45 a.m. – arrive at hotel and schlep massive bag full of new mustard sauce packaging up in the lift, lie down on bed for half hour, look out of the window and then leave

10.45 a.m. – 6 p.m. – spend entire day at the viewing facility preparing for groups, looking through stimulus, reading documents that keep being changed by the client every two minutes

6 p.m. – clients arrive and change everything that you've been working on all day

8 p.m. – 10.30 p.m. – German colleague moderates groups, clients talk German so you can't understand anything that's being said. They also hate you on

sight because you're too young/blonde/British/tired/
depressed. Sit behind a mirror manically typing up
everything the simultaneous translator is saying, then
try to make sense in terms of which of the dreadful
ideas is the least negative. Tell client your thoughts
whilst he/she looks at you with disdain. Leave for
hotel and feel sad, wishing you were a pop star,
novelist, playwright etc.

11 p.m. – 1 a.m. – order room service, send emails and
start to get grumpy emails back from the clients who
are unhappy because the people you spoke to were
wrong and they are going to ignore everything you
suggest anyway. Watch infomercials for strange vegetable slicing machines and exercise contraptions whilst
brain ceaselessly whirrs around and around and you
worry about whether you're going to sleep through
your alarm and miss your dawn flight home again

Okay maybe there'd been a couple of trips that had
been fun. New York, for example. And you got some
time in the day to walk around the city. It wasn't all
bad or if it was, why was I still here?

The last five years I'd stopped travelling – it made
me too anxious. I was glad when I only had to get a
train to Manchester or Leeds and if I was lucky, I could
return the same night and sleep in my own bed.

Then Phoebe became my boss and things changed. The mood changed. It felt like things were even more accelerated. There was rarely time to sit down and eat lunch, and sandwiches were shoved down your neck whilst typing with one hand. It became permissible to take client calls in the loo whilst urinating. There was no down time or if there was you were called into a brainstorm.

Phoebe walked past as I was writing notes in my book. Writing notes was a good way of looking busy and avoiding her attention.

'*MORNING REBECCA!*' she boomed. '*TRAIN TROUBLE AGAIN?*'

I was glad that everyone was wearing headphones and couldn't hear her.

'*Sorry,*' I said. '*I was on a client call and had to miss the first train so I could finish the conversation.*'

'*A client conversation with whom?*' she said walking backwards towards my desk, and looking down at my notes which so far said: must get a scented candle for Pete's mum's birthday and pick up coat from dry cleaners.

'*Um it was that cleaning wax enquiry. Remember? The one from a few months ago?*'

She raised an eyebrow and clearly didn't believe me.

'*Well send the brief over so I can have a quick look before you make a start,*' she said dismissively and walked off.

She didn't walk. She STRODE. She was Sheryl Sandberg (the famous female head honcho at Facebook), to the power of ten. Later I would need to invent a reason as to why the brief hadn't arrived. I would drop her an email, and say that some other agency had got it instead.

The other problem I had with work was the fact that there seemed to be resentment coming from the younger generation. The previous Thursday during one of our 'Share & Care Hours' (you had to take a colleague you didn't know out for coffee), a young man had informed me that Gen X were to blame for everything that was wrong with our country – the flagging economy, corporate greed and corruption, not enough cheap, good quality housing in urban areas. He listed everything about my generation that he despised, whilst I quietly drank my coffee and reassured him that I wasn't personally responsible and weren't these coffee brainstorms supposed to be uplifting for us both?

There was a part of me that felt that there was some jealousy perhaps – we'd had fun, it was true (the travel had felt exciting for a while) and we'd been hedonistic (yes, me definitely, from what I could remember) and raved and all that, and now this generation were spending their youth taking photos of their food. The only office banter seemed to involve food or food-related activities.

There was a new Korean street food shop opening.
There was a place that sold seaweed soaked in gin.
There was a stall selling kimchi that had been aged for
four years straight.

I loved eating as much as the next person, but where were the wild nights spent getting off with strangers? Or losing footwear whilst moshing at the front of a gig? Food was for old people who couldn't dance anymore. My generation had eaten chips and didn't worry about their 'carb-load'. We didn't find food sexy. We avoided it and spent our money elsewhere – fags and booze, mainly. Every time I went into the kitchen I braced myself for a lecture on the best coffee beans to buy (Jamaican, £12.99 a bag) and why I couldn't continue using Nescafé.

About seven years in, I'd started getting the itch to leave Mango-Lab. I had a few different ideas but none of them had much of a commercial angle. These included:

A Rock and Roll café, selling cupcakes inspired by seventies rock legends; a risotto takeaway business, with hot risotto delivered to your desk, 'Risotto to Go for the Days When Risotto is too Slow'; a vintage brooch dealership, this was very niche but at the time I lived in Ladbroke Grove, and admired Portobello market. I wanted to be one of those cool, bohemian women in long fur coats who sold knick-knacks and nattered to one another all day. That was the thing with cool jobs.

They were often poorly paid. Though some would claim my job was cool too, I guess.

Whilst it wasn't as bad as some industries, marketing could still be a relatively sexist industry. If you were a woman, it made sense not to put your neck out or say anything too controversial. If you were a man you had to do the opposite. Early on in my career there'd been a male colleague (long gone now – he'd been head-hunted to work in advertising), who constantly scratched his balls whilst waiting by the printer. After scratching for a couple of minutes, he'd then lift his palm and sniff. It was a low-down, dog-like behaviour, but nobody said anything as he was seen to be a 'creative genius' and said '*fuck*' a lot in boring meetings, which created a lot of excitement. I knew early on that this tactic wouldn't work for me.

A woman scratching herself and swearing wasn't the done thing. It seemed like men had more leeway to be themselves. Swearing became a bit of a trend. The ball scratching didn't take off but instead there was lots of expansive body language that the men used to take up as much space as possible. The women who did well were of two ilks; pretty and hard-working to the point of nervous breakdown, or un-feeling and robotic. I had built my career on being sort of okay-looking (blonde, blue eyes, enormous arse), and saying '*that's interesting*' a lot. I made very high quality cups of tea.

I listened to boring men and told them they were right just so they'd shut up. I sometimes imagined what size penises they had. Other times I drew pictures of penises on my writing pad as they spoke. It was a small form of rebellion. It was a counterpoint to being so nice and not itching my fanny by the printer. Phoebe was different of course, because she had the stamina of a horse, and didn't buy into the whole people-pleasing thing.

If people were thirsty in a meeting then their mouths could remain dry and their spittle stuck in the corners. If a man swore then she mirrored this language right back to him. She was the only woman I knew who could actually play golf (and enjoyed it). She was old school in that way and had gotten into it to infiltrate the old boys' network (most male clients still loved golf). She also did long distance running. If I ever worked late (this was rare), I'd catch her running past with her laptop jiggling up and down in her rucksack, wearing a neon T-shirt that said '*LET'S DO THIS.*'

Overall at Mango-Lab, even if you set the sexism to one side, the priority was 'high-quality strategic thinking', which basically meant well-written decks on Pot Noodles, fizzy drinks and eye creams, peppering these presentations pulled together on PowerPoint, which we called 'decks', with one or two words that the client didn't understand, so they came away with the feeling that you were cleverer than them and they were lucky to have listened to you for well over an hour.

Phoebe and I were the same age, but she came across as far more put together.

I really wasn't happy this particular Monday. That wasn't unusual.

I had a creeping sense of unease. I had become a ball of the stuff.

TWO

A FEW HOURS HAD passed and I was trying to write the final presentation for a project I'd just finished. The client wanted to launch a wipe that cleaned a baby's bottom and also made them fall asleep. The name of the product was 'Goodnight Bum' and there was some mocked-up packaging and a potential scent idea (Lavender and Tea Tree oil). It was ambitious but had legs, or at least that was my argument. You see parents will always seek out *anything* that promises sleep, and nowadays we all believe there's a product that can fix anything. I'd interviewed twelve groups of mums in focus groups. They all reacted the same way. At first, they'd found the idea appalling (they were worried about the cleaning/sleeping benefit – was there some secret/toxic ingredient?) but I needed to come up with a positive slant for this presentation. Clients don't like to be told that their idea is shit. It's just like when a child holds up their drawing for approval. You try and be diplomatic and find something you *do* like – *You've drawn a cat with eight legs. How lovely! It's a spider cat. Don't cry, love. It's brilliant!*

'*The 'Goodnight Bum' proposition is both challenging and disruptive,*' I typed into PowerPoint.

I sipped my coffee. I didn't have my headphones on, but there was complete silence in the office. I often wondered why we didn't all work from home. It would save a lot of money and wasted travel time. At least the quiet afforded me some thinking space.

'*The challenge for 'Goodnight Bum' is to find a sweet spot between calming and cleansing.*'

My phone buzzed with an incoming text. '*Bella has sustained a small head injury whilst hanging off the climbing frame but we applied a cold compress and she seems to be in good health,*' it said.

I felt a surge of panic. Nursery had been sending texts for some time now. I still felt it was more appropriate to *speak* to the parent, but then I also acknowledged that speaking was becoming far less common because it was so time-consuming. I resisted the urge to Google 'minor head injuries in small children,' and tried to focus. Bella was that kind of child. She was boisterous and outgoing. She loved to try new things.

Hopefully she'd never experience the *slog* and sheer *averageness* of my own life. She was in good health. All was well.

Back to the presentation and the phrase 'sweet spot' was a good one. I used it a fair amount. It made me think of 'G-spot' and was just as mythical – it was where the truth lay, where an idea suddenly sprang into life and resonated, where it made people *orgasm*. In life, I'd failed to find this blissful truth for myself. For now, I could hear the boy next to me playing MC Hammer through his headphones. It brought back memories of a night in South London in my youth when I'd snogged a boy called Freddie. Freddie had been a very good dancer but a terrible kisser. I'd gone out with him for four months before finally realizing the truth. I wondered whether this music had come back into fashion, or was it part and parcel of this irony thing, where anything shit was cool? What was Freddie doing these days? Had someone taught him to snog properly?

Was he working on a 'disruptive proposition to send a baby to sleep whilst you cleansed its bottom?'

'*Bella is still in good health,*' a new text buzzed.

'*Thanks for the update,*' I replied.

'*Log onto our portal for updates on our menus this week,*' the next text said.

Was this a real person?

And would they text me when they took her to

A&E? Or when she was in intensive care? I needed to call them to check she really was okay but that would mean staying an extra half an hour, and missing bedtime. Bedtime was the key objective – if I could get home by bedtime then my life wasn't completely messed up.

I tried to get back to work again.

'The idea is overwhelmingly negative,' I typed as this was closer to the truth, but this sounded, well, rather awful. *'The idea works on some levels,'* I concluded.

I looked up and the MC Hammer fanboy was wearing a baseball cap with the word 'TWAT' emblazoned across the front. He looked up for a second and then back at his screen. Many of these young folks thought I was an elderly person hired by the company to help with our diversity initiative. He had no idea that back in the day I'd been a hot shot. No, that wasn't true. I'd never been a hot shot. I wasn't strategic enough and I worked hard but not so hard that I ended up in hospital with nervous exhaustion.

A proper sissy pants, me. Besides not all of us can be Phoebe-Sheryl Sandberg-BIG-BOSS-PANTS. Not all of us want to be her right?

I checked my emails, and there was yet another one from Mum complaining that Dad was being anti-social.

I didn't know why she was surprised by my father's tendencies to lock himself away – they'd been together for forty-five years now.

> Your dad refuses to try line dancing with me. He says he's too busy but it's pretty obvious that he's just hiding away. I never thought my life would be so lonely.

Mum was prone to being dramatic. I could empathise as I could clearly see that there was very little to recommend getting old (unless you were rich and old). They lived in a different part of London, I rarely saw them. It took me two and a bit hours to travel from Acton to Beckenham where I'd grown up. It was quicker to take the Eurostar to Paris. Dad was usually tinkering in his shed with his model railway. He'd retired five years ago and had a history of depression. Maybe it wasn't depression but was just low mood. He'd set the railway up so it ran around the garden. Mum was a social animal and needed to be around people. Dad was happiest when he could spend uninterrupted periods alone. Mum was constantly experimenting with a range of different evening classes, from watercolour through to Mandarin. They were relatively healthy but each time I spoke to either of them there seemed to be the arrival of another ailment. It was hard to see how there could be much of a silver lining.

Both my parents had always instilled how important it was to work, to have a dependable income, to have financial stability. Sometimes I wished they hadn't.

And I went for a walk this morning and another big, frightening dog attacked Puddles. He's shaking with fear whilst I type this. I am at my wit's end. Love Mum

Mum was often at her 'wit's end' and Puddles was my parent's Yorkshire terrier. Puddles was an unhappy dog that shook when he went for a stroll (or more accurately a 'shake'), shook when he took a dump, and shook when you offered him a treat. He was constantly being attacked by mean dogs and lacked confidence (something we had in common perhaps?). I made a mental note to ring Dad. We usually talked about the weather at great length and then I'd ask him how he was *really* and he'd say he had a cold (which meant his depression was mild) or the flu (which meant it was pretty bad) or a stomach bug (which translated to needing more antidepressants). We never used the word depression and yet this time I was worried about his reclusiveness. At the same time, I envied the fact that he could avoid people for long periods of time with nothing but Classic FM blaring out of the old ghetto blaster that had resided in my teenage bedroom. He didn't have to get crammed onto a train or listen to sad men swearing in meetings and he could amuse himself fixing little carriages together with glue and drinking tea (he even had a kettle in there so Mum had enabled him to be more of a recluse). He'd spent his working life in academia and this was how academics were. They pootled and liked quiet. This behaviour was not out of the ordinary.

Lunchtime arrived, and like every other work day I walked listlessly round the local boutiques trying to dispatch the sad feeling that lived inside me. It was cold and windy, so I bought a bobble hat. A scented candle. A new pair of gloves. None of these items were satisfying, and I went back to the canteen upstairs, bought my protein and salad lunch, and hunched over my phone, trying to see what was going on in the world of Instagram. It seemed that everyone else was doing far more interesting things than I was. There were a lot of motivational quotes about how today was the day where my life would finally take off. Others were preaching the benefits of feeling good about our bodies (which felt rather obvious, I thought, but these posts always proved popular). I spent ten minutes trying to think of something witty to fling into the mix, and then gave up. I called Pete instead. He worked at a catering company that provided posh lunches for corporate clients. He hated it but was good and rarely moaned.

He accepted that part of life was doing a job you disliked. We were both very different in that regard.

'*What's up?*' he said picking up after the first ring.

'*Not much. I just had lunch. Are you having a good day?*' I asked. '*The nursery texted and said Bella fell off the climbing frame again.*'

'*Is she okay?*'

'*I think so. No she's definitely okay or they would have sent another one. How's work?*'

'*Bit of a pain. There's a massive order in for a conference tomorrow. I've been on my feet all morning but I'm going to buy some tinned tomatoes on my way home and make a nice prawn pasta for dinner.*'

'*Did you take the prawns out of the freezer?*'

'*I think so.*'

'*If you didn't take them out then we can't have prawn pasta can we?*'

'*If they haven't thawed I'll do that sausage pasta thing Bella likes.*'

'*I don't think the sausages are still okay,*' I said.

'*I'll check when I get in,*' he replied.

There were a lot of conversations about freezing and defrosting these days. I wondered if all couples were the same.

Yet I knew I was lucky to have Pete. He made delicious food. He still took pride in his appearance and hadn't lost his teeth and hair. He did more on the

27

domestic front than many other men – in fact some weekend mornings, it was a race to see who could get the washing in the machine first. There was sometimes a tinge of passive-aggressiveness to it. We had sex every two months but there were also long periods where we didn't do it all and watched TV. Yes I needed to practice more gratitude. The problem was it was hard work, this long-term relationship stuff. The practicalities of life took over and you were left with two people exchanging functional information on how to get from A to B. A bit like when you ask someone directions and then don't listen and walk the way you originally intended anyway.

An image of Pete popped into my mind. The night we'd first met in a bar in Ladbroke Grove. It had been back in the days before mobiles, before screens, when people looked at each other a lot more (I'd heard from younger colleagues at work that this rarely happened much anymore). I'd had quite a lot of beer to drink (back when beer was trendy for girls to drink), and a friend had introduced me. He was tall, had a mop of dark hair, and an Irish accent.

'He's bad news,' my friend had said. 'He just goes from one girl to the next.'

I was a woman that loved a challenge and I treated getting Pete like a project.

We'd spent that first night kissing in the corner. We

kissed a lot. I tried not to think about it now because it felt like two different people. It had been. Two people without a kid, without the stress of paying a mortgage and bills each month, without all the domestic hum drum that took over, without acres of TV to get through each day.

Just two people that really liked one other.

In the beginning our relationship had been exciting. Like all couples, who fancy each other, we'd taken every opportunity to have sex. We'd had sex in a park, in a toilet, in my old bedroom when I took him to meet my parents (my parents weren't there for the sex part). Pete had never been a massive talker and had grown up in a family where his mum talked enough for the entire family – the rest of the family nodded or shook their heads. Nevertheless we had that initial phase of getting to know each other, sharing key childhood experiences, music we loved – all that stuff.

Then, like many couples who have been together a long time, we stopped asking those questions. Pete often said things like *'You told me that story already,'* or *'I know how this one ends.'* And it was true, there wasn't much original content. And he hated my work chat. Initially I'd come back full of venom and stories about my day,

I'd download them the split-second I came through the door. I had that need to get it all off my chest. Pete was oftentimes looking to provide a basic solution to these problems, so he'd say things like, *tell him to bugger off*, or *just don't do that project if it isn't in your job description*. This was fine, but what he didn't understand was that I didn't want a solution. I JUST WANTED HIM TO LISTEN. And sympathise. Like a friend would.

'*You can't have conversations with your partner like you do with your mates,*' Kath said.

But this left me wondering what you could do with your partner if conversations and sex were often off the agenda.

What did that leave?

And so I stopped telling him these work stories. I stopped telling him the old stories (he'd heard them all). I stopped telling him. It made me sad but I wasn't sure what I was supposed to do about it. It didn't feel like something that dinner in a nice restaurant would fix.

On top of this we'd been through three miscarriages after Bella. Miscarriages can bring you closer together but they'd seemed to push us further apart instead. We wanted to stay together.

But life was tiring and we didn't have energy to put into it anymore.

After lunch, I went back to the silent, air-conditioned

tomb. The air con had been turned up so high that several of my colleagues were wearing thick blankets wrapped around their shoulders. It made the whole place feel a bit desperate – like we were in some sort of disaster zone, just trying to hold our shit together until somebody rescued us. I shoved my headphones on, and spent twenty minutes trying to construct a Spotify playlist that would encourage me to run more often.

Phoebe came back into my field of vision. She mouthed the words, *WHERE'S THAT BRIEF?* at me and I made a sort of shrugged shoulder, not sure where, gesture and she was off again. It was obvious that there was a need for more briefs today. We were very busy but not busy enough.

I whacked some KRS-One on. An old P. Diddy track. The minute those beats started I felt more energetic. Hip-hop made me feel like I could conquer the world. Hip-hop artists never struggled with their careers or worried that they'd spent too much on a bobble hat and would need to return it. I love hip-hop (classics from the 90s). This stemmed back to my childhood growing up in Beckenham – basically you either liked hip-hop or dance music and I tended to be more of a hip-hop gal. It seemed as if those lyrics were written for a white, middle-class girl dealing with boys who thought I was too tall and boyish for them and friendship dynamics which changed every two minutes. Now if you clocked me in my Boden skirt, grey roots just starting to show through, you'd think I was listening to Coldplay or some such dross but I retained my tiny sliver of youthful abandon through listening to LL Cool J, DMX, Dr Dre and Wu-Tang Clan.

There was something about hip-hop that was remarkably confidence boosting.

Like many females, I didn't over-index on confidence and was drawn to people who did. LL Cool J never woke in the morning with imposter syndrome. He didn't have to read positive affirmations to know what he stood for or what he wanted to accomplish that day. It's was awe-inspiring. One day I would launch a magazine and it would give advice from rappers to middle aged women. It would be called *Dope Housewives*, and would blow *Good Housekeeping* out of the water. Who wanted to look at Judith Chalmers in a floral jumpsuit or read articles about body brushing when you could read 'Snoop Dog's 10 Tips for a Hot Damn Sex Life?'. It was accepted that your tastes became more conservative, the older you became but why did this have to be so?

Eventually, I came back to the slides I needed to finish off. Some of the presentation seemed to be rather repetitive, but I could always hide those slides, or delete them once I'd finished.

I couldn't help myself and checked Instagram first, scrolling through another fifty images of women who were apparently '*killing it*', '*nailing it*', '*embracing the day,*' and the like. I wrote another slide. Then went back on social media. I kept this not-very-virtuous-circle going for the rest of the afternoon.

'*The synergy between cleaning and sleeping doesn't feel optimum for a bum product offering.*'

'*Today's the first day of the rest of your life.*'

'*A core barrier is the fear of toxicity next to baby's private parts.*'

'*The only thing to fear is fear itself.*'

'*The optimized proposition needs to reassure on natural-ness as some respondents feared rashes and reactions due to strong offensive odour of product.*'

I was increasingly feeling like I was just arranging words in different configurations, and they made very little sense. I took a few screengrabs from various baby websites and stuck smiling faces all over the deck. That jollied it up somewhat and made it feel a bit more accessible. At around three p.m. it was time for a team meeting. Darren was my team leader – I'd hired him just before going on maternity leave and he was now my line manager. It wasn't uncommon of course. Having a baby was not a good idea and your career rarely survived – unless when you came back you worked ten times as hard and denied the baby's existence. It was a thorny issue and one that showed no signs of going away.

'*So, are we all SMASHING it today?*' Darren said as the four of us settled around the table.

There was something about him that gave me a visceral response – a queasy feeling. He was a strange hybrid of 'macho surfer' and 'steely banker'. It was a horrid combination.

'*We are smashing it today,*' I said under my breath but this was far from the truth.

I'd only had one brief in two weeks, and had been finishing up this debrief for three days now (when usually I should have moved onto a new project already). On the table there was a young female intern who seemed about fourteen, then a lovely girl called Sam who had joined Mango-Lab after her gap year in Belize rescuing turtles, and the guy with the TWAT cap who I'd seen around the office, but who had only just been put on Darren's team. Then me – the Grandma of hip-hop.

'*Let's each take a turn and say the one thing we're proud of achieving today.*' Darren said.

Darren had whitened his teeth, and smiled a lot to make sure to get his money's worth. In my last appraisal, he'd told me to study the book *How to Win Friends and Influence People*. He'd learnt all his 'tricks and strategies' from it, he said. I needed to be more *like him* if I wanted to win in business. The thing was, I wasn't sure Mango-

Lab wanted a forty-two-year-old surfer chick who slapped people on the back without warning . . . but he was right that I needed to be more enthusiastic – my enthusiasm levels were not great. He also told me that my business-winning target had tripled. He delivered this news with a grin, and then slapped the table to signal our one-on-one had finished.

'*Great dude! Do you want to high five?*'

I just glared at him. I clearly didn't want to do that at all. It had taken me forty minutes to fill in one line on the review form which was all in Excel – I found it impossible to use at the best of times. I had the sense that Darren was trying to catch me out and make my life as difficult as possible. I didn't like the cut of his jib. Even by Mango-Lab's standards he was a viper. If I'd been Phoebe, I would have taken his advice on the chin and *manned up*. Instead I went into the toilet and cried, and then went to Pret and bought myself a cheese and ham croissant. I rang Mum and vowed to escape this terrible job as soon as possible. I understood we needed to bring business in but they needed to be practical about just how much a part-time mum could bring in on her own with little support.

'*You'll never achieve this huge figure Rebecca,*' Darren had said in one of our more recent catch-ups. '*You won't even come close but let's set the bar REAL high? Let's see where that tide takes you.*'

He'd grinned, flashing those ghastly gnashers. He delivered bad news whilst smiling like Jack Nicholson's character in *The Shining*. This might have come from his self-help book but it didn't work for me. Many were terrified of him.

'I worked until three a.m. on a debrief last night.'

'I typed the whole thing whilst cycling on my bicycle.'

'My Fitbit says I got one hour of sleep but I just had a twenty-minute cat nap so my metabolism is back on form.'

'I missed my daughter's birthday because I was winning this new project from Ribena and so she didn't mind.'

'I've worked out that if I nap for ten minutes at three p.m. I can keep working till ten and feel fine.'

These were typical Darren statements. People who are workaholics smell bad. This was something I'd noticed about him from day one. His body was slowly decomposing as he became a man/robot hybrid. When he sweated it smelt like someone had died. The human elements were rapidly being broken down. He often appeared from nowhere and was suddenly right behind you like he was floating around. His legs replaced by wheels because legs were useless and didn't transport you from one laptop to the next in quick enough time. Meanwhile in that same appraisal meeting, Phoebe had sat in the corner and taken notes the whole time he was speaking – *'This loser will probably last no more than six months,'* or something close. Maybe she drew penises in the margins too. And I tried to do these things – to be more enthusiastic, more dynamic, but it felt as if I was sinking.

They knew this of course and I felt like this was part of the plan.

We were back in the meeting. Darren was using the corner of a piece of paper to pick something out of his teeth.

'I'm proud that I took good notes during the banking groups and learnt some super interesting insights about people and their favourite financial services apps,' the intern said cheerily.

She was very pretty but would soon be very tired. I often witnessed their pink, healthy cheeks become hangdog and pale as the long hours drained the life force from them.

'Great work,' Darren said tapping his pen noisily on the table. *'Banking is one of my favourite categories. Well done Sasha.'*

'It's not Sasha,' she replied.

'Whatever . . . next dude!'

'I'm proud that I've identified a new paradigm shift in the pet food market,' said the TWAT.

I drew a little penis in the margin.

'I'm constantly surprised by the pet food category,' Darren said. *'Such rich behavioural data when you compare dry*

versus wet. There's definitely a breakfast innovation session in there somewhere if you'd be interested in writing it.'

TWAT nodded and then glanced at my pad. I worried that perhaps he'd noticed my penis drawing, so I quickly drew some branches coming out of the bell-end so it looked more like a blossoming tree.

'And what are YOU proud of this week, Rebecca?' Darren asked.

I could always sense sarcasm in his voice. I had violent fantasies which ended with me punching him in the face. I knew these feelings were irrational, but Darren had come to represent my failure and lack of popularity. I stared back at him, and thought about how I'd need to bandage up my hands properly to get a good punch in. How I'd never punched anyone before but this first punch would be very powerful. How his teeth would shatter one by one, like in a cartoon, and then fall to the floor. How I would perhaps pick these teeth up and keep them as mementos. How I would leave the office with them in my pocket and then make a bestselling rap album where I dissed Darren in every song. Then I stopped and felt a wave of panic. It wasn't Darren's fault that I was becoming less relevant. Or that I only had two clients commissioning business. Or that I didn't share his boundless enthusiasm for dog kibble.

'I feel like I've finally had a breakthrough on this baby wipe presentation.' I said, which was not true but no

one was going to read it apart from the client. Darren flashed me his *winning business smile.*

'Well there's a surprise. You're being AWESOME. Well done dude.'

'Rebecca, I'd love to run some ideas past you about the pet food market,' TWAT said.

'That's a great idea,' Darren said. 'Rebecca, remember we said you needed to collaborate more with the semiotics and cultural insights team moving forward? It would be great if you two could hit those waves REAL hard if you know what I mean?'

Darren had managed to make this sound rather pervy. That was another thing he specialized in – innuendo. I scribbled over the penis tree on my pad and nodded. I didn't like this TWAT but would play the game. If it helped me appear more dynamic and *with it* then so be it.

I went back to my desk. The meeting had felt a bit staged. Had the TWAT and Darren agreed ahead of time that we would collaborate? Who was this boy? A spy? A flash drive in a baseball cap? I continued writing slides and checking Instagram as before, but I suddenly felt like my head was detaching from itself, and travelling up to the ceiling. *Had the nursery texted but I'd accidentally lost the text? Was Bella really okay? Were the prawns defrosted or not? What about the sausages? And the non-existent brief? I'd lied about that and Phoebe would soon uncover the lie.* Once it reached the ceiling my head stayed resting on the plastic tiles, and softly bounced around looking down on everyone; the young people in their blankets; the green smoothies in massive plastic bottles; the headphones; the grey carpet; the photo-copier which was always broken and required a compli-cated access code; the herbal teabag stuck to the floor. I'd done a pill or ten in my youth and the whole sensa-tion would have been pleasant if I'd been in a nightclub back in the noughties, but here under the florescent lighting, with the tinny echo from headphones and relentless air con being blown down our necks, this was not pleasant at all. I had to hold onto the desk to stop myself from falling out of my chair. Was this a stroke?

I got up and half walked, half staggered to the kitchen. No one looked up from their laptop. It wasn't unusual. We were all alone with our emails and anxiety. Once inside the kitchen, I stared at the cupboard and repeated the instructions stuck to the door. *Dispose of ALL teabags in the bin provided. The fridge will be cleaned every Friday and all EDIBLES will be disposed of PROMPTLY.* My head was still not attached to my body. It was some-where outside seeking a blanket. I wondered whether I was dying. I tried to normalize my breathing. I rested my head against the cupboard. *I am okay. I am okay. I am okay.* I repeated. Then I turned around and the TWAT was right next to me.

'Are you feeling alright?' he said not unkindly. *'I read one of your blog articles and you'd written about the unique connection between cats and their owners and I wanted to try and tap into some of that for this proposal I'm writing.'*

'Yes,' I said weakly, could he not see I was dying right now? *'I will check my diary and be in touch.'*

I turned back to face the cupboard.

'I hate the instructions, everywhere don't you?' he said. *'Do you want a cup of tea or are you just chilling in here?'*

My head has come off and is floating somewhere next to the bookcase thanks.

'Chilling,' I said.

Now please leave me be. I really didn't want him to notice my hands shaking as I took the coffee out of the cupboard and deposited a spoonful into my cup.

Back at my desk I wrote an email to Phoebe and copied in Darren, explaining that I needed to go home as I felt like I was coming down with something bad. Before leaving I sat in the toilet and tried to compose myself for the journey home. It was frightening to feel so out of control. Was this a panic attack? A breakdown? Or was I about to drop dead?

'We used to have Molton Brown soap and now they're getting it from Tesco,' I heard a girl outside the cubicle saying, *'Do you think there will be redundancies soon?'*

I recognized the voice as one of the admin team.

'Phoebe's just won that big frozen food account,' another

voice said – it sounded like the receptionist – *It's massive. Phoebe is pretty amazing really.'*

'Phoebe is incredible.'

'I heard she only took one week for her maternity leave.'

'I heard she had no pain relief during labour.'

'She did a climb up Kilimanjaro a month later.'

'I heard her husband is very good-looking.'

'Their kitchen is huge – I saw a picture on Facebook.'

'She has lots of dinner parties and I heard that Piers Morgan came to one.'

'Well maybe we'll get Aesop in the toilets again.'

'I hope you're right.'

On the train, I stared out the window. I felt like you do at the end of a hangover. The feeling you get at roughly 3 p.m. My head was back on my body but my head was aching. I felt flat. I looked down at my phone and saw an email labelled URGENT.

Re: FISH FINGER INNOVATION OPPORTUNITY

Hey Rebecca,

I have some great news on a new fish finger proposition that the client wants to research next month. It's an exciting challenge. It fits perfectly with the goals and objectives we drew up with Darren at your last appraisal.

Hope you're feeling better already.

Phoebe.

P.S. What happened about that brief? Was it a false alarm?

Better already? I'd only just left the office! There was nothing about the email that made me feel better. I had ZERO interest in fish fingers. Who did? Well Phoebe was different. She could fake an interest in anything. This was why she was successful. She had the stamina of an ox. She never woke up with the sheets imprinted into her face. She never laughed and weed herself because her pelvic floor was shot to buggery. Okay, she wore terrible clothes and had no style but I was clutching at straws. All you saw when you looked at her was confidence and strategic prowess. She was *dynamic*. This was the word she constantly waved under my nose – the word she bandied about as if it was some sort of magic formula, but what did it actually mean? How could I be more dynamic if my head was flying off all over the place and everyone was talking like a surfer dude? I was sorely tempted to send her an email telling her to FUCK OFF. Wasn't this a benefit of getting older? Saying exactly what you thought and not mincing your words? This was what I loved about Mum. The older she got, the less she cared about anyone and the more sweary she became. I wished I could channel some of her now so I could overpower Phoebe.

I typed a reply.

AWESOME! I LOVE FISH FINGERS. Sorry, the brief was a false alarm but will definitely chase again next week. They said they needed to spend more time working out the objectives.

Rebecca x

She was also the kind of person who got off a transatlantic flight, and went straight to a meeting, then got straight back on the plane (perhaps turning her knickers inside out in the airplane toilet), slicked on a bit of lip gloss, readying herself to cook a delicious three course meal for her dinner guests when she got home. So it was true that she'd only had a week off for her maternity leave, and I'd also heard another rumour she'd come back with the umbilical cord still dangling out the bottom of her tights (she'd been *dynamic* right from the get go then). She lost her baby weight the next week by only eating nuts and drinking water. Her baby boy started talking when he was five months old. His first words were 'Yaki Soba' (his favourite dish from Wagamama). She did a successful pitch to an online retailer on her first day back in the office. She never drew penises on her notebooks (as far as I knew), and she was constantly giving me advice on how to be more productive.

'Rebecca – you need to get up an hour earlier and work on your emails.'

'*Why don't you use the commute time to ATTACK some of your top objectives? You can actually use your phone to record your TO DO LIST and you need never forget anything important again.*'

'*Have you tried that new productivity app called RELENTLESS? It means you can fill in every single moment of the day with tasks?*'

Both Phoebe and Darren were cut from the same cloth. Phoebe was the CEO and Darren the Managing Director but Phoebe liked to monitor me at close range. There had been a time, when I'd been doing better, and she'd been more hands off. So, the fact that she was so in my face was not good news. I sometimes thought they would have had amazing children together, who never had to sleep (waste of time), never got ill (illness was for wimps) and worked 24/7. The only difference was that Darren tried to pretend he was a nice person and Phoebe didn't bother with that at all.

I didn't like to fill in every available moment with work. It was bad enough that no one had dead time, that no one stared or observed anything because they were constantly on their phones. I still cried now and then when I left Bella at nursery and was then too teary to check emails on the way in. Unlike Phoebe, I had still looked pregnant eighteen months after the birth. My pelvic floor was a giant plastic bag flapping about, and I peed without warning. Each time I wrote a business proposal, I usually lost the project. I kept thinking how pointless this stuff was. Who cared about the positioning strategy for some ear buds? Or an innovation path for an Asian suppository brand? I felt like I had no insights to offer unless they involved my daughter and her sleeping habits. I watched colleagues' eyes glaze over as I talked about her. I wasn't *dynamic* it was true. Clients liked me because I was kind. I made them feel good by laughing at their jokes and asking about their family.

Some people are top strategists and others are . . . nice.

As I made my way out of the station, walking to the bus stop for the second stage of my journey, I still wasn't feeling right. There was an uneasy sensation working its way through my body. The email from Phoebe had only made it worse. The month before I'd just finished a project for a frozen yoghurt product. I had found it all so demoralizing. There were people dying in wars and famines, and I was contemplating whether this product should be called 'Milky Joy,' or 'Full of Milkyness.' Then whether it should have a cartoon dog or a koala as its mouthpiece. I knew this was where I was going wrong. I had to talk myself into it. I had to try and emulate Phoebe.

Then I remembered Dad and quickly left him a message. *'Dad, can you please pick up? Mum is worried about you. She says you're spending all your time in the shed and haven't come out in a while now. Ring me back or send me a text just so I know all is okay.'*

Back home I couldn't wait to see Bella but she was grumpy and tired, kept flailing about and kicking off about the fact that her pasta had tomato sauce ON TOP rather than ON THE SIDE and I'd mixed the broccoli in too. On the positive side, her head just had a small bruise on the side so the fall obviously hadn't been serious. Nevertheless I lost my temper and ended up shouting at her. Eventually things calmed down, I put her to bed, and spent some time stroking her hair. These were my favourite moments in the day.

'Mummy, is it nursery day tomorrow?'

'Yes it is darling.'

'I don't want to go.'

She sat up and flung her arms around me, planting tiny kisses on the side of my head.

'I know. But listen, just two more days and we'll be together again. We can do lots of fun things.'

I put her back into bed, and pulled the duvet up which she immediately kicked off again. I often came in in the night and found her lying on top of the covers, her tiny feet freezing cold.

'I don't like the grown-ups at nursery, they're horrible.'

'But you never want to leave when I pick you up.'

'They said I was a baby because I cried this morning.'

'Well that's not true. You're clearly a big girl.'

'They're monsters. They're horrible. Mummy isn't a monster.'

'Sometimes Mummy is a monster right?'

She closed her eyes, sucking on the ear of her bunny toy and fell asleep. I remembered the nights standing over her cot, willing her to sleep, crying with the tiredness of sleep deprivation. It was true that things got easier. It was perhaps a blessing that I'd never had another baby. I was too old to cope. She murmured in her sleep, and something tugged inside. I leant in and smelt her hair. This was *one of those happy moments*. These moments usually involved Bella. Moments when I felt like life had a bit more meaning and purpose. When I wasn't lost in a panic of information and things to do.

The prawns had been defrosted.

Pete and I watched TV like most evenings.

'Why is she running back into the factory when she knows the psychopath is in there?' I was holding a pillow in front of my face.

'She's not. She's going back to warn him – she wants to save him most likely.'

'Yeah but she's the one having an affair with the gangster. Why does she even care about the other guy?'

Pete didn't answer. He refused eye contact. He hated it if I talked during a dramatic moment.

That had been all the words for the day. No more content. In bed, he gave my arm a quick squeeze, rolled over onto his side, and started snoring.

That night I dreamt I was floating in the sea and I came upon a giant fish wrapped in plastic. He kept floating past me, mouthing the words DYNAMIC then lying very still, like he was in a coma. Was this the fish finger proposition? Was this my career? Was this Dad? Was this Bella? My relationship with Pete stagnating?

Three

*Your dad came out of shed for exactly one hour
yesterday. I am feeling lonely. What is the point?
Also I got a parking ticket in Sainsbury's car park.
How is that even possible? I thought the parking
was free? Is it free?*

Mum ☺

I needed to ring Mum and speak to her properly. I
popped it on the bit of ticker tape that ran through
my brain and it promptly disappeared down a chute
labelled –'the millions of things to do at some point in
the future.'

After dropping Bella off, I bumped into a mum who'd
been at the local park a couple of weekends ago. We'd

ended up having coffee – she was in the newborn phase and had that drawn-out, anxious expression that was characteristic of that time. Her name was Bryony.

'Love your trainers,' I said as we stopped near the station.

They were bright green with purple flashes. Despite looking knackered she had that ability to look dishevelled in an attractive way, her hair piled up in a bun on the top of her head, a big leopard print scarf wrapped around her neck. She was probably about twenty-seven. Her baby was wrapped in a dozen blankets despite the warm sunshine. I had been exactly the same. It paid to ensure your baby was as warm as possible and poor Bella had often ended up clammy by the time we got home.

'Thanks. I must take your number,' Bryony said. *'I thought we could meet up for another coffee soon perhaps.'*

I sympathized with the need to talk to another adult. When Bella had been tiny I'd have had coffee with the postman if he'd have been interested (he wasn't – instead he always shouted *'Oi Average! Cheer up!'* whenever he saw me on the street. I wasn't sure how my nickname had come about but guessed he was referring to my appearance in a casually sexist/offensive manner – ignoring the fact that he had one remaining strand of white hair that was plastered across his forehead. Last time we'd met, Bryony had told me she'd worked in advertising for a big London agency in Soho, but was now on six months' maternity leave (advertising was an unforgiving industry for mothers, much like marketing). She now had ambitions to be a photographer. She wanted to take photos of children that weren't cheesy, the opposite to those studio portraits where you get a family gurning holding onto a bunch of nonsensical props.

'*I feel completely rootless nowadays,*' she'd said with the candour that lack of sleep and a bit of welcome adult conversation tends to create. '*I need to find something that energises me again. I think having a baby really brings it all into focus. Why would I want to sacrifice spending time with Ralph to do something I hate?*'

It was a good question. It was one that puzzled me most days. Ralph was suckling from her breast. He was beautiful – white blonde hair and grey eyes, tiny fingers which wrapped around one finger, nails translucent and pale. Bella meanwhile span round and round in a chair kicking the bottom of the table. I'd always struggled with breastfeeding. Perhaps because of my age?

'*It's a phase. You'll feel better,*' I'd replied but I wasn't so sure.

At least when you were on maternity leave you could dedicate all your anxiety to raising a small person. Once you went back to work, it got mixed together with a whole heap of other shit (which in some ways was beneficial as it diluted the brutal levels of worry you'd previously dedicated to your baby).

We swapped numbers and agreed to meet up for a coffee. It was against my usual anti-social instincts but I sensed she needed a friend and so did I (I wasn't exactly swimming in them).

I got to work on time (no sarcastic comments from Phoebe) and after checking my inbox went with Simon/ TWAT HAT for a coffee to discuss pet strategy.

'*I definitely feel much better,*' I lied as I sipped my turmeric latte, which I was trying to convince myself was nice, but was *not* as nice as a regular coffee at all. I was hoping Simon would be impressed by my ideas, and would pass it on to Phoebe/Darren so they'd see how *dynamic* I was. The only problem was the day hadn't got off to a flying start. Bella had cried again at nursery, and I'd then spent five minutes looking for a nursery assistant who would take her from my arms. Many of the other children were crying too, and the whole scene made me sad. Why were we leaving these poor saps with other people so we could do jobs we hated? Simon was quite sweet though, and when I arrived he listened as I did my usual brain dump about my travel problems/childcare/woes/bad commute. He was softly spoken and intelligent. He also didn't talk over me like many of the other men at work.

'So how long have you worked at Mango?' he asked.

'Since the early noughties,' I said. 'I guess you would have been about ten years old when I started. Mad hey?'

And in a flash I saw that classic catchphrase, 'You don't have to be mad to work here but it helps!' printed on tea mugs and mouse mats everywhere. Was that what had happened to me? Had I been institutionalized at Mango-Lab and made crazy? Why had I never tried anything else? Bryony and the way she effortlessly considered a new career, simply moving onto something new, felt unimaginable.

'So how come Phoebe is your boss if you've been at Mango even longer than she has?'

I thought about it for a moment and chose to tell the truth.

'I think I just ran out of steam – something like that anyway – Phoebe has always been fiercely ambitious,' I wanted to change the subject because I wasn't quite sure how I'd managed to progress so little in such a long period of time. 'Anyhow, let's talk about this pet food presentation. I did a project a few years ago about scented cat litter so I could talk you through some of that?'

'That sounds spot on. Did it have essential oils in it? Also I always thought there was a subtle relationship between cat litter and cat food. They look the same but culturally we don't have the same amount of shame around *faecal matter that we used to. Perhaps there's a role for a product that fulfils two roles at the same time?'*

'An edible cat litter?'

'Something like that yes.'

'I haven't heard of such a thing and I can see a few barriers but it's worth identifying as a route forward.'

'The client is open-minded and wants NEW ideas. Do you think the accompanied feeding time depths were the best method?' he asked.

'Yes but I might have added some follow-up phone interviews. And made sure I got a good spectrum of pet owners. Highly involved, less involved – that kind of thing.'

'We don't call them phone interviews anymore,' he said. *'They're in-depth digital pow wows.'*

'Well those. You know, talk to the owners after they've used the product and get their feedback.'

'I like that. I wonder whether we should frame it as a litter or a food? I'll have to think it through.'

The turmeric was catching in my throat. I was tired. Perhaps I needed a supplement for women in their forties who struggled to be enthusiastic. I wished it was time to go to bed. The senseless back and forth. It was kind of enjoyable . . . sort of . . . like the sensation of peeling off old nail varnish from your thumb, and it coming off in one piece.

When you worked in market research for long

enough you realized that whatever category you worked in the stories you told the clients were, more often than not, the same. It was all about finding some sort of human insecurity or lack, then addressing this lack with your product. For pet owners, the lack was usually a guilt that they weren't spending enough time with their pet. It was the same for working parents. We all want to believe that we're doing everything we can for our loved ones. In an unpredictable world, this sense of control was important. There might be a terrorist attack at any moment but at least your cat had a nice smelling bottom and your baby had eaten three vegetables. It's the little things and all that.

I thought about Bella and what she might be doing right now. It was mid-morning and they'd probably be playing outside. I hoped she didn't have any accidents today. They usually asked me to log into the portal to check on her progress. I could never remember the password.

Did this make me a bad parent?

As we were talking, Simon's eyes scanned down to his phone screen to see if there was any fresh update on his news feed. He was continually showing me his screen to show some fresh horror that was kicking of – a primary teacher who was a rampant paedophile, a dead elephant with its tusks ripped out, a woman raped on a packed train, a terrorist chopping someone's head off. When I'd been Simon's age, I'd spent an inordinate amount of time listening to Radiohead and feeling sad but there was rarely a specific reason for this sadness (aside from the time I shaved my eyebrows off). I felt sorry for his generation because there were now so many reasons to feel unhappy. There was too much information on the stuff that was going wrong. If we'd been peasants we would have just muttered into our mashed potato whilst people far away were burned and villages pillaged. The culture of being constantly plugged in wasn't healthy.

'*You look a bit pale,*' he said as we both stood up to go back upstairs. '*Do you want to get a fish burrito later?*' he asked. '*I'm walking down to Borough Market at twelve and they're super tasty.*'

I nodded. It would be good for me to do something different and get over my cynicism towards younger people and their food obsessions. I was saying YES to life today. Yes to a coffee with Bryony! Yes to lunch with Simon! We went up to our desks and put our headphones on. The blankets still seemed to be out in force, and I wondered why nobody said anything or just went home where it was warm. Wasn't there a law about keeping employees at a comfortable temperature? It seemed today that they'd despatched with both air-con (which was a relief) and heating. Maybe the girls in the toilet had been right to worry that the soap wasn't posh anymore. This was all symptomatic of a broader money-saving initiative. Perhaps being kept chilly made your brain less sleepy. There wasn't enough time to worry about these macro things, and by the time I'd answered the fifty and then some internal emails about meetings, innovation sessions, new initiatives and brainstorms to land on the names for these initiatives, it was time for lunch.

Kath had sent me a text. She had three beautiful children who looked like they'd stepped out of a Boden catalogue. Back when I'd been romping around the capitals of Europe with my Top Shop blazer, and bag full of bad marketing ideas, she'd been bringing up kids, and being generally excellent at it. She thought my life was exciting and I thought hers was calmer and more authentic. We were both bored but she argued that at least I was getting paid for my time.

Hey high flyer? How's things?

Fine, I replied. I might be coming down with something – feel a bit yukky.

There's a lot of bugs about. Lara has an Instagram account. What do I do?

Motherwhelmed

Lara was her twelve-year-old daughter, and I was surprised she hadn't had an IG account for longer. We weren't the first generation to have no real idea what our children were doing.

Just follow her and ask her to keep the account private.

I think she's putting videos of her making slime on there.

I think that's pretty normal.

Is Bella okay?

She won't wear tights and keeps falling over.

I remember that phase too.

Ring me later.

Cool will do ☺

Later Simon and I walked towards Borough Market. It was a nice day, the sun was out, and I had that momentary pop of happiness that comes with realizing that you're not dead yet. Perhaps this was the thing. The small moments of happiness and nothing more.

When Bella squeezed me tight.

When I leant in and smelt her hair.

When the sun came out after a few days of grey.

The prawns being defrosted.

Leggings instead of tights – signalling a small parenting victory.

The market wasn't busy, and I picked up a box of raspberries (priced at six pounds so I set it back down). I thought about how much Bella would enjoy eating these and picked them up and paid for them. If you're a working mum, you basically have a child-ghost who follows you about all day, making you feel pain in your heart and angst about whether you're doing the right thing. It wasn't unusual for me to buy stuff for her to make myself feel better. I was sure we all did the same thing.

We ordered our burritos and I tried to eat mine but about fifty per cent fell on the pavement. I didn't like this trend towards eating whilst in motion. It wasn't enjoyable. It also made a mess of your clothes. Simon smiled. He had a wise face, and blonde hair that sprouted out the sides of his cap. He was wearing braces with his black skinny jeans and giant high-top trainers which had come back into fashion again. I had a feeling that he saw me as a benevolent granny type. Was he seeking some sort of mentor? I couldn't recall the last time I'd been to lunch with someone. Usually the dynamic types were cliquey and didn't want to come too close as they sensed I had a losing streak.

'So, *I read that report you wrote about "Scouting for Trends,"'* Simon said biting into his burrito. *'It was cool.'*

I was finding his interest in me quite curious. He'd never spoken to me before. There was also a side of me that felt suspicious. Was he a spy? Was he *Darren's spy?*

'Yes. We presented it at a "Global Youth Research Trends" conference in New York about ten years ago. It was fun,' I said trying to retrieve a bit of lettuce from my teeth. *'We met Thurston Moore at a bar in Greenwich village.'*

'Who's he?'

I started explaining about Sonic Youth, and how important they'd been as a band, (in fact I'd never really been into them but I got exasperated when people didn't know much Gen X popular culture). I stopped. It was hard trying to impress people with name-dropping if they had no idea who you were on about.

'I will have to look them up on Spotify,' Simon said. *'Maybe I can send you a playlist and you can listen to some of my favourite music?'*

I nodded but I'd had enough exposure to millennial music in the office. The speakers constantly played stuff that sounded like you'd heard it before. Where was New Order? The Smiths? The Cure? All the other great bands with 'The' in their name? Why did much of it sound like bad 90s dance music? I knew I sounded like my dad now but it really felt like everything was just regurgitated from the previous generation. It was impossible to create something new. But it was also clear that Sonic Youth wouldn't give me cut through. Thurston Moore was probably claiming his pension by now and eating lettuce sandwiches, avoiding crusty bread so his dentures didn't drop out, all that stuff. There came a time when you had to hang up those cool shoes and get down with the slanket-posse. I wasn't quite ready for my stand-up bath but I wasn't at the cut and thrust either. It was the mid-line. It was the pits.

Too young to surrender to old age and watch *Inspector Morse* all day long, and too old to be twerking and taking spice. I got back to my desk and re-read the fish finger research project brief that Phoebe had sent over. It would be an important project if it was part of a bigger frozen piece of business.

Everything about it filled me with despondency.

FISH FINGER INNOVATION BRIEF

Fish fingers have been a much-loved family snack for close to three decades but have recently faced challenges because of their lack of healthy cues. We want to rein-vigorate fish fingers and position them in the 'healthy, family, pleasure' quadrant so that families feel like they're making a healthy choice. Our ambition is to be the in the TOP THREE food brands in the next two years.

I underlined key phrases and thought about the possible challenges. Fish fingers were fine. Everyone loved them, even if they weren't entirely fascinating. Generally people loved them because they reminded them of their childhoods. I started jotting some notes. We would need to do some research groups to find out what current consumers of fish fingers thought, and then maybe some with people who didn't buy them to discover the barriers. I scribbled away some ideas and then added in a couple of ideas from the semiotics team (I still had no clue what they did but Simon had emailed me a few studies they'd undertaken previously on family brands), and in this way the afternoon passed by quickly. In this sense, work was good. It felt meaningless, but it was like doing an arrowword puzzle, and kept you from going senile. I sent the ideas to Phoebe so she could approve before I sent them to the client. When I looked at my phone it was five thirty and I hadn't got up from my seat for more than two hours. It had been a productive day. I had eaten an overpriced burrito. I'd talked about popular culture with someone younger than me who wore braces and wasn't a clown.

I managed to log into the nursery portal after three failed attempts. Bella had eaten chicken curry for lunch and made a kite out of an old washing up bottle and some string. There was a photo of her holding it, looking proud. I sent a copy to Pete with a text.

LOOK HOW PROUD SHE IS! X

I was missing these moments because I was trying to come up with a reason as to why people didn't eat more fish fingers. I felt the head detaching sensation but it went away again. I had to fight to stay afloat. My life was okay. I was okay. The office was okay.

I just needed to finish the baby wipe presentation and things would be okay.

I phoned Kath on the walk back to the train station. I often thought it would be quicker to just create a moving pavement on the walk from Southwark to Waterloo. It was a waste of energy to do the same walk. It made me impatient. There were so many offices here that the moving pavement thing would come. Perhaps we'd sit on the pavement and have our phones attached to our eyeballs so we could really *chill*. There was a sea of people streaming out of the three glass and concrete towers. Everyone was smiling like it was the summer holidays. And everyone was on their phones, ordering pizzas, scheduling waxes, texting their spouses to say they were off to the pub. This was the best part of the day, the going home part where you shook your blanket off and felt a tiny glimmer of sun on your face. It was possibly worth going to work just so you could get this feeling regularly.

'*How's things?*' she said. '*Have you done any 'blue sky thinking'?*'

'*I feel so old,*' I replied, crossing the street and narrowly avoiding a cycle courier who had a boom box attached to the back of his bike.

'*The boy I was talking to today didn't even know who Sonic Youth were.*'

'*Well NEWSFLASH LADY. WE ARE OLD. Do you know that I have a walking stick? My back has seized up and I can't walk!*'

'*How?*'

'*I was doing these HIIT sessions online, and I guess I was doing these burpees and going too hard and THWWAAKKK I heard something in my back. I've been told I can't do any exercise for six months. I* need *to exercise.*'

It's the only thing that is mine and nothing to do with children and all that shit.'

'Oh that's sad. Mind you, any excuse not to exercise,' I said.

'But I like to exercise,' she said.

'You'll be doing marathons next.'

'Not with a sodding walking stick I won't!'

'Well you'd be proud of me. I did one good thing. I arranged to have a coffee with a local mum.'

'A local mum! Wowsers! That's uncharacteristically social of you.'

When had I got this reputation for being anti-social? Was it still a hangover from having a young child and being too tired to face going out in the evenings?

'She's called Bryony and she's really nice and she's much younger.'

'Well that sounds promising,' Kath said. *'You need more local friends love. I rarely see you anymore. In fact I don't think any of the old crowd see one another. We're all too busy.'*

It was true. The only good thing was that Kath and I spoke on the phone. We didn't just text. It meant something. The people you *spoke* to versus those you *typed* to.

I thought back to our school days. They didn't seem that long ago. We'd spent our time sitting in Kath's bedroom, talking about boys, listening to music and smoking out the window. We'd started clubbing at fourteen, then everything was a blur of getting off with boys called Danny, Jody and Bobby, and then came university and quite a lot of parties and some drugs, then our thirties and Kath was popping out her children, and I was necking Nurofen Plus, and carrying enormous bags of ideas, before showing them to people who had no interest in them at all. The mudslide into our forties had come next and now we had walking sticks and no one had even heard of Sonic Youth FOR CHRIST'S SAKE.

'I'll ring you soon,' I said. *'Don't worry about the Instagram. It's just like that Talkabout phone line we used to use. Remember? It's like that but with pictures.'*

'But that was moderated by adults wasn't it?'

'Yes, you're right but do you remember those two ugly boys we went to meet in Clapham? One said he looked like Brad Pitt but he was actually very short with acne?'

Kath laughed.

'I think we walked straight past and pretended we hadn't seen them.'

'Instagram is just a modern version of networking, that's all.'

'You've made me feel better. I need to see you soon. There's a bottle of gin waiting.'

On the train home, my head ached and I felt it detaching itself from my body again and working its way down the carriage so it was moving towards the toilets. This time it happened without warning and I tried closing my eyes and enjoying the session. Wasn't it nice to be detached from reality for a few moments?

I checked my phone. A message had buzzed up from the nursery but I'd not seen it.

Bella almost fell over today but she is now in good health. No medical intervention was necessary. Please log into the portal to see the latest update on her health.

Hadn't I just logged in and she was fine? I would see her soon anyway. This was the problem with the continuous updates – there were too many 'crying wolf' occasions, so you became jaded and stopped worrying. What if something really serious happened?

After a minute, the sensation stopped and I opened my eyes. I felt normal again. I wasn't going mad. I called Mum, and she said that Dad had come out to eat lunch but had then gone back to the shed. He hadn't washed his hair in two weeks and was sleeping in his clothes. Apparently, he'd set up a makeshift bed in there. He was playing very loud classical music in the middle of the night and the neighbours had complained that it was keeping them awake.

'Did you have some sort of argument?' I asked. 'What kicked it off?'

'I'm worried darling. I think he's sinking into his old ways. I don't know what to do.'

'This is his personality, Mum. He doesn't like too much social activity. He likes to be on his own. It's fine. Stop trying to make him do stuff.'

There were times when I suspected I was actually more like my dad – it wasn't in my nature to be overly social.

'But the hair thing is driving me crazy. What if someone sniffs him in the supermarket?'

'There are plenty of smelly people, Mum. No one will notice. Just get him dry shampoo.'

'Dry shampoo?'

I explained the concept in detail (I'd worked on a project recently all about it – it was one of those things that was doing well because we were TOO BUSY NOW TO EVEN WASH OUR HAIR) and she promised she'd buy some. I wasn't sure why the head-detaching thing had come back because I was clearly being very successful today. I was solving problems, being social and managing to control the head-detaching feeling. If I could keep this up then maybe I'd get over

Anniki Sommerville

this bumpy patch (if that was what it was) and start some sort of upward trajectory.

I looked out the window at the trees draped in plastic carrier bags and felt my heart sink. I then got my laptop out and spent fifteen minutes wrapping up my baby wipe presentation. We stopped for ten minutes so it bought me more time. *YES, the IDEA of the baby-wipe-sleep-aid was flawed . . . but DESPITE these challenges it showed potential AS LONG AS it kept a focus on CLEANING benefits rather than SLEEP ENHANCE-MENT.* If the client was nice, and not too demanding, then things usually went well. It was only when they wanted innovative and weird methodologies (anything that had the word DIGITAL in it was usually a warning sign) that I felt out of my comfort zone. Perhaps I was going to be okay and wasn't losing relevance with each passing day.

As I came out of the station, I looked down at my phone and right on schedule i.e. AFTER regular work hours, Phoebe had sent an email. She wasn't happy with my ideas for the fish finger thing. She thought they were outmoded and showed a lack of strategic thinking. She just came out with her critique and didn't mince words. I bit my lip and used words and phrases like 'awesome' and 'thanks for the interesting feedback' and 'I look forward to collaborating on some interesting strategy'. I promised I would do better tomorrow. Then visualized her head being squeezed between the doors of an elevator. Her head would be hard and it would take a while to squash it completely but I tried to conjure up her expression, and how I would stand there with my turmeric latte in one hand just smiling (or maybe with no expression at all, which would possibly be more frightening). Just when I felt I was still relevant and could contribute, something would happen to tell me otherwise.

Pete had texted to say he'd collected Bella. As I turned into our street, I felt my blood pressure finally return to normal. We lived in a beautiful, leafy suburb. There were lots of families, a lovely park with swings and some climbing equipment, and it felt like the opposite of the glass monster I'd been freezing my ass off in all day. Our overweight tabby cat was sitting on the kitchen table. The early evening autumnal sun was coming through the French doors. Bella was playing with Pete upstairs. Dad would come out of the shed and wash his hair. I would write some more fish finger strategies. I had a beautiful daughter who would hopefully never work in an air conditioned brick like me. I also had breasts that were saggy, but not actually touching the floor. I could listen to Radio Four and understand about forty per cent of what was being discussed (less if it was the news but on *Women's Hour* I could understand more, as it was trying to be more accessible). I ate burritos. Perhaps one day I would be more like Bryony and change careers. Like just change . . . it might be possible?

I had no idea who was in the charts but I was the SAME AGE as Kate Moss and younger than Kylie Minogue. I would always be younger than Kylie. I hadn't seen any photos of her of late. Was she going to move into the Helen Mirren phase next? Or was she stuck in the middle like me? Not yet in the 'it's amazing that she can still speak and walk,' bit.

Despite these positive affirmations – *I am younger than Kylie. I ate a burrito. I am younger than Kylie. I ate a burrito* – I felt confused. This head detaching thing was perplexing. If I'd been Mum I would have Googled 'brain cancer' or some such but I wasn't a hypochondriac. Despite being self-obsessed (though, arguably, no more than your average modern woman), I didn't go to the doctor until I needed stitches or a limb fell off. I avoided them at all costs.

I heard a shriek coming from upstairs. Bella ran down, her face flushed and rubbing her eyes. She was excited to see me. She wrapped her arms around my head and squeezed hard. Another moment noted. It was enough right? We sat on the small, stained sofa in the kitchen (*I must replace it at some point),* and she told me about her day (drawings, fights, cake for one child and not for her because she'd called another child 'a bum hole'). Pete and I nodded at one another, and he went to fetch his iPad. I put Bella to bed (we chatted a bit first about unicorns and whether they were real and she told me how much she hated her the nursery grown-ups again). Then once she was asleep I sat stroking her hair, and when I came back down, Pete was still glaring at the screen. Technology wasn't good for couples who were looking for excuses not to talk to one another.

'How was work today?' I asked.

'Fine,' he replied.

'Anything interesting happen?'

'No.'

'How was my day then?'

'How was your day?' he said looking up for a milli-second.

'One of my colleagues didn't even know who Thurston Moore was.'

'Well they're much younger than you so it's hardly surprising.'

'Well thanks, I know that already.'

Suddenly I felt angry. There'd been a time when I'd have vented about Phoebe but there was no point. His advice was always the same – *'why don't you just tell her to fuck off?'* Pete had a low tolerance for office politics because he'd never worked in one. It was also boring. I knew it was boring. I was goddamn bored by it all too.

'*There's a new drama with Suranne Jones starting tonight,*' he said finally putting his iPad down on the floor. I sighed. We were back on familiar territory. We either talked about TV or food (but this seemed to be true of the population at large). Later on we watched a drama about a couple going through a marital crisis, and the female protagonist murders her husband by poisoning him a tiny bit each day. I secretly felt envious that they still had the will to even bother – I didn't think Pete and I could be bothered to murder one another unfortunately.

I hadn't said anything to Pete about my weird head-ache/dizziness. If I had said something then it might have gone something like this:

Me: I feel like my head is coming off sometimes and then it floats off somewhere and comes back again.

Pete: You need to get more sleep perhaps?

Me: No I think it might be something else. Maybe a panic attack?

Pete: What have you got to panic about?

Me: What are you looking at now (gesturing to iPad)?

Pete: Why do you bug me about what I'm looking at ALL THE TIME? I never ask you what you're doing on your phone and you're on it constantly.

Argument moves onto my phone addiction, Pete's need to chill out with his iPad after a long day, how I justify being on my phone and say it's 'work' but how it isn't because he knows I'm looking on ASOS at dungarees.

This was the problem. We were locked into a pattern. One said *this* and the other *that*. We were two store mannequins frozen into specific poses, unable to break out. There were rarely any surprises. It had been a long time since anything unexpected had happened. We were parents, we were tired.

I thought back to the miscarriages I'd had after Bella. Each one had been relatively early (before twelve weeks) but they'd taken their toll. We'd also had to do a lot of baby-making sex. I'd used ovulation tests and special lube that promised to 'nurture and support sperm on their special journey'. After the first miscarriage, I'd been eager to try again, almost as if getting pregnant would erase what had happened. When it happened a second time I felt a distance grow between us (apparently I was miscarrying because my eggs weren't top notch – the doctor said miscarriages were much more prevalent in women my age). Pete continued to be supportive, we entered a third phase of trying.

It felt like it was something we were toiling through together, like a fairground ride that we'd paid for but hated (but it was too late to get off).

'Can we just stop now?' he'd said as I told him it was a super fertile time again and I wanted us to have a quick bunk up upstairs.

'I want to give it one more try,' I said.

'But Rebecca, it's so depressing, look what it's doing to our relationship!'

'We're okay. We're okay aren't we?'

He made a face like 'no, we certainly weren't' but to his credit, we had sex that night, then the three nights after that (the more the better in that forty-eight hour window according to my online research). I couldn't seem to let it lie. I was trying to prove a point – I could get something I wanted out of sheer determination. When I miscarried again at ten weeks, it felt as if both of us had shut quite a lot of feelings away. We put the idea to bed (he did this more quickly and I resented how he seemed to be capable of moving on). I also felt like Pete was great in an emergency, could make cups of tea, rush to the shops get supplies, make a hot water bottle, but didn't know what to do when life rolled along without having to visit the 'Early Pregnancy Unit' for scans. Or have your partner bleeding in the middle of the night and call an ambulance, and the neighbours coming outside to watch her screaming as she was wheeled into the back.

Was that how it was in relationships? Did you just hunker down and *endure*?

We were both fascinated with our screens. Screens were so much easier to interact with. I wanted to scroll across Pete's face and see a different expression. I wanted to type *'interesting conversation that is not TV related,'* onto his forehead. He probably wanted to type *'find girl that doesn't complain about work and not having a second child'*.

By the time I'd brushed my teeth, and rubbed expensive cream into my face, Pete was asleep; his mouth making a strange flapping noise like a fish out of water. I'd read that many couples liked to have separate bedrooms nowadays – it was a nice thought but it worried me that I thought it was a nice thought. At least when we were in bed together our bodies touched now and then (even if was usually an accident and we moved away again as soon as it happened). Separate rooms also amplified the idea that you didn't want to be around the other person. You could argue that it kept the mystery alive or some such but the reality was that they just got on your nerves too badly.

Something was bubbling away inside of me – something not right. Tomorrow I would schedule a visit to my parents. I would start the day positively and not tell myself negative things as soon as I woke up.

Tomorrow would be more good moments, more moments of happiness than bad, sad, anxious, worrying moments.

I put my headphones on and listened to a positive thinking visualization. I tried to hide my phone under the covers so it wouldn't wake Pete up. He grunted at me to put it away, and I hunkered down under the duvet.

Just me and my little phone friend. Being mindful and positive together.

I am excited about my new future.

I am excited to embrace my new life.

I am going to be more positive.

I am open to new and different things.

Four

THE THING ABOUT BEING 'in your forties' is that you feel like you haven't much to look forward to. For a start, appearance-wise things go to hell in a hand-bucket. I was pretty much invisible to the opposite sex now. A couple of younger female colleagues had told me that it was rare to get chatted up these days so maybe it was society that was changing.

But there were simple truths that you couldn't escape.

- I could never be an 'enfant terrible'.

- I would never own my own swimming pool

- I wouldn't be able to get beads plaited into my hair on holiday, without looking like one of those old

Anniki Sommerville

women that gets beads plaited into their hair on holiday.

- I would always be referred to as 'good for my age.'

- If I got a tattoo, it would be seen as symptomatic of a mid-life crisis.

- A hangover lasted a week

Age wasn't just a number. We all wanted to be pumped up, youthful, dewy, glowing, energetic, sexy and dynamic. It was exhausting. My body wanted to age. My face wanted to be left alone to slide and sag. I sometimes thought ageing was easier when we just threw on a moth-eaten cardigan, collected stray cats and collected coupons from the back of *Woman's Own*.

Okay maybe I *was* still attractive. Two months ago I'd been eyed up by a man in his sixties on the tube but this kind of event didn't make me feel better. Old men were not ideal. I made a list in my head of exciting, dynamic and sexy older women who still got plenty of male attention.

There was Jennifer Aniston.

Kate Winslet.

Rachel Weisz.

These were all Hollywood actresses who were a different breed to ordinary middle-aged folk. I tried to imagine what it would be like to not feel quite so invisible, to still be able to arouse interest from the opposite sex, to actually make young men look at you with fresh eyes; for them to want to have rampant sex with you.

I concocted a fantasy letter in my mind to these ageless beauties.

Dear Jen, Kate and Rachel,
I love the way you're so sassy and look like you're in your twenties despite being well into your forties. I imagine you have good cosmetic surgeons and possibly have facials once a week and do yoga and HIIT training every morning. You may also be wearing heavy-duty support underwear but that's cool. I just wish you could be more honest about how you look the way you do and cut the rest of us some slack.

I want men to get erections as I walk past in my red swimsuit. I want them to cross their legs as I walk past because their penises hurt. I want Bradley Cooper to be hopelessly in love with me. I want to water-ski, and not have people laugh as I fall off and plunge underwater. I want to be a ballet dancer. I want to play the drums like Dave Grohl. I want to have a hit comedy series. I want people to laugh at the prospect of my comedy series before they've even seen it.

I want to feel there is MORE coming my way rather than less.

Love Rebecca x

I dropped Bella at nursery. My chin felt painful, and I realized I'd been too eager that morning in plucking out my chin hairs, and now had a bad rash. Bella cried and clutched at my legs like she was a baby seal about to be clubbed. Both the nursery assistants ignored me, and I ended up walking like a zombie from side to side trying to shake her off.

'Is there some way to turn off all the texts I keep getting each day?' I asked one of them (the slightly less grumpy one).

'Don't you want to know how she's doing each day?'

'Yes but is there an option to shut it off if my day is particularly busy? It's quite stress-inducing sometimes.'

They glared at me. This was the wrong thing to say. I was a bad parent.

'You can choose to ignore the texts I suppose,' one said.

'No of course, forget it. I love the updates,' I said.

I gave Bella a final squeeze and ran for my train.

As I left the building, Bella's cries were still reverberating in my ears. The tug inside, the desire to turn back and get her was too strong. It was wrong to leave your kid with a bunch of strangers each day but work demanded it. I tried calling Mum, but she didn't answer – she was probably at one of her classes. I needed some distraction and I also wanted to find out if Dad had improved any. I looked up at the trees and tried to remember the positive visualization from the night before.

Little moments of happiness. This was something to hold onto. Tiny fragments. This would stop my head leaving my body entirely.

I can imagine the life I want.

The office felt upbeat and people were chatting. There had just been a breakfast presentation by Darren on 'How Meat Substitute Represents a Massive Opportunity in The Fast Food Sector.' He was on a real high and was walking around clapping people on the back like he'd just won the lottery. His eyes looked haunted though, as if he'd put in another late night and had perhaps even slept in the office (there was a futon in one room and it was no secret that when the workload was heavy, you could sleep there for the night). I was happy to have missed this presentation, but also nervous that Darren would report back to Phoebe on my lack of initiative. Ever since the appraisal they'd kept me on the back foot.

Simon sat next to me and smiled. I asked him for some more ideas – *innovative, new, fresh ideas* for my fish finger proposal, and he talked to me about packaging, and how we should try and decode the packaging, and then look at the semiotic and cultural significance of fish in the wider world, and cod, how the notion of scarcity played out in society in general, and how this impacted on our perceptions of meat. I asked if he could type it all into my proposal (as I didn't understand what he was talking about and had tuned out for most of the chat). He agreed.

There was something sweet about this chap, and I wondered again why he was bothering with an old fruit like me, but he seemed to think I was eccentric – perhaps he liked that kind of thing. Perhaps I was his 'Helen Mirren.' Besides, Mango-Lab was just a temporary holding pattern in his career until he spotted something more interesting. He had a myriad of options because he was young and healthy and full of beans. He was a shark, and I was a giant fish finger with my head stuck in a plastic bag.

'*Would you like to go out for a drink?*' he asked. '*A few of us are going to the pub later and I thought maybe you'd like to come along.*'

'*Hey?*' I said.

I was surprised. I couldn't remember ever being asked to the 'yoof' drinks. I wasn't in that demographic anymore. Besides on the rare occasion I was asked I usually turned it down. I needed to get back to Bella and see her for that precious hour for bed (which was usually the most fractious, stressful hour of her day, so not pleasant at all).

'*The pub is super nice and they serve this street food from Korea which is delicious so we could grab some of that perhaps?*'

Korean street food? Drinks? I hadn't been for a works drink for months – in fact the last time had been Christmas and now it was almost May. Yes, I usually raced out the door at five thirty (or a bit earlier if the coast looked clear). Then again, maybe this was *exactly* what I needed. Part of the reason I was no doubt failing at work, and not being strategic enough was because I didn't hang out with these young people. I was feeling stuck in a routine – work, home, bed, work, home, bed and this would shake things up. I agreed I'd go along for a couple of drinks. I texted Pete. He said he was fine with it.

As I've already said, going out was extremely rare.

I spent the afternoon listening to a Spotify playlist of my favourite nineties hip-hop, and amending my fish finger proposal. *I'm gonna take this itty bitty world by storm. And I'm just getting warm.* I could feel the benefit of collaborating with Simon – he'd given me some fresh insights, and I was proposing a whole new digital platform whereby fish finger loyalists could upload footage of themselves and their families, and we could regularly check in and ask them questions. The head detaching from my body thing had passed and I felt better again. *Things could be much worse* (this would be the inscription on my grave one day).

I did a conference call to discuss the *sleep enhancing bum wipe* proposition and that seemed to go well, apart from the fact that I spent the last twenty minutes talking to myself, as both the brand manager and research and development team had been cut off. I sent them a short email saying sorry, and then marched across the office, feeling like I was in my very own shampoo/sanitary towel/probiotic yoghurt commercial.

Who said that women couldn't HAVE IT ALL? I was successful, had young colleagues who were interested in my point of view and I was 'nailing it'. Then I looked across the office and Phoebe was staring at me – it was hard to read her expression. She was either thinking about something or she was plotting to kill me and dispose of my body.

Sorry missed your call, Mum had texted when I got back to my chair. *Dad tried dry shampoo and smells better xx*

Well that was a relief at least. Later in the office toilets, I applied concealer under my eyes, and along the two lines that ran from my nose down the corners of my mouth. I would need to book an appointment for some sort of facial 'lift' soon. I sprayed some dry shampoo on my parting (which only amplified the grey fuzz), put a spritz of perfume on and brushed my hair.

I thought about Bryony and her jaunty top knot – it was a style that many of the younger mums wore. I tried to copy it but instead it made me look like Mrs Trunchbull out of *Matilda*, the Roald Dahl novel. I let my hair fall around my shoulders. Was I too old to have long hair? What was the cut-off point? Fifty? I was wearing a sweatshirt with a jaunty French phrase on it – *'C'est la vie'* – and I felt like I looked as cool as is possible. I would eat Korean buns with the best of them. I had all my teeth. I went back to my desk and checked my phone again.

I hadn't received any messages from nursery which was odd and I worried that perhaps they'd stop texting me entirely. I quickly logged into the portal.

Bella ate asparagus for lunch and did a painting of a sunset. There was a photo of her holding said asparagus aloft and looking chuffed. I was sad that I'd missed this first. When she grew up she'd always say – *I remember the first time I tried asparagus and my mum wasn't there because she thought that frozen fish fingers were more important than anything else.*

Perhaps I needed to go home and be there for bedtime.

Then I noticed the baby wipe client had sent a grumpy email about having missed the end of the presentation.

'*We missed the final recommendations because we were*

cut off the call. Was this done on purpose? We also failed to receive the full deck – did you send it?'

I sent an apologetic one back again and re-sent the deck (which I'd already sent the first time). I then worried that perhaps the recommendations weren't very good. I'd rushed them. In fact I couldn't really remember them at all. Each time I sent anything to anyone I had a moment of self-doubt. Then when I was in the loo, trying to tie my hair up so it resembled a *sort-of-different Bryony style*, Phoebe came in. She looked seriously pissed off.

'Rebecca, I've just been on the phone to your client. They wanted to speak to me because they were cut off before they heard your summing up. They also said your argument was all over the place and they had no clear direction on where to take the product.'

'But I just emailed them and they seemed fine.'

'When was that?'

She looked at me as if I'd just crawled out of the plug hole. Her hair was always unnaturally tidy. She probably used hair mousse. Did they still sell hair mousse?

'Just now. Honestly they seemed happy just now.'

'Well good but listen I've had to talk to you before about not being STRATEGIC enough. I hate to sound like a broken record, but you need to step up or we're going to end up having another awkward conversation.'

'Did you even look at the presentation?' I asked.

'Who do you think I am? A lounge lizard? A bon viveur? I've got SHIT LOADS to do and don't expect to have to check up on a senior colleague to see if she's doing her job or not.'

She went into a cubicle and slammed the door behind her. My mood took a nosedive. It was like being back at school with the mean girls who stole your bus pass, emptied your bag into the bin and tried to flush your face down the toilet.

'Have you sent that fish finger proposal to the client?' she called from the toilet.

I thought about her climbing Kilimanjaro. Giving birth and then doing a debrief. There was no point even trying to compete. She was the gladiator and I was the slave cowering beneath her waiting to have my head chopped off. She started singing in the toilet. It sounded like M People.

She was psychotic.

I imagined kicking her up the bum and how she'd cry. Then I considered my favourite rapper – LL Cool J – what would he do? Well, he would breathe. He would channel his negative feelings. He would make a bestselling album, and blow her one week maternity leave out of the water. I thought about different ways I could hurt her. I could tie her up and saw her legs off. I could get so much cosmetic surgery that I looked fifteen years younger than her. I imagined a scenario where I emerged from the toilet, dragging her by her hair. I knew this kind of repressed anger was unhealthy, but what choice did I have?

There was very little I could do for now.

Screw affirmations. It was time to sample the alternative and get drunk.

I got another text from nursery.

Bella said she was very tired today because she'd had a late night. Please log into the portal for more instructions on recommended sleep times for four year olds.

The Korean pub was noisy and there was no one in there older than thirty-five. I wished I hadn't agreed to come along. Perhaps I'd have one drink and I'd go home. I had put a lot of effort in these past few days, and that was the most depressing aspect of it all. I was working hard to take on board the feedback I was getting and failing nonetheless. Simon pretty much ignored me once we'd sat down with our overpriced bottled beers, and then they bought over these bun things, and they tasted revolting and I wished I was at home eating shepherd's pie on the sofa with Pete. Why did people want to eat something that tasted like cat food in a brioche?

'*I think I might go,*' I said standing up.

'*Don't go,*' Simon said, tugging me arm. '*Tell me about Sonic Youth again. Tell me about the bands you used to like.*'

'*Oh, I LOVE 90S RETRO,*' one girl exclaimed in a whiney voice. '*I love Whigfield and that song "Saturday Night,"*'

'*That was bad,*' I said. '*It was bad then and it's bad now.*'

'*I know but BAD is good, isn't it? God these tuna fish buns are scrummy. Simon, have you been to the new street food place outside Kings Cross? They're doing seaweed kimchi. It's lush.*'

I missed Bella and was worried that she was going to grow up to be a moron like this bun-eating upstart. I remembered that she'd been to bed late the previous night and hoped Pete had turned her in early tonight. I finished my beer, got up and ordered a gin and tonic, didn't bother offering anyone else a drink, and sat down. I was still thinking about Phoebe and her ominous warning.

'*I once went backstage and met Kim Deal from the Pixies,*' I said.

'*Who?*' Simon said.

'*KIM DEAL! You can't tell me you haven't heard of KIM DEAL.*'

'*Is she the one who died and was married to Michael Hutchence. The one on "The Big Breakfast"?*'

The girl sniggered. I was aware that I sounded really, really old. I was trying to impress them by using cultural reference points that were way out of date. Why didn't I try and stay abreast of new things? Why was I so resistant? Was this a symptom of getting old? I got up, drained my glass and walked towards the door. I was just slipping out and Simon came up and put his hand on my shoulder.

'*I want to help you,*' he said.

'*What?*' I leant in.

'*I can see that you're sad. I can see it because I feel the same way.*'

'*Was he making a pass at me?*'

'*I'm not sad,*' I said. '*I have a lovely family and a great job,*' but even as I said it I could feel a lump in my throat.

Perhaps this was what the head detaching thing was about. My real feelings were finally showing themselves after years of smiling in meetings, being ignored, and trying to be kind. I shook my head and tried to leave. Simon was a weirdo. And besides, didn't everyone know it was Paula Yates who'd married Michael Hutchence? As I walked off I heard a panting noise and was surprised to see he was following me.

'*Come back, come on. I promise it'll be fun,*' he looped his arm through mine. '*It's cool to have someone like you to talk to. Forget what I said about Kim Deal – please.*'

What did he mean 'someone like me?' An elderly person? A mum? Someone who actually knew who the Pixies were and could name at least three of their albums?

I headed back. I felt like I needed to give the evening a chance. Besides I needed to escape my own brain for a few hours. Pete would be okay. I never went out. There was no reason to feel guilty. And I was glad I did because during the next couple of hours things improved. My colleagues were actually remarkably well informed, even if they knew little about Michael Hutchence. Politics wise, they were far more know-ledgeable and better read than I'd ever been at their age (or even now, as I tended to get distracted by the celebrity news in the *Daily Mail* rather than read proper newspapers). We ordered three more rounds of drinks. One of the girls (blonde, pretty, not the one who liked Whigfield) suggested we go to a club, and I knew that was NOT a good idea as I'd miss my last train home, but there was a little voice inside saying *DO SOMETHING DANGEROUS.*

'*It's funny,*' I shouted in the Uber on the way to East London, somewhere I hadn't been in months, maybe years. '*I thought young people were boring because all you talked about was food but you're much brighter than I was at your age.*'

'*Thanks,*' said Simon. 'But *NEWSFLASH we aren't one homogenous group. We're actually individuals.*'

93

'*YOU ARE,*' I tapped his forehead cheerily, feeling emboldened. '*YOU ARE INDIVIDUALS! WELL DONE INDIVDUALS!*'

Young people were cool. I was one of them. Cool!

Back in my youth, I could count the times I'd really danced, like properly danced on one hand. I'd always struggled with being too self-conscious. I'd needed to drink a lot (or take substances) to shake off the feeling that I looked silly, and this meant that by the time I was feeling sufficiently confident to get on the dance-floor, my limbs would no longer cooperate. I felt a wave of people pushing me onto the dancefloor. This made things easier, because it meant I could be held upright by the crowd around me. It also meant that no one could see me dancing. I was no longer a middle-aged market research has-been. I was an INDIVDUAL being supported by the crowd, my tribe, my posse. I was hitting targets. Projects and clients were zooming all around me. I was flying First Class, drinking fine wine, then doing Pilates at 5 a.m. and getting fillers in my face and having a baby with my personal trainer.

I was like a young Helen Mirren but much better. I was more *dynamic*.

I was a Hollywood actress in my peak.

After an hour (or more perhaps) of dancing, I started thinking about going home and tried to calculate how much an Uber would cost, then whether Pete would be angry because it was now 2 a.m., and then whether the Korean bun was making me feel sick or whether it was just the thought of cat food in a brioche that was doing it. But it was all okay because I was out and I was having fun with a capital F. Simon wrapped his arms around my neck, and we jumped up and down. I looked into his face but everything was getting blurry. Was this my son? My son from a relationship many, many years ago? What was I doing dancing in EAST LONDON with my son? He leant in as if he was about to kiss me and that was the point that I felt the bun coming up, along with a pint of gin, and some pork scratchings I'd bought right at the beginning of the evening that weren't actually pork but roasted chicken balls or something. I pushed him away, and raced towards the toilets. The mouthful went back down and I turned to see Simon lurching towards me.

'Stop following me, will you?' I half gurgled, half whispered. *'Look if you want to snog me then do it now. Do it whilst I'm incapacitated and won't feel guilty about it tomorrow.'*

'SNOG YOU?' he said, confusion all over his face.

I was out for ONE NIGHT. I was in the East End which was practically another country. I was Alice Cooper with a snake wrapped around my neck. I was

Miles Davis tooting away like I owned the place. I was a guitar string vibrating into infinity, and soon it would all be over and I'd be the mum with the job she didn't like. I lunged towards him and planted my mouth on his. Luckily for him I was no longer nauseous but Simon's tongue felt weird, and not very sexy. Perhaps this was how it was now because all the kids used dating apps but never actually snogged anymore. They needed more practice. I could help them get more practice.

'*Get off,*' he said pushing me away.

And as he pushed, I stumbled backwards, and it was as if the crowd had opened because I kept falling until I landed on my back. All I could think about was how these kids talked about bloody artichokes and matcha lattes, and yet underneath it all, they were violent. I'd bumped my head but luckily there was no blood. I struggled to get up and people were staring, but not for long as nobody wants to see an old lady wiping spit on the back of her arm. It's not pleasant. I searched for the exit. I had a feeling Simon would never follow me again. I got into an Uber eventually and ended up paying eighty quid for the ride home.

I tried in the car to log into the nursery portal. I couldn't remember the password and couldn't face contacting them again to get a new one, then I remembered the asparagus. My daughter had eaten asparagus!

What a gem. I would hug her when I got in. I'd missed her so much. I spent the rest of the time looking at photos of her on my phone. She was really so beautiful. I realized I'd do anything for her. Why didn't I just feel happy that I finally had her? Why not? When I got in, I didn't bother drinking water or taking pain-killers. I took my shoes off, got undressed and fell face down into the bed. Pete was luckily deep in sleep. The cat was sitting on a pile of washing at the foot of the bed. I didn't even check to see if Bella was okay. The back of my head had a bump on it. The last thing I thought before I fell asleep was *that will be sore in the morning*.

When I opened my eyes, there was a moment when I thought it might be another day in the office. In fact, it was 'A Mummy Day' which meant I had no childcare and would have to get through the day and be a semi-competent parent. I patted the back of my head. It was definitely sore. I thought about the lunge. I thought about how appalled Simon had been. I was a horrible old letch like one of those film moguls. My heart thumped in my temples, and when I stood up my veins seemed to be pumping with toxicity. I peered at my phone. No messages. Just another email from Phoebe saying that she'd forgotten I wasn't in the office today, and so we'd have to catch up tomorrow. Hoorah.

'*Don't you want to know what I got up to last night?*' I asked as Pete got ready for work.

'*Can you get some potatoes?*' he asked. '*We've run out and I want to do mash tonight.*'

He pulled his jeans on, grabbed a T-shirt from the cupboard and said nothing.

'*Aren't you curious how my night went? Why I was out till three?*'

'*Not especially,*' he replied. '*You smelt completely toxic when you got in.*'

An image sprang into my mind of the two of us sitting in an old pub just off Portobello Road. We'd been going out six months and our favourite activity was talking rubbish and drinking as much beer as possible. Sometimes we'd row a bit at the end (because we'd had nothing to eat but a packet of dry roasted nuts) but then we'd usually snog before we fell asleep. We'd be too drunk to have sex, but then the following morning, we'd always do it.

Hungover sex was always the best – it was literally the only proper cure for a hangover (as long as you weren't so hungover that your head was splitting in two). Why did this stuff never happen these days? Would we be able to get it back if we arranged a babysitter and then spent an entire afternoon drinking?

(Our old haunt had probably been revamped and wouldn't be the same anymore).

'I thought we could have cod in pancetta with mash. But like I said I need potatoes.'

'I need potatoes,' I said.

'Be serious.'

'I went EAST and it took ages to get back,' I said. *'I had a terrible time. Never again.'*

I pulled him on top of me but he wriggled off again.

'East London is cool though,' I said. *'We should try and go there one day. It isn't anything like how I remembered it.'*

'God your breath stinks! Were you smoking too?'

'Maybe a bit.'

Moments of happiness. Small upturns.

I was still pissed obviously.

I wanted to tell him about how I'd bumped my head but worried that this would just make him more grumpy. I was aware that this wasn't appropriate behaviour for a forty-something market researcher. Perhaps this was why I was doing it. No it definitely was. He went downstairs. I wanted him to interrogate me, to fling my handbag up in the air and then rummage through the contents. I wanted him to be jealous. Like Ray Winstone. Not abusive but horribly jealous. Maybe to ravish me. Not to force me but to be forceful. To be suspicious. I wanted him to grab my phone and look through it for evidence. I wanted him to hold me down. Instead he went out, came back in and then picked a fresh pair of socks out of the drawer.

'Can you put a wash on? This is my last pair of clean ones.'

'Why didn't you answer?' I asked. *'Thankfully I'm fine,'* I said. *'Just in case you were worried?'*

But he'd already left the room.

'I had sex with two different people last night,' I muttered. *'I'm joining a cult and will be gone by the time you return.'*

No answer. He'd gone downstairs to make coffee. I emptied the washing basket from under the bathroom sink, then went in to check on Bella. She was just waking up. It would be a very long day.

'Mummy is a MONSTER!' she shouted as a greeting.

'Mummy is very tired and needs to do some washing,' I said.

'Mummy is a tired MONSTER,' she giggled.

I picked her up and cuddled her. Could I convince her to stay in bed all day? Could we play a game where we both slept and then watched TV and then slept all day?

Motherwhelmed

I wanted more conversation from Pete. I wanted more passion. I wanted to be a good parent. I wanted to be like Phoebe but not such an asshole. I wanted to be in the know like the younger people at work. I wanted to be more progressive and less grumpy, less stuck.

I wanted *everything*.

Five

I'D FORGOTTEN THAT TODAY was my coffee with Bryony. I walked into the café and spotted her immediately. She was in the corner, breastfeeding. She was wearing a pair of dungarees and a Breton top. She had one headphone in her ear and was writing in a notebook.

'*Rough night?*' she asked as I sat down, immediately getting out Bella's colouring book and pens in the vain hope that she'd be quiet for a few minutes so we could have a conversation. It had been a very noisy, busy morning. I felt like it was time for lunch but it was only 10 a.m.

'*Ralph didn't sleep at all,*' she continued without waiting for my answer. '*When do they actually sleep?*'

'*Well Bella started sleeping at around three years old,*' I said. *'I hate to depress you but she was up two or three times a night until then. I just got better at dealing with it.'*

I thought about Darren and how he'd use that additional time to his advantage – how he would watch TED Talks and read strategy books (and never watch reality TV or boxsets like I had). All I was capable of doing during those sleepless nights was staring at my phone or the TV.

'Oh God. I don't think I'll survive that long.'

'You're young! You're fresh. Imagine what it was like for an old bird like me.'

Bryony laughed.

'You're hardly old, are you?'

'I'm in my forties, let's put it that way.'

'Oh I'd thought you were younger than that,' she said.

'With this face?' I said making a circular gesture, taking in the lines, the pale, sickly skin.

'Mummy I want your phone.'

'No phone darling. You've got colouring to do.'

'Phone then colouring.'

'No colouring then phone.'

'Do you let her have your phone?' Bryony asked.

'Yes but I save it so I get maximum benefit. I do it as a last resort when she starts to go mad.'

I went and got a coffee. When I came back Bryony looked close to tears.

'*Do you think you can just hold him for a minute whilst I go to the loo?*'

'*Are you okay?*' I asked. '*Of course I can, hand him over.*'

She nodded and passed him to me. Feeling a newborn in my arms brought back all the memories of Bella's babyhood. I loved the warm and heavy feeling. The sounds they made. I wished I'd enjoyed it more (but had been too tired and anxious to appreciate the good things). It was a shame that early motherhood was so disorientating that you often failed to notice the positive stuff too. Bryony was gone for some time. When she came back her eyes were red. I remembered with Bella that I'd sometimes sat on the toilet for ten minutes just to feel a sense of peace and separation.

'*I don't ever get a moment to myself and then when I have ONE MOMENT I don't know what to do. Sometimes I just lie on the floor for ten minutes and stare at the ceiling. The house is a mess. I need to apply for photography courses but I can't seem to get my act together. There's no food in the fridge. I'm not sure what I'm doing. I'm not even sure if he's gaining weight. Does he look normal to you?*'

'*He looks really good,*' I said. '*He's like eight weeks now right? Well he's robust and he's definitely feeding. Bella never really took to breastfeeding and I had to start formula quite quickly but I can see you're making a real go of it.'*

'Do you think so?'

'I do.'

She smiled as I passed him back. It felt good to make someone else feel better for a moment, to step outside my own world, and the same incessant, whirring thoughts.

It was like logging into someone else's' portal and getting their perspective. I obviously needed to do it more often.

We talked about my job and how much I hated it. How hungover I was. Bryony laughed when I told her about falling over in the club. We talked about how her advertising job had been really sexist, and all the senior directors were men and the senior women were mad, mean or a combination of the two.

'I'm not sure what I'm going to do when Ralph is bigger,' she said. *'I want to try photographing families. I feel like I have this creative thing inside but have always been forced to watch other people being creative. I want to find something fulfilling, something meaningful.'*

'I don't know if that's possible. I mean jobs are jobs right?'

'You can't think like that anymore Rebecca. The world has changed. We want more from life right?'

'I've been in the same job for too long now.'

'It's never too late to change, right?'

'I guess but I never thought of anything better to do. And it pays well. And I can do it fairly easily.'

I was aware that these weren't good reasons to stay in the same place. Why had I stayed? Why had the time gone so fast? I had been consumed with having a child and that had sucked up a lot of time. I'd spent maybe ten years thinking market research was the thing I was good at (when I clearly wasn't or at least I was good but NOT GREAT). I felt sad that I'd wasted so much time. So much! What could I do instead? What? Bella was now happily playing on the CBeebies app on my phone. Ralph was back in the buggy and fast asleep. My hangover was starting to wear off.

'That's the thing. My generation had lower expectations,' I said eventually. 'We worked hard but didn't expect it to be fun. You lot are different. You want everything to be an elevated experience. You want everything to count and be meaningful.'

'YOU LOT? Who exactly are you referring to?' Bryony said sticking her fork into a slice of chocolate cake she'd been nursing for some time.

'You know millennials, young people.'

She laughed.

'How would YOU feel if I lumped your generation together and called you all GEN X?'

'Well that's what I am. I was born in the seventies. Okay sorry. I guess I am generalizing.'

I could feel myself growing impatient. Why was she disputing the fact that our generation were so different? She was in her twenties. She was young and had her whole life ahead of her. She'd never have to work the hours I'd had to or do all the drudge and the *slog*. She'd probably go back to work or she'd be lucky enough to change direction (she still had time) and yet I was stuck. Now it was rare for people to stay in jobs for longer than a couple of years. I'd been at Mango-Lab practically my entire life!

'I don't think of it that way. You're Rebecca. You're a mum. You live in West London. You hate your job. We may have more in common than you think.'

I didn't answer. She was beautiful in her complete and abject tiredness. She was also right. For the first time in a long time I began to see the way I pictured the world was rigid. I put people into tribes. I categorized. I classed. I judged. It was part of my job, thinking of people as specific *demographics,* but it had also flooded into my whole way of seeing the world. You are good. You are bad. You do this. You do that. It left very little room to connect.

'When you get those spare moments, those moments when Ralph is asleep' I said. *'Try not doing anything. Leave the course applications and domestic stuff. Try and see if you*

can watch TV or just sit and stare at a wall. All that stuff can wait. That's my advice anyway.'

'Thanks. I'll try. It helps having someone to talk to about it. It really does. I feel like I'm going mental some days.'

'I struggled. I was the same. I thought I needed to be DOING STUFF all the time. Rest. And don't believe that bollocks about sleeping when the baby sleeps. It never works. You can't'

I emerged from the café feeling proud of myself. Was I changing? It felt like I was doing something unfamiliar, reaching out to someone instead of dismissing them because they weren't the same as me.

Was it true that there were opportunities out there?

'STUPID OLD WOMAN!'

Unfortunately I'd become so absorbed in my conversation with Bryony that I hadn't noticed that Bella had had about forty minutes on my phone. Forty minutes was too long and it meant that the moment you took the thing away from her she went bonkers. She was shouting at me. She'd never called me OLD WOMAN before but it was interesting that it was happening in public, with people outside the café watching and in full view of the local high street. I tried to back out of the café, dragging Bella by her parka hood. The people staring were chiefly women who had forgotten the misery of mothering small children, and were peeved at having their *latte chit-chat* about watercolours and patchwork and expensive Saga holidays disrupted with abuse. Bella didn't have tantrums often, but when she did, she threw herself into the enterprise with a full commitment. Taking the phone away from her was a dangerous move but the alternative was that we walked down the street with her clutching it – this would bring more judgement from other people (i.e. she's screen-parenting) or she'd drop it on the pavement and I'd have to get my screen replaced again (this had happened before). Bella grabbed my arm and twisted the wrinkled skin on my forearm. She tried to retrieve the phone from my coat pocket. I thought about Ralph and how passive and floppy and gorgeous he was. It was true that new mumhood was relentless but this part was no walk in the park either. I held her at arm's length as she tried to bite me.

'*You are behaving very badly and it is unacceptable,*' I said but my voice was deafened by the traffic driving past.

Mum would have issued me a smack right now but that wasn't in my parenting toolkit as smacking was akin to chopping someones arms off these days. *Yes there'd been that one time but never again.*

'*I want more phone, I want lunch!*' she said.

'*Listen there are lots of things I'd like to do right now. I'd like to have a lie down. I'd like to watch TV. I'd like to drink a cup of tea which is actually boiling hot. But do you hear me complaining?'*

I could feel the pleasure of my conversation with Bryony wearing off to be replaced with guilt instead. I wasn't parenting well today and it was all because I was hungover. The bump on my head wasn't dangerous but it was throbbing and my throat felt dry. I only had limited time with Bella and had to make the most of that time. Instead I'd sat in a café, chatted to another mum and then handed Bella my phone so I could have some peace.

If I logged into the portal today the report would not be good.

Bella did not eat anything healthy and was entertained by a screen all day.

She didn't eat asparagus or do any crafts.

Bella looked up at me and screamed. We were progressing very slowly up the street. Me hunched over, trying to keep her at arm's length so she'd stop biting me but also out of harm's way and the busy road. Sometimes it made sense to stick to your guns and sometimes, on days like this, well it would have just been easier to let her walk holding the phone all the way home. Screw the judgers! I grabbed her arm and pulled her behind me. Bryony was right. We DID have more in common that I'd first thought. Motherhood was the grand equalizer. It took every woman back to zero. It obliterated your ego. It wasn't pretty. We battled down the high street, with me holding Bella by the arm and her feet scraping along the ground. The giant mum-god tutted loudly in my head. NOT GOOD PARENTING. NOT GOOD. There was a big part of me that wished I was dead. My head was throbbing again – I'd found a small scab at the back where I'd fallen. That lunge and the counter-attack kept playing on my mind.

'Hey, everything okay?' a voice piped up.

I just wanted to make it home. At home there was a TV with hours of child-friendly entertainment on it. We would eat a sandwich and watch a film and forget this whole debacle. I looked up to see one of the mums from Bella's nursery. It wasn't a mum that I wanted to spend lots of time with. I didn't know her well and had no idea what her name was, but her kid always had a lump of snot stuck to the end of its nose. Despite this fact she always boasted about how many meaningful activities she did with this kid – gathering sticks in the forest to make dollhouses, pressing leaves into papier-mâché vases, painting stones. I had never engaged with this stuff. I had grown up in the era of TV and still felt it was the best entertainment option available.

'*Someone is VERY overtired,*' she said gesturing at Bella.

Her obedient (snot-faced) toddler stood next to her, staring in bemusement as Bella smacked me over and over on the thigh.

'*You're very tired, aren't you poppet?*' the mum asked Bella cheerily, bending down.

I hated these mums. I liked the fact that Bryony wasn't one of them, or hadn't had time to become one of them perhaps. This woman was telling me, *YOUR child is tired because YOU didn't get her to bed on time and YOU aren't getting her to bed on time because YOU are selfish and YOU are selfish because you haven't noticed that your child is tired in the first place.*

The gormless snothead stared up at me.

'*She is a bit tired,*' I said.

'*Yes, I can see she's tired. What time does she go to bed?*'

Oh no it was the sleep competition coming up now. Who slept the longest? Who had the best sleep routine? Blah blah blah.

'*6 p.m.,*' I lied.

It was nowhere near that time.

'*In fact, sometimes we go to bed at 5 p.m. and she sleeps through till 8 a.m. the following day.*'

'*Ooh well that's nice and early,*' the mum said through gritted teeth, disappointed that I had a clear bed routine in place. '*Maybe she's tired because she's sleeping too much?*'

'*Mmm, can they actually do that?*'

Bella continued to slap me on my legs.

'*I AM THE ONE WHO IS ACTUALLY TIRED,*' I said eventually. '*She's young and has young cells that are constantly regenerating. All of mine are dying as we speak!*'

Her smile quickly faded, and she grabbed her child's hand and walked away.

'*AND BLOW YOUR KID'S NOSE*' I shouted after her. '*BECAUSE I DON'T NEED TO SEE THAT SHIT.*'

She would no doubt tell all the other mums I was having a breakdown, that I was a bad parent, that I was mean and horrible. For now, in the fug of my hangover, I didn't care. These kinds of mums were the pits.

This passive-aggressive mum judgement was exhausting. *Oh, mine is doing ballet, and mine is doing karate, and mine is doing Mandarin, and mine is the lord of the world, and mine is advanced for her age, and mine is reading Harry Potter even though they are only five, and mine is a complete pain in the arse, and is biting me but I don't want you to point that out because I am just about getting through this day and only need to be hugged and loved and made to feel better.*

My phone rang. Bella had ceased with the physical assault and was now doing some low-level crying.

'I know it's your day off,' Phoebe said.

This was NOT really a day off.

'I think the fish finger project is a no go — you made a good effort, and I looked through the docs late last night but I don't think they have the budget . . . anyway we have another lead and it needs immediate work. In fact, the prop needs to go before Friday. I wouldn't ask but know you need this opportunity and besides — it'll be a good learning opportunity.'

'I'm sorry,' I said looking down at Bella and feeling full of remorse, maybe she was getting too much sleep? Or not enough? Or something else that I hadn't dreamt up yet? There was NO WAY I could now go home and sit on my laptop for hours.

'But I can't really do any work today because I've got no childcare in place and it's not going to be possible.'

There I'd been assertive and set clear boundaries.

'I'm a mum too Rebecca,' she said. *'We just need to find some of that precious wriggle time. Did you download that app? The productivity one I told you about a few weeks back?'*

Today (aside from my coffee with Bryony) was essentially all about standing under a shower and being showered in shit. This was my penance for going out, sampling youthful hedonism and all that jazz. I contemplated lying face down on the pavement, so that someone would call an ambulance, and I'd be taken to a clean, hospital bed. I would have to work on this new pitch tomorrow and clear my diary of everything else. I hung up, with Bella still sniffing and looking miserable. Where was this 'wriggle time'? How did people fit everything in? Where was my expensive nanny on speed dial so I could drop my parenting duties with no notice and get my head back to the grindstone?

Once we got home I managed to fix some lunch, and then instead of the TV (the slacker option) I got the Playdoh and some other bits and bobs out on the kitchen table. I played some Joni Mitchell (a singer who always made me feel nostalgic for my own child-hood), and I tried to do some role play but it was tough. I wanted to sleep and now that the pain had subsided, the fear and anxiety had set in. Then for some reason Bella wanted a nap (maybe because I was being a bad parent and she wanted to escape into a lovely unicorn world of colours and lovely things), and she took herself off and lay down on the sofa. She had stopped regular naps a year ago. I felt guilty again. Perhaps we hadn't got the right balance on the sleep front. But no she went to bed at seven and woke at five thirty. It was fine (not for me it wasn't but there you go).

I sat in the kitchen with my notepad and made a list.

Things to feel happy about

Bella – even though I am inconsistent in my parenting

Pete – even though I am a rubbish partner and was out late last night and tried to kiss a colleague

Bryony – she seems nice and someone I could get along with. A new friend!

The cat – even though it keeps shitting in the garden and hiding it near the playhouse where it cooks in the sun and stinks up the place

The fact that I'm not dead and can walk about and haven't lost my hair from stress like that girl at work

My parents are still alive even though Dad is behaving in an unpredictable way again

I tried Dad. He picked up on the second ring.

'Are you okay?'

'Why wouldn't I be?' he said grumpily. 'Your mother's got me using this damn shampoo nonsense and it makes me sneeze. Gives me allergies. It's like I've got fleas or something.'

'You could just wash your hair.'

'I'm not a child Rebecca. I don't need to be told what to do!'

I'd probably distracted him from his train-building work. It was a bad time. Then again why didn't my parents ever ask me HOW I WAS DOING? Would it be all about taking care of them from now on?

'Mum said that you're spending too much time in the shed again.'

'What's wrong with my shed?'

'It's good to try other things too. Like maybe a dance class or something else?'

'Why would I be interested in dancing? I've got sore knees. I can barely get out of my chair without groaning. Wait till you're this age. It's not easy. You won't be dancing put it that way. Stop listening to your mother. She's mad. She's always been mad. She wants to spend every waking hour with other people. She can't be alone for five seconds without saying she's lonely.'

I could now hear loud, mournful classical music playing in the background.

'Anyway,' he continued. 'I've managed to hook up another segment of track so the railway loops around the vegetable garden and over the pond. You'll have to come and check it out when you visit next.'

He wasn't really listening anymore. He was locked into his own little world. Perhaps it was better that way when you got to that age. Why was it so bad being anti-social? I could relate to it. I could relate to the idea that you were seen as being a failure because you weren't enthusiastic and blasting new ideas all over the place.

However it also annoyed me that my parents seemed to forget they had a granddaughter. I had to remind them. Okay, once they remembered, they seemed quite fond of her but they'd never be those grandparents in the park doing fifty per cent of the childcare for free. I wasn't quite sure this was fair but it would have been nice to have the offer, and besides they had enough on their plate and were baby boomers. Baby boomers were selfish, Gen X were worriers, and millennials liked gourmet food. Each generation had their own characteristics, right? At least Dad sounded sane on the phone. It was one less thing to think about.

I scrolled through the TV planner and sipped on my tea. This was a little pocket of 'wriggle time' (Phoebe's favourite term) where I *should* have been reading work emails but I'd recorded four episodes of *The Real Housewives of Beverley Hills*, and this was my only opportunity to catch up. It was no accident that Phoebe had contacted me on my day at home – my non-working day. She always *forgot* which days I was contracted – in fact she went out of her way to get in touch when I was at home.

I texted Mum.

Dad is fine. Leave him alone for a bit. He just needs time. He's not mad social like you are xx

The programme was like pure, escapist, amber liquid pouring over my tired, alcohol-ravaged brain. THIS was why I no longer watched or read the news. Who wanted to feel even worse about their life? Who wanted to know about all the misery when they were ageing, getting chronic back-ache and struggling to have it all? Surely it was better to use media to escape. And wouldn't my life have been better if I'd married a wealthy man?

And how had I managed to get to forty-two and not own my own swimming pool?

'You're not hedge-fund-manager-wife material,' Pete had once said cruelly as I was complaining about the fact that it was always me who had to generate the biggest income. I'd threatened to leave him and find a wealthy fella. The thing was, it was true. I'd never been out with anyone who had money. My waist wasn't small enough. My cheekbones didn't stand out. And, besides, these rich housewives looked exhausted underneath their tight, shiny faces. It was a lot of work to maintain that perfection.

I Googled 'facial injectables,' after the programme had finished, and marvelled at all the before and after shots of women with sagging, sad faces turning into plump, happy, successful types. There was a video of a woman getting an eye-lift treatment which made her look wide-awake and took about ten years off her, at least. Before I could reconsider, I emailed one of the clinics, based in Harley Street. Almost immediately I received a chat message from the clinic and made an appointment.

Perhaps this was the step I needed to reinvigorate my flagging career. My flagging life. I felt inspired by Bryony. Perhaps I'd forgotten that life was about possibilities. This was what I admired about her generation. However, I felt like having a weary, haggard face didn't help me come across as being someone dynamic and in the cut and thrust of marketing. My competition all had faces like babies, all plump and dewy. They also had boundless enthusiasm and didn't think Darren was a total nob (they would, give them time). It was worth finding out about these things. The price might be an issue but when was the last time I'd done something *for me*? Sure I had a big addiction to scented candles and ASOS blouses but proper investments in my confidence?

I was slightly worried as didn't like the stuffed cheek, hamster faces of some of the older women I saw on public transport now. Was it better to look defeated or weird? And if all the other old women did it, then where did it leave you? The only woman on the tube who looked like Alf Garnett? I knew that society had changed and forty was the new thirty *blah blah blah* but there were times when I caught glimpses of myself (especially if my camera phone was pointing upwards) and I just looked like a hag. Simple as. Age wasn't really a number.

We all wanted to be youthful, dewy, glowing, energetic, sexy and dynamic (but not look weird). It was exhausting. I sometimes thought life was easier when we just threw on a moth-eaten cardigan, let our hair go grey and were done.

What else would make me happy then?

If Phoebe died.

Or failed. It was simple really.

I wanted her to fail.

Maybe if my life was more exciting?

But no, I hated noisy clubs and bars.

I hated young people too.

I wasn't really sure how you defined *excitement* at my age

Was it getting to bed early so you could get an extra hour's sleep?

Was it taking up running?

Learning a new skill?

It all sounded so tedious
More sex?
But that was too much hard work – you had to shave your legs, exfoliate, wear nice underwear, try and remember what to do.
I texted Kath.

I kissed a boy at work. And I went for coffee with a young mum friend.

WHAAAATTT?

Well didn't really kiss but tried to. I fell over and bumped my head.

WHAAAATTT? You are HAVING A MID-LIFE CRISIS MATE.

I don't think so. I'm okay. I'm just trying to figure out what to do next.

It's good to hear you're out of your comfort zone. You've been there some time.

Xx

xx

I didn't feel any guilt about the kiss *lunge*. I felt a bit humiliated but the thing was I wasn't attracted to Simon. The kiss had been a road-test to see if I WAS still attractive (turns out maybe no). That night, Pete and I watched a programme about an unhappy couple, and this time the man ended up turning into a zombie and the woman ended up getting eaten alive. We went to bed. I made a mental note that we needed to have sex soon or things would get weird. We'd done it a few nights before but we'd both found it an effort. Sex became more of a chore the longer you were together. You knew you had to do it in order to keep the relationship ticking away but it felt like hard work. It was hard work. In a way it should have been much easier, we knew one another's bodies, we knew what we liked but instead it felt stilted and awkward. It was trying to shift from the parent/friend/team dynamic into something else entirely and then slip back into that comfortable/snoring/frozen prawn thing again.

'*I feel like a piece of meat*,' Pete had said during that whole phase of trying-for-a-baby sex.

'*Look I'm the meat*,' I'd said after we'd done it and I was lying with my hips propped up on a pillow (this apparently helped the sperm swim more effectively to their destination).

'*Can't we ever have sex without having this baby thing hanging over us?*' he'd said pulling his dressing gown on.

'But what would be the point?' I replied.

I was always suspicious of couples who said they did it three times a week. They were probably on drugs. I also hated women who said *'ooh my husband can't keep his hands off me.'* That made me think their bloke was an old, randy octopus, rubbing himself up and down against every available object. There was a breed of monkey called the Bonobo and apparently it had sex all day long with every other monkey in the gang.

'Is your husband a Bonobo then?' I wanted to ask.

There was also an expectation that if you didn't have sex with your husband then it would be within his rights to have an affair. But what if YOU were the one who had the affair? Or what if you just went off sex? (which felt like me right now) Why was this the yard-stick for a functioning relationship anyway?

Sex could be a good moment yes but it felt like such an effort – you needed reminding WHY it was so good. Sometimes I felt like Pete and I had simply forgotten. Also there was so much great TV! And online shopping. There were lots of good books. Then there was the stuff you had to do like work. And parenting. And what about all the dust that needed wiping up? And the crumbs under the table? And the Playdoh squashed into the carpet? And the toilet that didn't flush and hadn't flushed properly for over a month so you had to always poo downstairs?

In the medieval times there'd been no shampoo and everyone had smelt awful with rotten teeth, but there'd been no distractions in the evenings. Sex was probably one of the few things you could do in life that made you forget that you were going to die aged thirty-five from some sort of plague. In a competition sex would always lose against TV because it required so much more energy.

In the future we would become silent, fat beanbags with one long scrolling finger and eyes the size of dinner plates. If we wanted orgasms, we'd plug into an app and a giant hologram of David Beckham, would scroll all over our body and we'd be done in three minutes.

Nevertheless the distance growing between Pete and I was troubling. It didn't feel right. I just had no time or energy to fix it right now (and no idea where to actually start).

That night I had bad dreams. I was trying to keep up with someone who was running away. I wasn't quite sure who this person was but it was maddening. The faster I sprinted, the further they were. The person was time or it was Phoebe or it was my relationship. It was perhaps all three. I had no time to meditate or reflect or set my intentions, because you can't quite do that when a small person climbs into bed and then kicks you in the ribs until you get up, empty your bladder and shuffle downstairs to make tea (then realise it's only 5 a.m. and that's why you're struggling to wake up because IT'S NOT TIME!)

'It's the middle of the night!' I shouted as we stood in the kitchen.

It was still darkish outside.

'Peppa Pig' she demanded.

'You are not watching TV at this time in the morning. GET BACK INTO BED.'

This was not a moment of happiness. This was not at all.

She threw herself onto the floor and started to rotate her legs round in a giant circle so it looked almost as if she was breakdancing, except it was accompanied by a wailing noise that made my hair stand on end.

'GET BACK INTO BED!' I screamed, crouching down so I was right next to her ears as they rotated past me.

She continued wailing and I tramped back up the stairs.

'Thanks arsehole,' I shouted at Pete who couldn't hear me because of the ear plugs (he said it was because I snored but it was really because he made fish noises that kept even himself awake).

I tried to get back into bed but Bella had followed me and was telling me all about a girl at nursery who had a brother who was a penguin, but nobody knew he was a penguin, because he only turned into one at night.

By the time I got into the office, I was feeling like the initial grumpiness of the morning had now been amplified ten-fold. I'd had to stand up for the journey, endure a terrible, tinny din coming from two sets of headphones on either side of me, been pushed and jostled as I got off the train, and then waited too long for a coffee which, by the time I raised it to my lips, was lukewarm. The inner parts of my eyes, the bits that looked like pale apple pips were itching, and I had nothing to look forward to but shame and writing a giant proposal.

Horrible, horrible, horrible, I texted Kath as I sat down in my favourite chair in the office (it had a Post-it note with my name scrawled on it and had been adjusted so it didn't make my old-lady-back ache as much as all the other chairs did).

Same, same, same, she finally texted back.

Nothing has gone right since I got out of bed this morning.

I thought about Bryony and how she'd probably just be trying to get Ralph to have a mid-morning nap. I didn't miss those days but then there was a strange longing to go back there too. I scrolled through Instagram, and everyone was putting playful quips about caffeine on, or how we needed to be more positive about our bodies, or how we needed to embrace imperfect parenting, and not put so much pressure on ourselves. WOMEN OF THE WORLD – I wanted to shout – WE must PUT PRESSURE ON OURSELVES TO SURVIVE! It was hopeless telling women to chill out when there was so much stuff to get done. Who was going to do this stuff? If you wanted money and a career, and a family then you couldn't languish on the bottom of the sea like a flat-fish, just shooting a small tunnel of sand-shit out of your butt. Quips about coffee were okay but how about a solution for women who could no longer muster up enough enthusiasm to go into work each morning? Women who had dads who no longer washed their hair? I took it back about technology. It was all a giant pool of crap.

I looked around. I'd sat down at my desk without saying a word to anyone. I was hooked up to a TED Talk podcast about *'How to feel less isolated in the modern world.'* The millennial robots were all plugged into their headphones and drinking strange green mixes. There was no sign of Simon. Would he ever speak to me? Would Phoebe find out that I'd behaved like a wally?

The pitch brief that she sent off couldn't have been much worse – even if it'd arrived in a sealed envelope with dog poo. It was *new product development for a major sanitary towel brand*. I'd worked on a similar project before, and had been exhausted and drained after listening to grumpy, hormonal women moan for hours about their dreaded curse in extended focus groups that lasted a week. I seemed to remember that the whole experience had made me menstruate for nigh-on ten days. I got my head down and started reading through the background.

'*Hey dude! New brief! Well done. Sanitary towels are such a cool category yes?*' Darren said as he walked past my desk.

He was wearing very tight cycling shorts and I could just make out the outline of his bottom which was tiny and like a seven year old's. He's possibly just finished another client briefing – making it his tenth of the week. Underneath it all I was jealous. I was jealous because he had the sheen that made clients like him. It was all fake but for some that didn't matter. It was a bit like the Botox. As long as you looked engaged and enthusiastic, like you were still in your twenties, all was fine (Darren didn't look like this but his teeth definitely gave him a youthful dynamic). I started making some notes in the margins – mainly just writing the word *periods* over and over again. How long would I have periods for? Were they going to stop soon? When did the menopause start? Did I want to have another baby? Would that be possible? It had been so hard with Bella that I doubted it. I looked up and Simon was standing next to my desk.

'Can I have a word with you in private?' he asked quietly.

A sound came out of my mouth that was like a creaking door, and I nodded. I had no ready-made explanation. I'd been drunk – simple as that. I was going through some sort of crisis. I was ageing and bitter. Were those valid?

'Listen,' I said as we sat down in the canteen which was near enough deserted aside from two depressed looking bald men in black polo shirts with the words – TEAM WORK IS GREAT WORK emblazoned across the front. 'I'm really sorry. I never meant to behave like that. The thing is I don't get out much, and I got carried away . . . I'm also under a lot of pressure. I'm sure you know that Phoebe and Darren want to get rid of me. I'm sorry.'

It felt good to get some of this stuff off my chest. Simon nodded.

'It was awful, but I forgive you, okay?' he said. 'To be honest I was worried about you. You drank an awful lot.'

'I know. I was out of control.'

'But maybe that's a good thing now and then?'

'Thanks dude.'

'And I'm gay – didn't you realise?'

'Really?'

It had never crossed my mind. I wasn't very perceptive

anymore. On bad days, people were just round shapes, with holes in their faces where noises came out.

'I thought everyone knew. I have a boyfriend called Mark and we've been together for eighteen months.'

I had been deluded, in so many ways.

'But you don't act gay,' I said.

'What kind of gay men have you been friends with in the past?' he said. *'I mean that's actually pretty offensive.'*

'I'm sorry but I thought there were more OBVIOUS signs.'

'What – like a hankie hanging out of my back pocket? God Rebecca, you really DO need to get out more. Gay culture is not 'The Village People'. You're actually being pretty homophobic.'

'Sorry. I sometimes open my mouth and this terrible stuff comes out. I think I get it from my mum's side. She's always been horribly tactless.'

'I'll forget you said it. Do you want help with that sanitary towel prop or are you okay with it?'

'I hardly think you're the expert are you?'

'Well if you do, you know where to find me,' he said. *'God the food in here looks awful. What's that over there? Lamb hot dog on a stick?'*

He walked off back to the office. Simon had a point. All my references were from my teenage years. I had nothing *modern* to bring to the table.

He really was just a genuinely nice person. He was

like Bryony. He was just more dynamic than me and had a better ability to move with the changing times. Perhaps I needed to suck some of that energy up. Be less rigid. Less grumpy. More dynamic. Phoebe was right. Perhaps that was what was wrong with me.

Perhaps it wasn't a breakdown.

Six

THAT NIGHT WAS ANOTHER bad night of very little sleep. At three in the morning, I remembered that Mum had once warned me that the older you got, the more troublesome your nights became. Ageing = anxiety. The thoughts rained down on me. I tried to visualize them as birds – I'd read somehow that this was a good thing, to make your thoughts into animals – but these were big, ugly birds that pecked at my nose. The more I tried to wave them off, the more they insisted on sticking around, pecking at my feet, some reaching as far as my knees with their hard little beaks.

My job is awful.

I haven't got any ham in the fridge for sandwiches after swimming.

My fringe is going grey.

I remember that time when I wore jellybean sandals with socks to secondary school and everyone laughed at me.

The time I danced with that boy and fell over and everyone laughed at me.

The time I walked across the office with my skirt tucked into my tights and everyone laughed at me.

Will my relationship survive?

Where has my red tassel earring gone?

Why is my head coming away from my body?

Am I really a bad parent?

Is Dad going to be okay?

I kept on mumbling to myself until Pete started shaking me.

'Becca, you're talking in your sleep,' he said.

I didn't tell him I was awake, that my mind was in crazy-land. It was very strange but we started kissing and then had sex. We were both half asleep which made the experience better in a way. When we were conscious we got too annoyed with one another. It was all too easy to focus on Pete's jellyfish snoring. Afterwards I realized I was full of positive thoughts about Pete. I wasn't feeling so resentful anymore (I was never really able to pinpoint what this resentment was but it was always present). Yes he was a kind, faithful, sexy man. He didn't talk much but that was okay. He'd been nice not to lecture me after my late night out. Perhaps our relationship would be okay.

'*Do you think we should put some time aside to talk?*' I said the next morning whilst he was boiling the kettle.

Bella was making shapes out of Playdoh and had been up since five. I was feeling like it was already lunchtime again.

'*I guess,*' he replied pouring water into his mug. '*I mean that would be a good idea. But also what do we need to talk about?*'

'*US. The fact that we watch TV but rarely have a proper conversation?*' I said.

I could feel my heart rate was increasing and I needed to do some alternate nostril breathing (this was a method to calm yourself down that Kath had told me about. You needed to remember which nostril was which but once you did, it was remarkably calming).

'*What do we need to talk about?*' Pete said picking up the newspaper and sitting down at the kitchen table.

'*Why are you always reading? Why can't you ever actually look me in the face?*'

'*Oh God, don't start this again will you?*'

'*Start what?*'

'*You are always trying to change me. This is ME. I like reading the paper okay?*'

'*I know but I want you to LOOK AT ME.*'

'Well it's rare for you to look at me too you know,' he replied.

This was true. Why didn't I look at him? What was wrong? I felt like after all the time we'd been together I knew what he looked like already. He never changed. He was older, yes, but I knew his face better than I knew my own. Bella was looking back and forth at each of us. I needed more than the alternate nostril breathing and sex once every few weeks. Our relationship wasn't okay. The sleepy sex had been a step in the right direction but were we really going to sleep walk through the rest of our lives like this?

'*WHY WON'T YOU TALK TO ME?*' I shouted and without thinking I picked up a plate and hurled it across the kitchen.

It smashed against the wall and Bella screwed up her face and started bawling. I stormed upstairs and sat on the side of the bed. My heart was beating fast, there was a lump in my throat, my head was fully detached and flying up towards the solar system, whilst my inner voice was ranting inside. Was this the menopause? Why was I SO FURIOUS with Pete? I could hear him talking in a soothing voice to Bella but she was sobbing. What kind of parent was I? Mum and Dad had rowed occasionally but it was always taken upstairs, and they returned when it was all wrapped up. Yes there was the odd resentful snipe here and there, the hangovers of rows I hadn't witnessed yet but not this. The truth was I'd come to the end of my tether. It was like trying to bang a nail into the wall but the plaster came away each time. Eventually you just gave up and used Blu tack instead. I wasn't quite sure what that analogy really meant but I knew I was done with hammering.

Bella came upstairs and sat on my lap. I kissed her head and rocked her back and forth.

'I'm sorry, Mummy isn't angry. I was just being silly.'

'You broke my Paw Patrol plate,' she said, her eyes weepy and red.

'I'll get you another one.'

'Daddy said you have your visitor.'

'No it's not my visitor darling,'

'It's the bloody menopause then!' Pete shouted from downstairs.

'No listen . . . It's nothing serious. Mummy is A MONSTER. Remember some days we get in a really bad mood.'

I scooped her up in my arms and swung her around the room.

'THEN WE TURN INTO A BIG FAT MONSTER!' I screamed.

Bella laughed with relief. I heard the door slam downstairs and felt a pang of guilt. I'd just erased any good vibes that had been created by the sleepy sex. I'd erased it all with one smashed plate.

Happy moments with Pete. I tried to conjure them up in my mind.

The time we'd stayed by the seaside and had fallen asleep in the afternoon sun, then gone back to the hotel and had sex twice in a row and ordered chips and chocolate cake from room service.

A holiday where we'd hired a boat and gone out to an island near Corfu. We'd spent the day snorkelling and listening to an old radio Pete had brought with him.

The day Bella had been born. 'I'll always look after you,' he'd said, his eyes full of tears.

I needed to hold onto these moments.

On my way into work I tried to summon up some positivity. It was all about what kind of day you decided to make it. It could be okay or complete shit. It was all up to you (and luck – you could be ploughed down by a motorcycle courier whilst thinking through your positivity list but that was beyond your control). The journey into work was slightly more interesting as I watched a girl opposite me on the tube apply a full face of make-up. She started with moisturizer, moved onto foundation (applied with a brush?), then blusher, then something that looked like silver eye shadow (was this contouring, something I'd only read about online?) and then mascara, then more blusher and more silver stuff and finally lipstick. All of it done whilst the tube was in motion. All of it done with an audience. These younger women were audacious. They were fearless. It gave me hope for the future.

The office was always busy on a Friday. Simon had sent over his suggestions for the sanitary towel brief (I wasn't really sure why he was being so helpful), and I spent the day inputting his points into PowerPoint slides with lots of stock images of women bungee jumping and meditating.

We would do some digital work, then face-to-face, and finally we'd get some core territories that we could recommend to our German client – a client who was looking to launch a COMPLETELY NEW PRODUCT into the UK market (they always wrote the important bits in CAPITALS to make your heartbeat race and underline the stress factor). The more Phoebe stayed away from me, the more my confidence grew. It was the definition of a bad boss really. She was very good at undermining and spreading insecurity but bad at offering any encouragement. It was as if encouragement was a weakness, something that wusses needed, something to be frowned upon. Then, around eleven o'clock, just as I felt like I was making good progress, Phoebe appeared out of nowhere, with a tan-coloured roll-neck, and red knee-high patent leather boots (she wasn't blessed with good fashion sense but you couldn't have everything, right?). She picked up the paperback on my desk and sneered.

'HOW TO BE YOUR BRAVEST SELF,' she said. *'Do you really read this tripe?'*

'Sometimes. It's actually pretty good,' I replied.

'Success is about turning up,' she said. *'It's about taking risks. It's about being dynamic. It's strategy. It's effort. If it was just about being brave then we'd all be millionaires.'*

'Well, we can't all be you,' I whispered under my breath.

She shook her head, put the book down and looked at my screen. Thankfully I was no longer scrolling through dungarees on the ASOS website (Bryony looked so good in them and I needed to get another pair). I instead had my sanitary towel proposal up on my screen.

'So you've got all the pitch done then?' she barked.

'Just about to press send.'

'And what about the baby wipes? Have you re-written the final debrief for the client?'

'Not yet. It's on my list.'

One of the young female interns looked up and looked away again.

This may happen to you one day, my pretty, glowing, happy one. When you get old. When you lose your dynamic, pretty face and youthful enthusiasm.

'Good,' Phoebe picked up the book again. 'Well *STOP* reading this nonsense. Read Lean In. *Have you read it? It's great.'*

She walked away. Phoebe had recommended this

book to me several times. Like *How to Win Friends and Influence People,* I could tell it wasn't my cup of tea. There were people who related to these kinds of books but they weren't me.

The people that inspired me were Iggy Pop, Kim Deal, Courtney Love, Grace Jones, Kate Bush, or writers like Dave Eggers and Zadie Smith or people who were honest and open like Oprah. None of these people worked in market research. Perhaps this was where I was going wrong. It seemed as if it had taken an inordinate amount of time for me to come to this realisation. *Lean In* is for you Phoebe – yes but I don't like Sheryl Sandberg . . . no, wait, that's not fair, I don't know her but for some reason I associate her with those women who have had empathy lobotomies. I associate her with squeaky shoes, power bobs and checking emails on the beach whilst learning to bodyboard. I associate her with relentless work. My hands were now sweating. Maybe Phoebe had a point – many of these books didn't help and I often forget them before I've even got the end. But there was something reassuring in the notion that life *could change*, that *you* could change, that you wouldn't be muddled forever.

She is trying to get rid of you. She hates you. A little voice started up in my head as I opened the baby wipe document, and started to meticulously go through each slide, looking for ways to tighten my argument and make it less vague. *You took a whole year off to have a baby. Your pelvic floor is floppy. You don't wear blazers because they make you look like a feminist, stand up comedian from the eighties. You cry at the drop of a hat. You will never be a trail blazer. You will never go to lunch with Sheryl Sandberg.*

The concept of a wipe that both pacifies and cleans a baby's bottom is highly positive and we recommend progressing this proposition forward to the next phase of quantitative testing.

I finished up the re-written slides and sent them to the client. I had done all I could.

A text from nursery again.

> *Bella ate mackerel for lunch today and then made a piñata out of leftover newspapers.*

When had she ever eaten mackerel? There was a child who lived with me who begged for my phone and wanted Hula Hoops and then this other child, who ate fish and did crafts every day.

Was I a role model because I spent my time away from her writing up my thoughts on bum wipes? Or did she want a mum who baked cakes and did the washing whilst hand sewing all the name labels in her clothes? Did Phoebe's three children look up to her? When did they see her? She was always at work. I knew that she Facetimed them from her office now and then. I knew she did that when she travelled. Darren too. Darren had a watch with a video link up and he spoke to his kids whilst he cycled and listened to management strategy books on Audible. This was the key to success. Multi-tasking.

I continued finishing up the sanitary towel proposal as my shoulders grew more hunched and uncomfortable and my bum more numb. I had worked for three hours without moving. I'd had to fetch a blanket from one of the receptionists because my teeth were chattering. I hoped they were monitoring my computer, so they could see just how much work I'd done. I'd only spent ten minutes on ASOS today. Every now and then Simon would walk past as if he was checking to see what I was doing. I took a break, remembering to take my pass with me because otherwise they didn't let you out of the building, then mooched about downstairs, bought some soup, ate the soup, and called Kath. Sometimes I needed these little personal interactions to break up the day.

'This morning I've had to make packed lunches for two children who refuse to eat anything but ham,' she complained. 'Chris left for a cycle ride at 4.30 a.m. and will return after bed AND I need to bake cupcakes for a children's party tomorrow.'

'Well not to be competitive but I had a scare with Phoebe and just ate a thimble-full of soup from Pret that cost five quid. On a plus note I did have sex last night. Oh and I've finally finished a proposal for a massive sanitary towel project. It may be the project that saves me.'

'Who would want to launch a massive sanitary towel?'

'Basically if I win this then my job should be out of the firing line.'

'I never knew that towels could be so important. Well, I guess they are if you haven't got one and your period arrives. Your job is odd. I still don't understand it.'

'And I've booked an appointment with one of those clinics – you know the ones where they make you look much younger.'

Kath sighed.

'Are you having me on?'

'I need something to make me feel better.'

'That's ridiculous!' she replied, then paused. 'But let me know how much it costs, right? The wrinkles around my eyes are dreadful. Suddenly we're actually old, right?'

'We are called "mid-life", I think.'

'Sounds shit like mediocre, medium, meh.'

'To top it all I keep getting this feeling like my head is detaching itself from my body.'

'Have you been to the doctors to get any tests done?'

'Why is it a symptom of something terrible?'

'Did you hear about Shelley? She was only forty–one and got a brain tumour.'

'God I hope it's not one of those. I never even thought about it. I just thought it was anxiety.'

'Go and see your GP, get some tests. Now listen, if you're wearing a long, knee length skirt, would you wear thick black tights? And if you did, could you wear white trainers?'

'Why do you ask.'

'Because you're still working in town and know about fashion. In the suburbs nobody knows these things. What do the girls in your office wear when it starts to get cold?'

I went back to the office and had some time to do some admin, so ordered Bella some tights from Boden (nearly forty quid for three pairs), and then looked to see if there were any herbal supplements that would lessen the impact of the menopause. I also Googled 'head detaching itself from body whilst at work,' several times but nothing relevant came up. There were some grisly articles about accidents where people's heads had come off, but nothing in terms of the specific feeling I was getting. I booked a doctor's appointment.

Perhaps if it was bad news, I would leave Mango-Lab and finally do something I liked. What would it be though? I needed to brainstorm with Bryony. Bryony still had that delicious sense of optimism. It was noisy in the afternoon and nobody seemed to be working. Beck was playing through the speakers, and there were a few beers on the trolley that had been put out early by Darren (who'd just won a job for a trainer brand researching new designs in four European markets). He was being even more annoying than usual and kept doing the running man in the middle of the office, then asking whether anyone wanted to 'hit the clubs.' I had learnt my lesson and wasn't going near another nightclub again. The mid-afternoon break was spent discussing the latest French crime TV drama, and I hadn't watched any of it, so I nodded along, trying to look engaged, and then asked whether anyone had watched *Curb Your Enthusiasm* (everyone had, everyone loved it – I sometimes worried that I was becoming the main character – Larry – always bitter, grumpy and cynical so it felt good to laugh at these tendencies). There was a long discussion amongst the team about the toiletries in the ladies' loo, and when we'd get Aesop back in. This was where companies got it wrong. They thought it was all about strategy and collaboration and giving new names to meetings and meeting spaces, when people just wanted really nice soap and a good chat about TV.

For once work felt bearable and I realized it was

because we'd taken our headphones off for the afternoon and talked to one another. Talking to younger colleagues began to convince me that maybe they weren't so dreadful after all. I had made a lot of assumptions without actually bothering to check if these were true.

So another rare moment of happiness. *Talking to people you worked with and realizing you have something in common with them*. Perhaps things weren't so complicated after all.

On the journey home an email pinged and the sanitary project had come in. Things were looking up! The client, Sven, loved the proposal and was *excited to be working with us*. I would have punched the air if I hadn't felt so tired. Life was like this. It was shit and okay, shit and okay – yet I still hadn't got used to it.

I went to call Mum to tell her the good news but then knew that she'd mainly want to talk about Dad and his introvert tendencies again so I hung up. I wanted to try and stay buoyant for a bit longer.

Seven

'*SQUEEZE THIS RUBBER BALL tightly and we'll be done in five minutes,*' the lady said.

I peered up into her face as she hovered over me with the needle. Her skin was incredibly smooth, but I suspected she had very good genes more than anything else. I felt a sting between my eyebrows as she squeezed the skin together, and then pushed the needle in. I thought I heard a tiny, popping noise which was perhaps the rational, feminist side of my brain dissolving, and then there was another three or four stings and it was done. I'd always said that I'd never resort to Botox and yet HERE I was. I felt embarrassed but also triumphant; like a toddler that had done its first poo in the potty. She held a mirror in front of my face and I was relieved, and a little disappointed at the same time. I looked *exactly the same* but now had red lumps around my eyes and forehead.

'It'll take a few days to have an effect,' she said, taking the rubber ball from my hand. 'The muscles don't stop moving right away.'

'Will I be able to smile?'

'Of course,' she laughed. *'This is only a tiny bit. We call it 'baby Botox.' Just a refresh. Like you've had a good sleep and not been working super hard.'*

'Will it swell up?' I asked, thinking of some of the scary images I'd seen on Google.

Women with massive, bloated faces. Or with eyebrows that curved up to their temples. I hadn't really researched this at all. I'd just dived right in.

'No. You'll love it. Nobody will notice.'

'Well, I want people to notice,' I said, climbing down from the reclining chair. What was the point otherwise?

Her clinic office was wallpapered with before and after images of women. This was a factory for erasing disappointment, hard times, bad career choices, and failed relationships. I'd read somewhere that if you smiled then you naturally felt happier, and I hoped this procedure would give me the same result. If I couldn't *feel* happy then I could at least look happy, and then perhaps the rest of my attitude would change and I would start being more successful.

This was how I justified what I was doing anyway.

I rubbed concealer over the red spots and headed into work, texting Kath on the way.

I got Botox.

She didn't reply.

She would either berate me for being stupid (we'd always sworn to steer clear of this sort of thing and grow haggard and saggy together) or she'd ask me where and go and get some herself. As I exited the tube, I got a text back.

You are officially a wanker.

I smiled. This was something I appreciated about Kath – she always blew the wind out of my sails – in a good way. It felt like we were fifteen again and blowing smoke rings out of her bedroom window listening to De La Soul.

The day passed without incident, but I ran into the toilets to check that my face wasn't expanding in some sort of ghoulish manner. I texted Bryony to see if we could meet for another coffee. I'd been thinking back to when we'd last met and how I'd felt more positive in her company. I needed more of that kind of person right now. I raised my eyebrows and frowned and the muscles were still in order. I smiled and those muscles all looked normal, too. I started to think that perhaps it hadn't worked at all. Perhaps the grumpy vibes were too heavy to fight against.

I then did something supremely silly. After swearing not to go out after work with colleagues . . . I did it again. When Simon asked me out to celebrate winning the sanitary towel account, I agreed. I was sure you weren't supposed to drink after Botox, but that didn't stop me. I would only drink a small amount. Pete was at home and could get Bella. Bella had done some good craft today and eaten mackerel. I'd won a big project and that rarely ever happened.

All was well in the world.

'Sniff it quickly.'
'It's making my eyes water.'
'It's too strong. I may actually have a heart attack.'
'I never do drugs. I think you're a bad influence on me.'
'I've done far worse than this, Simon. We'll be fine.'

Rewind a few hours and a few of us had headed to a pub in Soho, and then downstairs into a venue where a band was on stage. They reminded me of Depeche Mode, and had very tight trousers and semi-BDSM gear. I stood right at the front but couldn't seem to get into the music. This had always been my problem – even when I'd been younger, I'd found it exceptionally hard to lose myself. Instead I looked up at the lead singer and tried to figure out whether I fancied him or not. He had a top knot. He was attractive but very self-conscious. Too polished. Too much practice and not enough spontaneity. Simon stood next to me and I swayed next to him. I'd been a fool to imagine he'd fancied me in the first place. I practiced wiggling my eyebrows up and down and there was still some movement. When would the Botox finally kick in? The music was giving me a headache. I ordered more drinks. I hadn't eaten much and more drinks weren't the best idea.

Two or three hours passed. All the other work folk had gone. They had debriefs the next morning, and groups happening, and innovation workshops. Simon and I moved on to another bar. It was late but I wasn't sure of the time. I'd texted Pete to tell him I was going for a celebratory works drink but that had been many hours earlier. And now Simon and I were hunched over this toilet seat and we were sniffing something that could have been coke or could have been something else. I'd found it on the floor and had shoved it in my pocket. This wasn't my usual behaviour but I'd had a day of making rash decisions. I was thinking about being more open and progressive, fighting my rigid, traditional ways. The coke/talcum powder had zero impact. Even the drugs weren't as effective as they'd been in my youth. It was a shame, as I'd wanted to get high or at least feel something – to escape out of my head without *my head detaching,* so to speak.

'Did you feel anything from that stuff?' I asked Simon as he slid into the booth with yet another vodka and coke.

'Nothing,' he said, wearily shaking his head and scrolling through his phone.

'Do you think I look young? Or younger than I did a few days ago?'

'I can't see any difference at all. Why?'

'Okay so how old would you say I was if you didn't know me.'

'Forty.'

'Jesus!' I said, slamming my glass against the table. *'That's awful.'*

'But you told me you were in your forties so that's good right?'

'If a woman asks you this question then always pick a number and then knock ten years off it.'

'Okay so you look thirty-five.'

'What so the number in your head was forty-five?'

Simon sighed.

'I don't want to play this game.'

We sat in silence for a bit. I watched some people, trying to calculate their individual ages.

'Are you on Grindr?' I asked leaning over his phone as he started tapping at the screen.

I raised my eyebrows up and down. Yes, they were still operational – even now. Even with a skinful of booze.

'No, definitely not. You seem to think that gay men are only into one night stands. I have a boyfriend remember? I'm settled and happy.'

I was feeling weird. Was this Botox? Or the *stuff*? I dabbed my nose with a tissue. I was too much of a lightweight. I had zero tolerance. There came a point when the bad, ageing cells were simply too tired to fight the toxins and the poisons flooding your body. And today had been especially toxic.

'I don't really know what I'm doing staying out like this,' I said, taking a sip of my drink. *'I hate my job,'* I said. *'I hate my life. I hate everything.'*

'Oh, here we go. Why don't you take Phoebe or Darren's advice and just be more aggressive?'

'Is that what they say about me then?'

'Well no but . . . well they did mention in a meeting that you need to be more robust and less emotional all the time.'

'Did then now?'

I felt humiliated at the thought that they saw me as some kind of floppy, hormonal woman with no backbone or business acumen.

'How come you're so enthusiastic?'

I raised my eyebrows but they were starting to feel heavier. Or was I imagining it?

'It's good at Mango-Lab Rebecca,' Simon said. *'There's*

loads of opportunities if you play the game. You just need to work harder and the rewards will come your way.'

'I haven't had a pay rise in some time,' I said.

'But maybe you don't try hard enough anymore?'

'I'm not interested. It's all nonsense.'

Simon grimaced.

'Then you need to find another job and stop wasting peoples' time.'

I couldn't help feeling like he'd talked to my bosses and was quoting them verbatim. Perhaps he was a spy, a plant, someone pouring company messages into my brain so I complied with the values.

'You're just not prepared to kiss up to people,' Simon said tapping his hand on the table.

'When you get to my age it becomes more difficult,' I stopped myself from slurring and concentrated. 'You get angry. You can't tolerate the same things.'

'But it's just WORK – it's not life. You use people to get what you need and then you move on. I won't be here in five years' time. I'll have my own company or I'll be living in another country. This is a stepping stone.'

He put down his phone. He was scrolling through his work emails even now. He was very different to me. He had the stamina required. He knew what he wanted. He was like Bryony. She was tired now but would recover, pick herself up and move onto something better. Was it too late for me to do the same?

Could this be a stepping stone to something better? Simon was right. I had made everything much more difficult and challenging. Could I change now? Could I just smile on through?

'*You look thirty-nine,*' he said smiling. '*I lied.*'

For some stupid reason that made me feel better than anything anyone had said in a long time.

Perhaps work didn't need to be so heavy and cumbersome. If you just tried to get what you needed and then did something else.

I would be very hungover tomorrow.

It seemed as if growing older was all about realizing that fun could never really be fun without a whole heap of comeback. If you got off with your friend's husband then she'd never speak to you again (when we'd been teenagers we'd regularly shared boys and compared notes). If you drank rum then you felt suicidal the next day, whilst your kid blasted you in the ear with a fart gun. It was all boring and tedious, and even if you tried to throw caution to the wind, (like tonight), then you'd end up sitting in some dingy bar talking to a colleague about how much you hated work. Where was the joy? Where was the jumping into the swimming pool with all your clothes on? Or snogging a rock star? Or leaping up and down on the bed and ordering pizza at three am? (okay, this was a snippet from an advert I'd seen, surely?) And now I was starting to see that much of my life had been wasted in the corporate world. I had been a round peg in a square hole. All those mornings, sighing as my alarm went off at 3.30 a.m. because I had a flight to Munich at five, all the nights in hotels on my own watching infomercials for the latest abdominal exercise contraption. All that time should have been spent getting off with rock stars and being reckless. Except who did that?

'I'm off,' I said.

'I'll order you an Uber,' he said.

'Why do you want to hang out with me?' I asked as I stood up and grabbed my bag.

I could already feel the comedown from whatever it was we'd shoved up our noses.

'I want to learn from you I guess.'

'I'm not Yoda. I'm useless.'

I suspected there was something else going on. It was a strategy. It was a plan concocted by Phoebe and Darren together. Simon was giving them notes each day. Hadn't he said that he sat in on meetings with them? That he wasn't going to hang around for long? That he would probably get what he could and move on?

The journey home was a blur. Pete and Bella were both fast asleep. I went in to see her but a bit of sick came into my mouth, and I had to stand over the toilet and retch for a while.

I looked in the bathroom mirror. One eyebrow looked ever so slightly higher than the other. I was worried that perhaps this wasn't normal and I'd forever look like some kind of Bond villainess.

When I awoke my head was hurting, and I was sticking to the sheets in a clammy sweat. I recollected standing in the garden smoking a Vogue Menthol (I'd had a packet in my knicker drawer for years and smoking one felt akin to taking heroin these days). I had a terrible taste in my mouth. I rolled onto my side. I *then* remembered that I'd been locked out and had had to hammer on the door for twenty minutes until Pete had come down. He'd been wearing his black, towelling dressing gown with the hood up, and for a moment I'd mistaken him for the Grim Reaper. He'd hissed a snide, derogatory comment, and went back to bed. I'd gone out into the back garden and looked up at the night sky.

It was beautiful when you really studied it, the stars all fresh and glimmering and light, but it was hard to look at anything without other thoughts coming into play. I must have fallen asleep on the sofa with the *Kardashians* on because I woke again at five, and the screen had gone blue and the cat was asleep on my back. I crawled upstairs and into bed. It wasn't quite the moment when you accept that you need to surrender to a higher power but perhaps it was. The 'drinking and taking drugs,' route wasn't for me. I wasn't Keith Richards. I would be dead if I continued like this.

But where did that leave me? Bodybuilding? Religion? Running? More stuff injected into my face? Or something creative? But what? What creative? Did it really matter? Surely anything was better than my current job.

Bryony had texted back and said we should meet that weekend for lunch. I felt a tiny burst of pleasure. There was something about her that made me feel good. I couldn't quite figure it out. *Hope* perhaps. Pete got out of bed and went downstairs without a word. He had every right to be mad but I wanted a man that barred my way and shouted and threatened (no maybe not that). I wanted passion. I wanted a shaking finger in my face and the sense that he cared about the choices I made. Not this silence. Not the aggressive tidying (it always seemed to imply that I wasn't on top of things, that he was having to step in and take over because the house was a mess) Was part of me trying to goad him into being more emotional? Probably. He was very even-tempered and the only time he lost it was when he drove the car. Then he went ballistic and used terrible language. I wanted to see this in our relationship (the passion, feeling, not the swearing part or rude hand gestures).

I went into Bella's room. A child was a good distraction when you had troublesome thoughts.

'I love you,' I whispered.

This was clear enough. I knew that my daughter was the best thing that had happened to me. Did I want another? Why did that thought keep popping into my mind? Because soon it wouldn't be possible. Soon time would have officially run out. And besides babies were so exhausting. You could never actually do the things you wanted to do and had to pretend that standing in a park freezing to death or listen to some mum drone on about how weaning was fun.

These things were fun:

Smoking a Vogue menthol

Drinking

Dancing

Doing something you loved

Playing footsie under the table with your other half and then rushing home to make love

These things were not so fun:

Pushing a swing

Motherwhelmed

Listening to a mum brag about her child's excellent handwriting

Doing washing

Loading the dishwasher

But then ultimately there were these small happy moments (I kept coming back to this thought – that happiness was not a state that you stayed in for long, that it was very transitory), where the universe showed you what perfection felt like. You rubbed your face into their hair, felt their arms tugging around your neck and then they said they *loved you*. I was starting to recognize them more now.

Would I swap all my independence for another child? What would happen to my job at Mango-Lab? I was sure that a second maternity leave was a sackable offence (no it wasn't but it would definitely sound the death knoll on my career). Did Pete want more children? I had a feeling that he might but he definitely wouldn't be up for that miserable trying-to-have-a-baby-sex again.

This morning he was in the kitchen making breakfast, each move steeped with self-righteousness. He was cross. Cross that I was always asking him to talk to me. That I was going out late. Why didn't he say any of these things to my face rather than just huff and puff? Okay perhaps I had become a female version of Jeremy Clarkson – maybe a more rock and roll version, maybe one with better fashion credentials, but an asshole however you looked at it.

'*I had a horrible dream and the child-catcher was trying to eat me Mummy,*' Bella said looking up with her pale, grey eyes.

My internal organs were churning. There was black grot in my nose. My head was pounding.

'*There's no such thing as the child-catcher darling. It's just a film, a scary film,*' I said.

'*Did you get me a new plate?*' she asked, wrapping her arms around my neck.

'*I will. Mummy hasn't seen any yet but I'll look on the computer.*'

'*Your hair smells bad.*'

'*I know. I need a shower. Shall we get up and have a shower?*'

This was one positive of parenthood. You had to get on with it.

'*I don't know how she manages,*' I heard other mums say sometimes when talking about a mum working full-time with three young children.

She doesn't have *any choice* I'd think. You had to keep up the pretence that you were in control and had some semblance of being responsible. You gargled with mouthwash, ran a brush through your hair and *sucked it up*.

Was I simply struggling or was this a proper mid-life crisis? I had a clearer picture in terms of what it involved if you were a man; they wore ponytails, more leather than was normal, and got a younger girlfriend. Or they retired to sheds and made train sets and stayed there for twenty years. Or they surrendered, and lay on the sofa staring into space. Or cycled like mad as if they could exercise their way out of ageing? Or they went to Butlin's weekenders and pretended they were eighteen. But what did women do? I was flirting with this mid-life crisis but wasn't fully immersed. This had always been my problem – sitting on the side lines observing, watching, never letting myself go. Even in my hedonistic days, when I'd gone to raves, I'd sat in the corner wondering why my nose was so large and my legs so short and fat. It was impossible for me to really LOSE it. I would never experience the high of being completely untethered and running through like a wild half woman/ half horse. I couldn't even skinny dip without cowering over bent double (this had happened once in my early twenties – everyone else had run into the sea completely naked and I'd lurched behind them like Quasimodo).

Pete left for work without saying anything. I made Bella and I breakfast, and noticed he'd left the dishwasher full of dirty plates. This was his dirty protest as he was usually so on top of things. This was the way couples played out their silly dramas. It wasn't about hurling plates at one another, instead it was about leaving the dishwasher stacked with dirty filth and leaving for work in a huff.

'I don't want scrambled egg,' Bella wailed pointing at the dried-up concoction on her plate. *'I don't like the yellow bit.'*

'So you want white scrambled egg?'

'No I don't like the way it feels in my mouth.'

'So a hard-boiled egg then?'

'Without the yellow bit inside.'

'I am not making you an egg with no yellow bit inside. The yellow bit is good for you. It's full of protein.'

We stared at one another. A breakfast stand-off. One of us would need to back down.

'Well have some cereal then,' I replied and took all twelve boxes down from the cupboard.

I pointed at the Cheerios and she shook her head. I pointed at Weetabix and she did the same. I tried the Shreddies but she wasn't interested. Eventually we landed on the chocolate cereal that was full of sugar and crap. It was all about compromise. Even now I was trying to please Bella and didn't put my foot down often enough. I'd got my job at Mango-Lab because I thought it was THE thing to do, the thing that made me a proper, respectable grown up. I'd wanted to do something more creative with my life, but I was lousy at drawing and could never master how to make a hand look like a hand versus a spider.

Motherwhelmed

I lay on the sofa and put CBeebies on. Bella lay on top of me and we cuddled. She still sometimes had that sweet smell when you sniffed her hair. I closed my eyes and tried to focus just on that for now.

Luckily there was no going into the office today.

Eight

IT WAS SATURDAY MORNING and Dad emerged from the shed looking like he'd aged five years since I'd last seen him. His trousers were held up by a piece of dressing gown cord, and his hair was greasy, and piled up on his head with a red and blue bandana from his motorcycling days. The dry shampoo had dyed his scalp white (I needed to tell him it wasn't a replacement for having a shower now and then). He had also grown a beard.

'I told you he wasn't well,' Mum said, shaking her head as we walked up the garden path and into the house. *'He isn't eating properly. Sometimes I look down there at two in the morning and the light is still on. He's not sleeping at all.'*

I felt guilty because she'd been sending me emails

and voice messages but I'd been too preoccupied to get in touch. Work had been taking over my life but not only that . . . this creeping sensation that I only had a finite amount of time to get my life sorted.

'*Perhaps you shouldn't have allowed him to drag his futon in there,*' I said. '*There's no real reason for him to come out now.*'

'*Well there's no proper toilet,*' she said. '*But he did have a look online. I checked out his search history and he'd been Googling "portable toilets".*'

Dad still had a futon leftover from the nineties and insisted it was comfortable when everyone knew it was like sleeping on a table. He'd also started storing crackers and nuts like an elder squirrel so he could actually hibernate in there for some time.

The problem was I could relate to it all. What would be better than just hiding away? No more pretending everything was okay, no more struggle, no more conversations. I was seeing a bigger version of it in the office. Headphones. Email. Less banter. We were all retreating into our own virtual sheds. Why hadn't been able to read the tell-tale signs that things were going downhill? Dad had been on antidepressants for some years, but it wasn't a cure, and it was important to keep an eye on him. If he didn't sleep properly, or get enough outdoor time then things got worse. He retreated.

'How's it going?' I asked when we sat down in the front room – trying to keep it as light as possible.

There was a pot of tea and some Jaffa Cakes on a plate. I forced three of them into my mouth. I'd left Bella with Pete, and was taking advantage of being able to eat biscuits without her asking for one too. Pete was still in a mood with me. We had barely said three words to one another since my night on the town. Men who liked to retreat was obviously a theme here.

'Well I just need to get this final plan sorted and we'll have the best railway system in the whole of South London. I've got a touch of flu perhaps but nothing worse than that.'

'Will you stay for lunch?' Mum said.

I saw the familiar line etched between her eyes. I tried to frown back but it wasn't happening. The Botox had put paid to that.

We ate lunch which was sardines on toast with mashed potato on the side and some pesto pasta. Mum always prepared a bunch of stuff that never combined well. We ate in silence. Mum kept getting up, walking around the kitchen, adjusting the radio volume, and sitting back down. I tried to make a few comments about work and stuff but stopped. Nobody enquired after Bella. I studied Dad's face. His skin was sallow. He looked like he'd lost weight. I touched his wrist.

'*Dad, you would tell us if things were really bad?*' I said. He didn't answer.

'*I'll show you the circuit track I've made around the compost bin,*' he said.

'*I told you he was sick,*' Mum said and started crying. '*All he talks about is the damned trains.*'

'*Well at least he has something he's interested in, hey Dad? Why is it any different to you and your evening classes? He's just immersing himself in a hobby.*'

'*What and never washing his hair? Or eating dinner with me? Or watching TV? Or even making conversation? I might as well be on my own.*'

'*I can't help feeling this is more about you than Dad,*' I said.

We were talking as if he was still in the shed and not sitting at the table working his way through some pasta.

'*Stop trying to make light of this,*' Mum said grabbing a napkin and blowing her nose. '*You turn everything into a stinking joke to get yourself off the hook.*'

I didn't say anything. There was more than a shadow of truth in this – I couldn't afford to invest energy and time into this problem when my own life was sinking into the mire. For now, I needed to go easy and try and do what I could. There was no point raising the fact that the more Mum pushed Dad to be social, the more he ran away. I also begrudged the fact that I was constantly put in the position where I had to balance both of their needs – Mum's desire to control and Dad's to escape and be left alone to his own devices. For a moment I got the realization that their relationship was not all that different from mine and Pete's. How had it taken me so long to put this together? I was often trying to change Pete – make him more talkative; more socially engaged and the only difference was that Pete disappeared into his iPad rather than a shed. Pete needed time on his own. He didn't like talking unless it was strictly necessary. He loved his family but was happiest sometimes in his own company pottering about.

'Why is your way the RIGHT way?' he sometimes said when we argued and he had a point.

There was no rule book that said you had to talk about everything all the time. Our most common clashes were the result of me trying to fit him into a particular mould. Just like Mum was doing. This felt like a bit of a Eureka moment.

Oprah would have been proud of me, put it that way.

I rang Dad's GP after lunch and booked him an appointment for the following week. I felt like there wasn't much else I could do. We hugged and he agreed to take a bath that evening.

'I don't know why she's making such a bloody fuss. What's so wrong with wanting time on your own?'

'She's just worried Dad and you do look pretty awful. Listen even if you're spending time in the shed, you still need to look after yourself.'

'There's nothing wrong with me.'

'Well go and see the doctor just in case. It might be worse than a flu right?'

Like many men he wasn't comfortable talking about his mental health – physical ailments were far more acceptable.

'He'd never come out if I didn't force him to,' Mum whispered before I left.

And Pete is the same, I thought to myself.

I am spending too much time forcing it.

✶

'*Now pull your left arm around your head and stretch, feel every muscle reaching for the sky*,' the teacher said.

Sunday morning and I'd booked in a yoga session. I was one of those people that dipped into yoga once every six months or so. When I went to a class I loved it but also felt supremely demotivated because everyone else was more stretchy. Today I had just about managed to get one arm up, but then we were expected to twist our wrists so our hands were pointing to the back of the room. It seemed that for this to happen you would need to have wrists that rotated 180 degrees. I looked around and everyone seemed to be fine with this concept

'*Focus on yourself. The person, the one you never listen to,*' the teacher said.

Who was this person inside? I visualized a small female Gollum. Pointy teeth. Self-obsessed. Hurting people left, right and centre. Not particularly good at anything. Flatlining in her career. Inconsistent as a parent. Bossy and demanding as a partner. Someone who would never get their shit together. A bad daughter who ignored her parents and their increased vulnerability.

'*Now into svanasana or downward facing dog.*'

The teacher glanced up at me. My palms were sweaty and my hands slipped off to one side. I pushed my bum into the air and felt a twinge in my leg. You needed to be patient and persistent with yoga. This wasn't a competition. Maybe this was the lesson. To stop competing and just let things happen. *Namaste* and all that.

'*Honey, you can put your arm down,*' the teacher shouted across the room, and suddenly she was right next to me and I could smell her lavender and hemp deodorant.

'*My hand's shaking,*' I muttered, trying to swing my arm into the air again.

'*You're just not used to using these muscles,*' she replied, trying to twist my arm higher. *'Enlightenment doesn't happen in half an hour.'*

I felt pain but not a good pain. I persisted nonetheless. Thirty minutes later and it was my favourite part. The lying down part. The lady next to me was breathing heavily.

What was going on inside her brain right now? Was she breathing hard to show me how good she was at breathing? I was wrong. It was competitive after all. Even breathing.

Bryony looked better than the last time we'd met. Pete was at home reading the papers having some alone time, and so it was just us in a local brunch café which was filled with small children and anxious parents trying to stop them from dismantling the place.

'Ralph is finally sleeping better,' she said. *'I feel like a new woman. It's incredible how awful lack of sleep makes you feel. I started questioning everything.'*

'I remember that with Bella,' I said sitting down and guiding Bella into the chair next to me. *'I used to just say the words "I surrender" over and over to myself. It felt like death. Lying down and just about to fall asleep and then hearing them cry and getting up again.'*

We ordered our food and I got some colouring books from the selection by the door for Bella to play with. She was tired and not as fighty as usual. There were times when I looked at her and realized she was still a baby. I pushed a bit of sticky hair off her face.

'*No scrambled eggs for me,*' she said. '*Scrambled eggs are disgusting.*'

'*No okay you're having pasta yes?*'

She nodded.

'*So how's it going with the photography?*' I asked Bryony.

I expected her to say that she'd had no time, that it was just a pipe dream, that she was too tired to think about it, and it would be easier to go back into advertising because it paid well etc.

'*Well good actually,*' she said, her cheeks glowing.

Ralph was at her breast suckling and she was a vision of motherly togetherness (I knew these moments were deceptive and that you could often look like you had it together when you were falling apart inside).

'*I've started this Instagram account and given myself a handle – @familyreality – and started taking some photos of Ralph and uploading them. I had an old camera that used to belong to my sister so it's just experimenting right now but I've started to draw up a pricing sheet so I can get an idea of what I'd charge for a half hour session.*'

'*WOW you've been busy,*' I said, impressed.

She'd done more in a few weeks to create a new career direction then I'd done in years.

'*I was hoping I could take a couple of photos of Bella and you today perhaps? For free of course. Just to build up my portfolio. I want them to feel natural.. The kind of photos you can't get on a smartphone. I mean nobody actually prints those up anymore but these are the kind you'd want to keep in an album.'*

'Sure,' I said.

I was feeling low. I had that typical woman thing where another woman's success was pushing me down instead of inspiring me to get my shit together. I had a feeling that the age gap between us was too vast. Yes I made a heap of generalisations about younger people but the truth was they were more optimistic, more expansive than I'd ever been. Perhaps this was why I was so bitter? They looked to the future rather than getting bogged down in the past.

'And how's work been for you?' she asked, moving Ralph onto her other breast as our food arrived. 'Your bosses sound horrible. Well familiar and horrible. I remember you mentioned someone called Darren and he sounded just like one of the creatives at work.'

'Does he have white teeth too?'

'Yes and he cycles everywhere.'

'Does he shout memos into his smart watch?'

'Come to think of it I think he did.'

'It's definitely a type,' I said.

I chopped up Bella's pasta. She wasn't speaking much but was behaving impeccably.

'I won this big sanitary towel project,' I said. *'Which is good news as I'm constantly being told to buck my ideas up.*

I don't really have any clients you see or not ones that commission regularly.'

'I used to work on San Pro when I was at the agency,' Bryony said. *'We found it really challenging. It's tough trying to stand out when there's so much own label doing copycat versions of the same thing.'*

'Well hopefully this won't be too bad,' I said. *'We've got to come up with some new concepts and product opportunities.'*

We were quiet for a while and I realized my mood was plunging down even more. The more I talked about work, the more I realized that my heart wasn't in it. Who actually gave a fuck about sanitary towel product development? Was this really what I wanted inscribed on my gravestone?

Rebecca invented a highly absorbent towel that will possibly never biodegrade and will be piled up in some landfill long after she's gone?

'How did you manage to get all that stuff done and look after Ralph?' I asked.

Bryony looked puzzled.

'You do far more than I do! What do you mean? I'm at home all day and have access to a laptop. Ralph naps more now. It's ideal. Being in an office is never conducive to actually working things through. There're too many distractions.'

'I never managed to get anything done with Bella in the

early days. I was lucky if I brushed my hair and got out of the house. It's probably because I'm older. Less physical resource, less stamina, all that stuff.'

We were silent for a bit. There was a boy at the next table who was sticking dried pasta to the floor and then flattening it with a fork.

'It's funny,' Bryony said wiping her mouth with a napkin. *'I've noticed you're very hung up on your age. Do you do that on purpose? One of the first things you said to me was how old you were, how you were 'past it' and the weird thing is when I talk to you it doesn't feel like that at all. I think you need re-position yourself.'*

'That sounds a bit wanky.'

'Yes it does but at the moment you've kind of created this role for yourself where you're a failure, you're looking at the past all the time, you're too old to change and yet I feel like you have loads to offer, like you're funny and wry and perceptive and aren't the grumpy old bag that you've described to me at all.'

'So I need to re-position myself?'

'Like a brand. Like we do with clients all the time. Who do you want to be? Stop focusing on what others are doing or not doing. I am starting to realise that I'm never going to be like many of the mums out there. I'm never going to puree sweet potato at three in the morning or get Ralph's feet imprinted in clay and hang them above my bed. And that's okay.'

I marvelled at just how mature Bryony was. She had bypassed all the insecure, anxiety phase of motherhood, was coming out the other side, and Ralph was still very young. Was it possible for me to *not* feel jealous of her and learn something? After we'd finished eating, she put Ralph in the buggy and took some photos across the table of Bella and I.

'I'm going to send these to you and you'll be my first client,' she said.

'Well at least let me pay you something,' I replied before we left.

'Give me something small or why don't we just try and meet up regularly and encourage one another?'

'So you'll give me input into my brand positioning then?'

'I'll have a think, yes, but I think you already know what's wrong. You need to focus on what's right *instead of all the stuff that's going wrong.'*

I nodded. I walked out of our lunch feeling lighter. I had to carry Bella most of the way home and she was super heavy, but it was okay.

It was a moment, definitely a moment.

Monday morning and the office had a bad vibe, like offices everywhere no doubt. I tried to re-access the calm I'd felt after lunch with Bryony but Phoebe called me into her office. I hated these face to face meetings. These were the ones where she usually said mean things because nobody else was around to witness them (to be honest she didn't care much whether anyone saw or not but she was definitely more frightening in private).

Perhaps I would do as Simon suggested and *play the game*.

She had four empty coffee cups on her desk, and a lot of angry scrawl on her writing pad. She'd obviously been in the office since five (she sometimes exercised at the gym at four thirty. I knew this because she'd dropped it into one of our conversations when she'd argued that I needed to be more time efficient). I offered up my best, most enthusiastic face. I could see Darren through the half-blurred glass. He seemed to be doing yoga stretches on the floor. I realized they were a team but not a conventional one. Usually you had 'good cop and bad cop' within management duos but they were both bad instead. Phoebe was obviously more senior but increasingly Darren was being given more of a spotlight. I actually preferred Phoebe in some ways because she wasn't such a phony.

'*Rebecca, we're approaching a turbulent period,*' she said, tapping her pencil on the table and narrowly avoiding one of her well-manicured finger nails. '*We need to see* each and EVERY team member delivering in the next quarter.'

'Well we've just won the sanitary towel innovation project,' I replied.

'Yes I heard from Simon that he was quite pivotal in the winning of that particular account. He said he'd written most of the proposal.'

For a moment I was shocked but then remembered his words – play the game. This was what he was doing. Buttering me up on the one hand and then dobbing me in to Phoebe. I would try and keep my distance from now on. What had I actually said to him? I struggled to remember now as I'd been so pissed.

'The thing is Rebecca you should basically be running THREE of these projects at the same time,' she said. 'We need more productivity. More collaboration. More innovation. We all have to up our game.'

'But what does that mean?'

'It means you need to work harder. Get here earlier. Why can't you drop Bella at nursery at six thirty?'

'Well two things,' I said. 'For a start the nursery only opens at eight and then there's the fact that she's still asleep.'

'Well what about a nanny? Get a nanny and you can leave whenever you want. Also you can stay a bit later instead of running off at five o'clock each night.'

'I don't have enough money to stretch to one of those.'

'*I think we pay you pretty well don't we?*'

'*But where would she sleep? In the garden?*'

'*See this is what I mean. This attitude of creating problems,*' Phoebe sighed, got out a mirror from her desk drawer and applied blusher to her cheeks, then a slick of pink lipstick. '*I want solutions. We want SOLUTIONS. Do what you have to, PLEASE.*'

'*I'm trying,*' I said. '*I'm definitely trying.*'

My initial smile had kind of dried on my face like a splat of grey gum on the pavement.

'*And what's wrong with your eyebrow?*' she said.

I instinctively reached up and tried to pull it down. I didn't think it was that noticeable but perhaps it was. I'd tried to do something to stay ahead of the game and ended up looking ridiculous.

'So you're saying I need to re-position myself?' I said borrowing some of Bryony's language.

'Well it's a bit late for that don't you think!' Phoebe said laughing, typing into her phone and no longer even looking at me. 'But actually yes, YES, that's exactly what I mean. You've gone out of fashion and feel a bit dusty. You need to get some sales behind you and remind people what you're actually good at.'

'*So what kind of brand am I then?*'

She looked up for a moment, her face thoughtful.

'*You're a German cleaning brand that nobody has heard of and has slightly, garish, incomprehensible packaging.*'

I felt my heart sink. I had thought she might say something a tad more flattering, to try and salvage my ego a tinsy bit perhaps. I glanced into the next office and Darren was rolling around the floor on his back. He had a special chair that hung him upside down each day. He said it made him think more efficiently but I suspected that it made him even more of a moron.

As I left her office I could feel my shoulders slump, and the smile had gone. *MY PRIORITIES ARE NOT FUCKING SANITARY TOWELS! I AM NOT A GERMAN CLEANING BRAND! I'M A HUMAN BEING!* I wanted to scream into the dead, cold air. And the stupid Botox couldn't erase unpleasant emotions. I was now one of those plastic dogs you see in the back of cars, nodding my head and smiling when I was falling apart. I had a wonky eyebrow. Perhaps it was permanent. Phoebe had sucked all the confidence out of me. She'd mown me over like *Flat Stanley* in the kids book that I read to Bella each night. I went back into her office feeling more emboldened. I would tell her exactly what I thought of her. I would finally put this whole awful thing to bed.

'I'm going to contact that baby wipe client,' I said my voice quiet and wallflower-ish. *'And there's that toddler shower gel account from last year.'*

Phoebe nodded but didn't smile.

'Fine whatever. Spare me the details. Just get on with it. I've sent you an Excel sheet to fill in. You can log in your time. We want to keep an eye on just how productive you're being each day.'

Did they have access to my computer? Did they know I went on ASOS for at least half an hour a day? Or that I usually took more than an hour for lunch and went around sniffing candles in Oliver Bonas and staring at the river, contemplating whether to go for a lunchtime dip (never to return?)

'Lean in, Rebecca! Lean right IN!'

'I don't like Sheryl Sandberg,' I said.

'Sheryl Sandberg doesn't like you much either,' she replied.

We were told to be confident, to be authentic, but successful women like Phoebe were horrible bitches. The nice women, the ones who retained their identify, who didn't pretend they were some power-jerk from the 1980s were seen as flops. I would never be an alpha-female. I had too many insecurities. I also couldn't afford a nanny.

Besides who was Phoebe calling dusty? Sheryl Sandberg was hardly cut and thrust anymore was she? Hadn't Phoebe got the memo?

'Well anyway,' Simon said as we sat in the airless meeting room catching up on the project that was going/not going to save my career. *'We'll get some women in our groups using pads and some others using tampons. Then we can compare the two experiences through digital*

pre-tasks and follow up in the groups to see whether there's any difference in terms of gaps.'

'As long as I don't have to do the digital pre-tasks as I have NO IDEA what you're talking about right now.'

'It's like WhatsApp. Have you heard of that?'

Yes that at least reassured me. We all knew WhatsApp – it was the easiest way to communicate with groups of people without having to meet them face to face. The nursery mums all whipped one another into a frenzy, usually over a teacher's birthday/dress up day/ collection or because there was a last-minute bake sale that needed organizing.

'Anyway,' Simon continued. *'I'll handle the digital stuff with one of those interns. Harriet is nice. Or maybe Penny.'*

'Which one is Penny?'

'The blonde one with the pretty face.'

'They're all blonde with pretty faces.'

'I'll point her out when it's 'Blue Sky Thinking Breakfast' tomorrow.'

'Listen,' I said changing the subject. *'I'd really appreciate it if you didn't feedback on me to Phoebe all the time. I don't want you telling her everything I'm up to.'*

'I don't remember doing that. I mentioned that I'd pitched in on the proposal but that was it.'

It was all about *playing the game.* I'd be more guarded around him now. He wasn't to be trusted.

'*Well I need to show Phoebe that I'm nailing it. So I'd appreciate it if you were more helpful. Or just behaved like a friend instead of a conniving bastard.*' I tried to raise my eyebrows to make a point, to show how desperate my cause was right now. '*I don't really know who they want me to be.*'

'*It's all about authenticity now,*' Simon said. '*Be yourself. Stop trying to be Phoebe. You could never be like her anyway.*'

'*You're right I couldn't but I don't think they want the authentic me either.*'

The authentic me didn't want to be here anyway. Simon took a sip of his drink. It was bright green and had tiny black seeds floating in it.

Authentic me was unpredictable. Emotional. Moody. It wasn't a woman running through an airport with a wheelie bag and shiny hair and breath sweetened by mints. A woman who got up at four so she could exercise before her first breakfast meeting that kicked off at seven. A woman who would be buried standing up because she thought sitting on a chair was for lazy people.

Me was a wild haired, tired creature, a grunting, fucked-off mess of a thing.

I logged into Bella's nursery portal.

Bella tried rocket in her salad today. She made a keyring out of sand. She also met a fireman and she tried on his hat and climbed up into the fire engine.

All these things. I gazed at the photo of her in the hat. It covered her eyes so just her nose and mouth stuck out. She was grinning. On work days I only saw her when we ran to nursery together. At night I saw her for an hour before she went to bed. How did Phoebe cope with never seeing her kids? Or did she just work to some method where she maximized the time? Was she better at making those moments count? I could see a parenting manual somewhere with that kind of title. Seeing kids had become a thing on a list of things. Like getting your hair blow dried, hanging upside down to invigorate your brain cells and logging how much sleep you'd got.

It wasn't a definition of success I subscribed to.

Later that evening, Pete and I sat on the sofa. We were just about to kick off a new boxset series which was all about a violent race of angels that turns into vampires and then take over a farm and fight in lots of ultra-violent ways. We hadn't been talking much since my last night out. Pete was on his iPad as usual. He had a semi-serious addiction to online retail but it manifested itself in strange ways. He always ended up buying the same grey or dark grey sweatshirts. He now had about fifteen of them stacked on the chest of drawers.

'I've never found the perfect one,' he'd said. 'It needs to be grey but not too dark and then no logo anywhere and the right fit. Baggy but not hanging off. Not too high in the neck either.'

It seemed like a relatively low-risk behaviour compared to some of the other things he could be doing so I tried not to nag him about it. Besides who was I to nag? I was all over online retail like a dung beetle on an ox turd.

'Do you think we should have a proper chat?' I said as he whizzed through the adverts that nobody watched anymore.

'Oh please can we stop it with the proper chat thing again? What do we need to talk about?'

'Well I feel like things just haven't been normal between us – don't you get that feeling too?'

'I get the feeling that you can't stop picking the same scab over and over. There is nothing wrong with our relationship. It's fine. We're a normal couple. We're tired. We're a bit overwhelmed but what do you want?'

I wasn't sure what I wanted. I thought about telling him my Ray Winstone, passion fantasy – the one where he got really worked up and told me to stop going out, be around more, how I was HIS WOMAN and all that but I realized it didn't sound very feminist. What did I want? More chat? By the end of the day I'd usually had my fill of that. So what else? For him to surprise me? But then when did I ever surprise him? He'd been asking me to darn one of this sweatshirts (it had a hole under the arm) for six months and I'd left it on top of the washing machine. I never prioritized him. I always put Bella first. I could see this stuff but couldn't articulate it.

'You're not going to start going on about another baby are you?' he said suddenly.

I was taken aback as I didn't think we'd talked about it recently but then remembered a couple of weekends previously and how I'd brought it up when I'd been in the loft clearing out stuff.

'I want to keep some of this stuff, just in case,' I'd told him.

We still had bags of Bella's baby clothes up there, and her Moses basket, and untold other baby paraphernalia.

'Is this what this crazy behaviour about? You couldn't have another child so you've decided to become Keith Richards?' Pete snapped.

He was always quick to get angry. I hated confrontation so naturally avoided talking about things. This was how we got into the whole *TV-zombie thing* in the first place.

'I did everything I could to support you when you were pregnant. I held your hand when you went for those scans.

I knew how awful the miscarriages had been, how you needed a shoulder but where was MY support?' Pete said.

'Hey hang on. This isn't what I wanted to talk about,' I said but it sounded wrong.

This was TOO much talk. Where was it even coming from? I wanted to talk about what I wanted from this relationship but I didn't want him wading in about how he'd been disappointed in the past. I needed to darn that sweatshirt. Okay I needed to make more of an effort too. I forgot that sometimes but there was just SO MUCH to do (well we were watching TV now so we obviously weren't that rushed off our feet).

'So let me get this right,' Pete said turning the TV off (I couldn't remember a time when he'd actually done this – was this the passion I'd been longing for? Was I lined up for a good session of ravishing?), *'You want to talk but you want to decide WHAT we talk about. You set the parameters. You call the shots.'*

'No it's okay let's not talk then.'

'No come on. You've got my full attention now. Let's talk. Work – you hate it, I know. Bella – you think you're not a good enough parent. You have this cool new friend Bryony that you like a lot. Dad – your mum's nagging him to death so he's hiding away from her. And me? What's going on with me, Rebecca?'

I realized I had no idea what was going on with him. What was it? I had come to see Pete as a piece of the furniture. We were co-parents. We did chores. We argued about chores. I rarely thought about his work or how stressful it was (and he was on his feet all day and working with people he didn't get on with but rarely said anything). I hadn't darned that sweat-shirt! I was a feminist, yes, but I'd neglected Pete completely. A feminist could still darn her partner's shirt couldn't she? What else had I done to show him I loved him?

'*Actually, can we watch TV now?*' I said.

'*No let's get it out. You want to talk about our relationship.*'

He was too loud. I wanted to watch the zombies killing one another.

'*The fact that you never talk to me.*'

'*WHAT AM I DOING NOW?*'

'*Shouting!*'

'*Okay so you want to talk but only if the talk works for you. And it has to be quiet because you don't like shouting but it's okay if you do the shouting?*'

Yes that was exactly it. I wanted us to talk but it had to be on MY TERMS. I could see I was being unrea-sonable but I was powerless to say that. There was always part of me that needed to have the last word. I found it hard to admit I was wrong. Bryony had been right. I was fixed in my opinions of the world.

I wanted everything to fit my criteria. I was just like

Mum but was it abnormal to long for a more decent level of conversation with your other half?

Pete went upstairs for a couple of minutes, then came back down and put the TV back on. In the zombie show, several people had their heads chopped off. The main female character had her legs eaten, but managed to have a baby which the husband fled with before she died. I ate a Mini Magnum. Just before going to bed, I rang Mum to see how Dad was. She didn't pick up. I started fretting about what that meant and then went to bed. I was just like Mum trying to mould Dad into the person she wanted him to be. It was the same pattern.

Yes I was pushing Pete into his very own shed.

In bed my thoughts churned around.

No amount of focusing on *my breath*, or trying to think of a giant, open sky full of possibilities would help. My hair was stuck to the back of my neck. Pulling my dressing gown on, I came downstairs and poured myself a glass of water. I clutched the kitchen counter as my head detached from my body again. It went up, up, up, up, until it grazed the ceiling where a long, grey cobweb was hanging in the corner, it then thudded into the opposite corner where some Sellotape from Bella's second birthday party was still stuck over the French windows. I tried to breathe, but my head had gone and left me. I opened my eyes and squinted out into the garden. An orange pair of eyes glinted back at me. It was the cat.

'*Help me*,' I mouthed. '*Help*.'

I went into Bella's room and sat on her bed. She'd stuck all the good behaviour stickers she'd won at nursery on her headboard. *Good effort! High five! You're Awesome!* I leant in and kissed her. Bella was the thing that kept me grounded. She didn't have to say anything. She just existed. What was wrong with considering another baby? Wouldn't that just bring more happiness into our lives? Yes it was exhausting and draining but it was worth it. What else was actually worth it? Not giant sanitary towels. Or edible cat litter. Or baby wipes that sent your kid to sleep. It was these moments. Everyone knew it but behaved as if STUFF was the priority. I was the one promoting all this STUFF. I was not being authentic in any shape or form. I felt a shudder go through my body as my head came back again. I tried to pretend that this head detaching thing was normal, and then I lay on the sofa and perused the TV planner. TV was the only thing that would drag me back to normality.

✳

I must have eventually fallen asleep back in my own bed, because I dreamt I was having more Botox, and then dermal fillers were being injected into my cheeks, and the fillers were like filling me up with air. They were making me light and happy, and young and dynamic, and I was floating into the sky, growing more and more youthful, until I faded away into a cloud . . . as a five-celled embryo.

When I woke up my cheek was stuck to the sheet, and I had that disappointment that you get when a dream is wearing off and real life is taking over. *I am enough. I do enough.* I am young and full of collagen and fresh and my life is all about Snapchat and batshit. The corners of my eyes itched like mad due to lack of sleep and the prospect of a day at the market research coalface filled me with dread. Pete came downstairs and we seemed to be speaking again but it was back to what was frozen and not frozen, what could be rustled up for dinner, whether it was too cold to hang washing outside. He then announced that he was staying in bed because he had a bad headache (he got these every few months and they usually meant he'd been working too hard). I thought about Bryony and how she'd said that I was too fixated on being middle-aged. Could I push beyond that and stop comparing the past to the present?

'*I don't want to wear tights,*' Bella complained as I tried to wrestle her into a pair. '*Too itchy!*'

'These ones have a teddy bear on the bottom,' I said.

'Teddies are for babies.'

'How about leggings?' I said taking a deep breath.

'I don't like leggings. I want bare legs. Daisy has bare legs.'

'It's autumn. It's getting cold. You can't have bare legs.'

'I want BARE LEGS.'

'I won't get you a treat on my way home from work.'

'I don't care.'

'Okay bare legs it is.'

I sprinted alongside Bella as she flew on her scooter to nursery. Her legs looked like they were going blue from the cold. I'd secretly stuck a pair of tights in her bag and would brief the nursery when I arrived. No doubt they'd text me with an update as to how cold she was and what a crap parent I'd been. She had to be prised out of my arms by two nursery assistants. Sometimes it felt like the arguing about clothing was just delaying tactics so we could spend more time together. That thought made me sad. My wonky eyebrow had settled now. With a face full of Botox I could smile regardless of all the shit hitting the fan.

✦

I texted Kath a few times but she was too busy to reply. She'd taken on a new role as a teaching assistant and had to leave her phone switched off most of the day. It felt like everyone else was moving on to do the things they were meant to do.

'*The doctor has upped his medication,*' Mum said as I did the final walk to work. '*He's taken to his bed because the track he ran around the compost bin was chewed up by a fox.*'

'*Is it fixable?*'

'*No. The fox chewed the whole thing. It was like the time he ate his flip flops. He thinks it personal. I'm worried he might get up on the night and try and attack it.*'

I didn't know how I could help. There was part of me that sympathized with Dad and his need to hide. I also knew it was impossible to change someone – I'd tried with Pete but we'd been together a long time and he was exactly the same. On top of that I'd not heard anything from the baby wipe client when I'd hoped there might be a new brief. And the toddler shower gel client had gone to Bali – her LinkedIn profile shot was her doing yoga. That meant the sanitary towel project was my only business win (and it wasn't really being seen as a win because Simon had taken most of the credit).

'Hey DUDE!' Darren flew past me in the lift, stepped inside, realized it would just be the two of us in there and then stepped out and pretending his phone was buzzing.

It seemed that he got nervous when we were one-on-one. Then as if things couldn't get much worse, Phoebe stepped in. She didn't look up and was staring at her phone – answering four million important emails whilst juggling childcare, a summer holiday to Tuscany, dinner with a client and a waxing appointment. She'd always reminded me of the Muppet with the blonde hair and hippie headband who was twinned up with the cool blue Muppet who played the saxophone. I had Googled this Muppet several times – it helped when things got tough at work, brought her down a peg or two. They could boss me about, belittle me but they'd never OWN my brain. Bryony was right. There was no reason why I couldn't go off and do something new. I just needed an Instagram handle and a business idea. Why was it so hard to think of something? It was hard because my brain was consumed with towels, wipes and cat litter. Emails that asked me to come along and *brainstorm the future of ice cream*. Emails about Friday socials and how the coffee machine had been replaced and could now make both lattes and mochas. How someone had drunk all the almond milk and failed to replace it. How the toiletries in the bathroom were no longer Aesop. How there might be redundancies soon. And then there was Phoebe breathing down my back, just waiting with baited breath for me to fall on my face. And Darren, that would really make his day. And Simon? A boy who pretended to be my friend but dobbed me in at the earliest opportunity.

My phone buzzed.

Bella has had to play inside at breakfast playtime because she is not wearing suitable clothing.

I sent a text back.

There are tights in her bag. Please put these on. She refused this morning. Thank you.

There are no tights in bag.

I HAD PUT TIGHTS IN THE BAG!

I sighed. I would need to log into the nursery portal and send a complaint. No perhaps I'd just try calling them. It had to be some sort of misunderstanding.

'*How's it going?*' Phoebe said looking up, as the doors opened on our floor.

She'd ignored me the whole time but that was okay as I'd done exactly the same back. *Play the game.* That was the idea anyway.

'*I'm trying to remember if I put tights in Bella's nursery bag,*' I replied.

'*There's an app for that. And like I said if you had a*

nanny she'd be doing that kind of thing for you. It frees up your brain to think about other stuff.'

'*I can't afford a nanny,*' I said but she hadn't heard.

It wasn't so much that we couldn't afford one – it was just that there was nowhere for her to live. And yes it was more expensive than the nursery – the nursery that never stopped sending me texts.

'*You must try going out in Peckham,*' Phoebe said as we walked into the office.

I struggled to keep up with her. It wasn't that her legs were long it was just that she moved everywhere at top speed. Loitering was a waste of time. Conversation and banter was a waste too.

Peckham was a dump. I'd grown up not far from there. It drove me mad that everyone was talking about it right now. Phoebe had bought a house there and thought she was the first person in the world to have noticed it had tapas bars and cafés where your kids could run riot. I didn't mind areas being rejuvenated (though I wondered where all the original inhabitants had been shunted off to) but hated being lectured about them when I'd practically lived up the road my entire life.

'*Perhaps you wouldn't be late every morning if you moved to Peckham,*' she muttered.

'*I grew up around there,*' I said. '*I swore I would never go south of the river again.*'

'*Ramen bars, tapas, pop ups. Everything,*' she said. '*You're missing out. Oh and what about the baby wipes? Or the toddler shower gel? Any news?*'

I shook my head. I felt like there was a clock over my head and if I failed to deliver a new client soon, I'd be ejected right out of my seat and land head first in the Thames.

Another text as I sat down at a desk. The office eerily silent again with just the gentle tip tapping of keyboards and the odd blast of tinny music issuing from headphones.

Bella will not be joining us for outside lunch play because she is not wearing suitable clothing.

I PUT TIGHTS IN HER BAG.

I typed back.

There are no tights in the bag.

YES THERE ARE.

I quickly picked up the phone and dialled the nursery.

Press one if you want to register for the nursery. Press two if you have an enquiry about holiday dates. Press three if you want to pay for the upcoming trip to the zoo. Press four if your child is ill or has nits and is going to be absent. Press five for any payment enquires or to give notice of cancellation. Then just a dial tone. There was no way to speak to anyone.

I texted again.

I PUT THE TIGHTS IN HER BAG.

No reply.

God was watching and today was under the impression that the shit storm needed to be dialled up a bit more. I checked my emails. Nothing interesting from clients. No new business. There was a whiff of desperation in the air. I was obviously not the only one struggling to create leads. I thought about Bryony and how she was following her dream, how she was using her leave to create some different options. I needed to keep channelling that energy. It was positive. What had she said? That I was funny and wry? What did wry mean anyway? How was I going to re-position myself when nobody was interested?

Simon and I sat together in the 'brainstorm zone' (which had hideous blown-up photos of gurning members of staff wallpapered all over the walls). We got a plan together for the massive sanitary-pro project (now given the snappier name of *Project Ziggy*).

'*The groups are very long,*' he said. '*Three hours, and*

Sven wants to keep twenty minutes between each one for questions and changing stimulus.'

'When will I eat?' I said.

'I guess you'll have five minutes before we start.'

'And are you moderating too?'

Simon shook his head. *'I think it's best if I'm the strategic head on this one. I can keep my distance, keep Sven happy and then come in if he has any questions whilst he's watching.'*

'But that means I'm doing nine hours moderating each day.'

'Phoebe says that's your core strength and I agree. You're a great moderator. People really like you.'

And they don't like you, I thought. It was so infuriating to be talked down to by this whipper snapper. I tried to remain calm but I was finally getting the measure of him. He wasn't a friend or ally. He was just as bad as the rest – worst in fact because he'd lied about his intentions, pretended to be interested, but was essentially using me to forge his way ahead.

Simon left to go and attend fieldwork for a new range of dried packet sauces, and I got a call from an old client who wanted to talk about a project looking at innovation in frozen sweet potato products. This was good news even though the client would probably ask for loads of different costs and it would take me ages to pull it together. I emailed Phoebe to tell her the good news. I tried to ring the nursery again. I logged into the portal but my password wasn't working. Had they locked me out because Bella wasn't wearing the right gear? I typed out an outline guide for the digital pre-tasks.

Dear respondent,

Thanks for taking part in 'Project Ziggy'. We are thrilled to have you feeding into our fascinating study. First off we'd like you to film your bathroom cupboard so we can see which products you currently use when you're menstruating.

Now which sanitary products would you find it hard to live without?

Imagine A WORLD WITHOUT pads. What about a world without tampons?

Tell me if your head has ever fully detached itself from your body

I picked Bella up and she cried as soon as she saw me.

'*I didn't go outside all day long,*' she bawled. '*All my friends were playing and having fun.*'

I cuddled her and went to find the manager. She was notoriously grumpy and I was actually quite scared of her but the whole tights thing was ridiculous. I found her in the kitchen talking to another staff member.

'*I've been trying to call all day,*' I said. '*Bella had warm tights in her bag. Did you look?*'

'*There were no tights when we looked,*' the manager replied.

She was wearing exercise gear and was obviously just off for a run. I wondered if she had kids and whether she understood how crap it was for them to stay inside and watch their friends playing all day.

'*What are these?*' I said pulling the tights from the bag and waving them in her face.

She looked at them suspiciously.

'*They're not clean. We don't put children in dirty clothes.*'

I bought them up to my nose and sniffed.

'*They're perfectly clean. Smell!*'

She wrinkled her nose.

'*They've got blobs all over them.*'

'*They are drawings of fried eggs. They're fucking BODEN!*' I screeched. '*Sorry I didn't mean to swear but they're perfectly fit for purpose.*'

Bella looked up at my twisted face (half twisted where there was still movement) and started crying again.

'*We do not swear in the nursery,*' the manager said.

'*I'm sorry,*' I repeated. '*It's just it's been a long day and I feel sad that Bella's not been out all day. She needs to get out. We all need to get out don't you think?*'

The manager walked out without another word. I was worried that I'd be expelled. Was it even possible? It had taken a long time to find a nursery that was near the station and had a nice garden. The staff were a bit moody but then again many people who worked with young children were. I would be too.

I carried Bella all the way home in my arms. I held her close. All that time I'd been worrying about work and she'd been locked inside like an animal. I'd paid eighty quid for someone to berate her because she wasn't wearing the right clothes.

I spent the evening perched on the sofa, scrolling through Instagram and hating everyone. One mum had uploaded a photo of her kid eating some sort of witchy quinoa casserole and had written underneath, *'So joyful that my beautiful daughter loves my wholesome dinner.'* Another had commented, *'God, how do you get her to eat that?'* and the mum had replied saying, *'She rejected sweets at an early age. We're terribly fortunate but she's really good with food and never eats Haribo.'* This was the same child that ran around the park with neon, blue bubble gum dripping down her chin. The same child who picked up a plastic spade and beat other small children around the chops with it. Who came up to you when you told it off and said *'I'm not listening. You're not my mum.'* The one who'd you once whispered in their tiny, misshapen ear; *'If you don't stop hitting my daughter, I'll tell your mum that you're eating gobstoppers and she'll force-feed you more of that yukky rice.'*

I drank a lot of wine. I didn't even bother to check on Pete who had retired to bed with a headache. There was nothing that could fix my mood. No TV programme. No nothing.

I got a text from Kath.

So sorry I've been busy. School life is mental.

I wanted to explain about the shitty day I'd had but didn't know where to start. I wanted to talk to her but knew evening calls on a weeknight were out of the question these days.

Good luck with it – I texted back.

I felt lonely. I drank another glass of wine and then went to bed feeling woozy. Pete was making the flapping noise again. I kicked him in the calf a couple of times and he stopped but after a couple of minutes it started again. I got up and went into the garden. I'd got three Vogue Menthols left in the pack. I smoked one, two and then three. I felt sick. I needed to escape. I was trapped. I texted Bryony.

Can we meet up again soon?

She replied right away.

I'd love to mate. Why don't you come to my house at the weekend and we can chat?

I started to type some more and then decided that YES would be the most appropriate answer. She didn't need all the detail on the tights and the portal and how shitty work was. I had a sense that Bryony believed in me – she thought I could create a different future. She didn't see me like the people at work saw me, like an old dinosaur who needed to be put out to pasture. She saw something else.

I'd booked a doctor's appointment for the following morning. It was chiefly to talk about the panic attacks/head detaching experiences but as usual I was telling him everything that was going wrong physically because I only visited the GP once a year at most.

'So describe your symptoms,' he said looking into my eyes.

The conversation with Kath a while back had worried me – reminded me that everyone our age was getting checked out because things like cancer were coming onto the horizon. I'd not felt well in weeks. And the past few days I'd had some sort of stomach upset. It felt like stress and I hoped perhaps he'd give me a prescription for some kind of sleep medicine or calming tincture.

'I can't sleep,' I said. *'I look at other people and wonder how they do it. How do they keep getting up and carrying on as normal?'*

The doctor looked a bit like Josh Homme from Queens of The Stone Age. I tried not to think about this, but it was distracting as he was possibly one of my biggest crushes. Josh Homme didn't work in market research and didn't give a shit about sanitary towels either. He was cool and rock and roll and lived his whole life in the fast lane. I had taken the wrong path. I had settled for less.

'Do you ever think about suicide?' he asked tapping into his keyboard.

I tried to picture what he was writing on that pad. *Old woman. Not unattractive but has hefty legs. Wears clothes that are too young for her. Delusional. Thinks she could have been a rock star.*

'Sometimes I get this sensation that my head is coming away from my body,' I said and he looked away from his screen and back at me. *'I know my head isn't actually coming off but it feels like it.'*

'I can put you down for some talking therapy, but the waiting list is very long. It'll take maybe four or so months, and then we can get you a prescription for some light anti-depressants. It's not unusual for women your age to feel depressed. You see, you might be entering the perimenopause phase.'

He ran his hand through his short, red hair and then stood up.

'WHAT?'

'Well you're in your forties and you're experiencing a lot of low mood, low libido and stress. It sounds like you could be entering the menopause.'

'I'm not ready for the menopause,' I said. 'I've not lived my life yet. I want to start a new career. There's a hundred things I want to do.'

'Maybe you'd like to try Zumba? I've heard it's really good for ladies your age.'

Did he think I was ninety? It had only been a couple of years ago (okay, maybe more), and I'd been dancing to drum 'n' bass. I'd been smoking weed and setting the dancefloor on fire with my moves (no, this had never been the case). Now the *perimenopause*? The warm-up to the bit where all your juices ran out of your body, like a roasting chicken on a spit, then you slowly turned into a scorched Weetabix, your essence, your female vitality, your sex and gizzards leeched out of your body so your only thrill was wiggling your hips in an embarrassing Zumba session. I would die before I'd do Zumba. He went out of the room and left a load of pamphlets behind – one of them said 'Zumba your Way Out of the Menopause'.

I felt tears well up in my eyes. Work, Pete, Bella's tantrums, none of them mattered. From here on in it would be towelling kaftans, mainlining evening prim-rose oil, and foot spas for Christmas. Then Murray mints, night sweats and heading off to the supermarket at five thirty in the morning dragging a dilapidated shopping trolley behind me to buy salad cream. Slankets. A Yorkshire terrier with an under-bite called 'Shorty'. *Inspector Morse*. Arrowwords. Imperial leather soap worn down to the width of a finger nail. Yardley's Lavender Water. Funny, sentimental ornaments that you bought in H Samuel because they made you cry. Collecting thimbles. Or teaspoons. Or hankies. Going into pound shops, and bulk buying handfuls of tooth-brushes, despite the fact that you had no teeth. Leaning in with a permanent grimace whenever someone spoke to you because you only heard ten percent of any conver-sation. Cider vinegar in the morning for constipation. Suppositories when it got really bad. It didn't matter what they tried to tell you – it was awful and none of it was anything like being Helen Mirren. I knew it and Dr Josh knew it too.

'Or the other thing we need to rule out is that you might be pregnant?' he said studying me more closely. *'Can you get a urine sample bottle from reception and then bring it back in when you're finished?'*

Pregnant? Was is possible? On the one hand he was telling me my fertility had finally hung up its sad, old trousers and retired, and on the other that I might actually still have eggs that could create a small person. I walked to reception in a daze and got a urine bottle. In the toilet my hands shook as I tried to pee and I ended up with only an inch of liquid inside. Could I possibly be pregnant? It was true that Pete and I had had sex not so long ago but with Bella it had taken SO LONG to conceive, with so much hopeless trying. The doctor obviously had to rule it out and then he could get on with his menopause tests. The menopause made more sense. I felt moody all the time and my chin was sprouting hairs. I got sweaty in public places and nobody understood my cultural references anymore. I sat in his office staring at the floor. I had strolled into this appointment without much thought. Now I was about to get some life-changing news either way.

I stared at the clock. The room silent aside from the sound of a plastic pack being ripped open.

'Congratulations,' he said turning away from the sink and throwing both latex gloves in the bin.

'What? Is it the menopause?'

'You're pregnant. A few weeks already I'd say. Have you had any nausea?'

I stared at him as if he'd just been fired out of a cannon. As if he'd just completed a stunt where he rode a motorcycle over fifteen double decker buses. As if he'd just sneezed into his hand and wiped it on my hair.

'No I mean I don't think so. No more than usual anyway.'

I often felt sick walking into work but that was just normal, right?

Motherwhelmed

'So it's not the menopause at all! On your way out make an appointment with the local hospital. We need to get you some folic acid too.'

I was forming a human inside of me.

Was this a moment of happiness that would pass in an instance? I wasn't sure.

Nine

D R JOSH HAD SWAPPED the pamphlets about menopause for slightly less jaunty ones with titles like 'Geriatric pregnancy; Survival Tips,' and 'Forty Plus and Pregnant; The Worrying Statistics.' I backed out the door in a trance. Pete and I had sex once every month, so what were the odds of this happening? I'd been led to believe that I was too old to conceive naturally, but there were obviously exceptions. When Bella had been two, I'd watched as all my mum friends had their second babies but I'd dismissed the possibility. I'd found it a real struggle the first time so had never expected I'd get pregnant now.

As I walked home, I made a list of all the bad things I'd done in the past few weeks.

Motherwhelmed

I'd drunk lots

I'd injected poison into my face

I'd taken coke (except, maybe it hadn't been coke,
  because I hadn't felt any noticeable difference at all)

I'd smoked some Vogue Menthols

I'd been under a lot of stress

'I'm sorry,' I whispered to the squidgy, tiny person growing inside. *'I never thought this was even possible.'*

I couldn't believe it. Then I was also worried because I'd had miscarriages before. This might just be another one of those. Could I cope with that devastation again? And stretching out before me were hours of moderating. How was I going to survive? Nine hour days. No food. No time to chill out. And how was Pete going to take the news? And how would Bella feel? I was failing at parenting one child so how would I ever cope with two? There was no point getting attached to the idea just yet. With Bella's pregnancy I'd been so, so cautious. I'd become permanently attached to my Nutri-bullet. I'd mulched spinach, kale, berries and then chorfed it all down, gagging because it smelt like bog water and tasted dire. It had taken three years to get pregnant. I'd done every-thing – digital ovulation kits, legs in the air for half an hour, acupuncture, foul tasting Chinese herbs, reflexology, positive thinking. Then when I'd got pregnant again, I'd tried the self-same technique. I'd cut out all the bad stuff, done gentle yoga and read books about mindfulness. And then each pregnancy had ended in miscarriage anyway. The healthiness hadn't made any difference at all but then again Bella had been born fighting fit and was rarely poorly. Perhaps this time it was a sign. Perhaps the fact that I'd been drunk, that I'd not been preoccupied with getting pregnant, meant it would be healthy. Yet still there was a voice inside that questioned whether I'd cope with another child. Here I was STRUGGLING. Unable to stay on top of work, being an excellent (or even average) partner, always feeling tired. But no, I needed to stay positive- this baby could represent an opportunity. Something good to focus on. Something that wasn't sanitary towels. I could devote myself to motherhood in earnest. I'd breastfeed for five years, grow my armpit hair, and give up on the rat-race. Phoebe could swoosh about in her cold, air-conditioned hell hole. All those career bitches. Mum bitches. The feminist bitches. The thin bitches. Fat bitches. Young bitches. All bitches everywhere.

Dear God,

Thank you for giving me this surprising news. I thought I was barren but you have proven me wrong.

I think this is good for me. I think maybe this is a sign that I need to slow down and finally appreciate life. I promise if you let this pregnancy proceed in a healthy manner, I will stop smoking and hanging out with young colleagues and will finally learn how to bake a good cake.

Love Rebecca x

I rang Mum and left her a message to call me back right away. I needed to work out the best time to tell Pete. Were we talking at the moment? I couldn't quite remember. We'd only had sex once in the last two months and yet I was pregnant. It was completely against the odds. A miracle of sorts.

I thought about all the different parenting fails I'd committed.

I'd set fire to Bella's packed lunch box by accident and flung it into the garden in a state of wild panic (poor Bella weeping and traumatized – thinking I'd done it on purpose).

Then the time I'd been so sleep deprived and mad that I'd considered throwing Bella in her Moses basket across the bedroom because she wouldn't stop crying.

Even recently I'd wanted a lie-in and had handed her an iPad and fallen back to sleep. I'd awoken to the words; *'No you're the MOTHERFUCKER,' 'NO you are,' 'Listen there's only one MOTHERFUCKING VAMPIRE IN THIS TOWN AND IT'S ME, SUCKER.'* Then some terrible gurgling noises as someone got their neck chomped open. She had accessed my Netflix account and was watching a horror film.

'Are they speaking Polish?' she asked, her tiny eyes crinkled up.

'Yes ALL Polish,' I said, snatching the iPad away from her.

I'd felt bad the rest of the day and tried to compensate by making cornflake cakes (which everyone knew was the slacker-parent version of baking. Mary Berry NEVER made cornflake cakes). I worried about the kind of lessons I'd taught her that day – that swearing was okay, blood-sucking criminals were real, and Polish people were foul-mouthed? How could I be trusted with another child?

Bella was with Pete who'd taken a day off work and so I decided to do a supermarket shop. I needed to be pragmatic and get on with things. The giant list of stuff to do didn't take care of itself. The theme in the local supermarket was Hungarian, and everything had pork in it – even the yoghurts. There was a mother pushing her toddler backwards into a buggy, and each time it stood up, she pushed it down, and it stood, and she pushed. I watched, pretty much hypnotized. Motherhood was the pits. The best bit of the day was the bit when they finally went to bed, and you could sit on the sofa. I thought back to my own mother and how tired she'd been. There had been times when she'd not had time to run a brush through her hair. And this had been with ONE CHILD, not two. I was getting the head detaching feeling again. I put my basket down and left the supermarket again. I'd filled it up with bananas and nothing else because pork didn't appeal to me today. Having another baby would kill me.

On top of this, Phoebe was looking for any excuse to get rid of me. Darren would be triumphant. My career officially OVER. Simon would step up and take my place despite the fact he was fourteen and had never moderated a group. They didn't need humans to moderate anyway. Soon it would be robots doing the same thing. I was surrounded by digitally savvy teenagers – all of them prepared to work for nothing more than a stand-up desk, and a free breakfast now and then. I'd be tossed onto the LOSER MUM pile. I'd be sent to out-of-the way places to do projects on financial services and car air fresheners. I sat down in the local café, ordered a cappuccino, and thought about how Pete would take this news. I texted Bryony (it was funny that my instinct was to get in touch with her rather than Kath).

I have some interesting news for you when I see you.

Oh have you found a new job? I hope so.

It's bigger than that. I'll tell you Saturday. Can I bring anything with me?

Just some wine. Or some fizz. I'll make some tagliatelle – would Bella like that too?

Sure, see you then.

I would need to flag up that I wasn't drinking. I wasn't sure how she'd react. She'd told me my life held lots of opportunities but another child was perhaps not the one she'd been thinking of.

I listened in to one of the conversations going on at another table. A young mum was talking to her friend who was also carrying a baby in a sling.

'*I don't know why he won't latch,*' she said to her friend. '*I've bought this bottle that looks like a nipple. It was advertised on Amazon so I'm hoping we can do some top-up feeds.*'

'*Top up feeds are DANGEROUS. I don't want to stress you Lauren, but the minute you start, you're on the road to formula.*'

She said the word *FORMULA* as if it was glue or bleach or something really bad.

'I thought it was okay. I mean they wouldn't sell formula if it was actually dangerous, right?'

'Look how much additional crap they put in there! And look at the packaging – don't you think it looks toxic. And it's not even biodegradable. And then it makes them really fat. Like you can always tell when you see a formula baby – they're enormous!'

She gestured with her hands, making a big, round tummy sign, and then puffing out her cheeks like a hamster.

'But she won't latch.'

'I know. You need the easy way out I guess . . . I think Zowie latches because he's got this super laid-back personality. I mean don't you think Lily is very anxious?'

'Does she seem anxious? Oh God, is she really?'

I'd been in this self-same situation many times. People said things to you that took your breath away. There was a lot of throwaway casual cruelty that went on, especially under the guise of being a 'mum-buddy'. Everything about motherhood was analysed. If you didn't breastfeed for two years, then your child would be a delinquent. If you breastfed for longer, you were a hairy-armpit weirdo who had a compost toilet and made their own candles out of ear wax. If you bought food pouches instead of mushing up your own gunk, you were lazy. It was tricky to work out the things that mattered, and the things that didn't. Was it okay to close the door, and sit on the toilet seat and meditate for five minutes whilst your baby screamed it's head off? Was it okay to watch a reality TV show when they were a newborn or were they already absorbing negative vibes? (I worried I'd done some damage with Bella this way). Could you put headphones on when you walked around the block with them in the buggy because they couldn't see or hear properly anyway? (This had been the only way I'd survived those long, boring walks, listening to Kate Bush to make the time go past more quickly).

Everyone was finding their own way.

The best moments were those when you connected with another mum, and realised you were both feeling the same thing – but even then there were times when you could put your foot in it, and fess up to doing something unacceptable. This was how I felt with Bryony. It was how I'd probably have felt with Kath if we lived in the same postcode and hadn't fallen into a text relationship. When you found the right mum you realized that it was okay to screw up, that there was no agreement in terms of what was a small screw up and a MASSIVE one. Yes I'd had times when I'd stood over Bella's cot, hunched and desperate, at three in the morning and I'd wept. I'd called on the power of Oprah

(I'd always found her voice soothing and knew that she'd be able to talk me out of any bad situation) to save me from the torment of another night of trying to guess what this tiny person wanted from me. Motherhood was a process whereby every part of yourself was rapidly dismantled and you were then reassembled in a slightly different configuration. I felt a prickle of fear. Was I really going to do this again?

'*I think Dad's better – he's actually washed his hair,*' Mum said as I carried the shopping back home again. She was talking into my ear. '*And he made a nice lasagne. He's cooking which is a good sign.*'

'*What about the fox?*'

'*He didn't talk about it all day yesterday. In fact he said he's going to make friends with the fox and put the track somewhere else, somewhere less accessible.*'

'*That sounds promising.*'

'*I know – it's funny how these things take care of themselves. I better go. I need to get some storage boxes from Aldi. They'll be sold out. I've already been up three times this week to buy some.*'

'*Mum I've got some news,*' I said.

'*Is it your job? Have they finally let you go? I warned you that might happen –*

you can't expect to work part-time and stay ahead of the competition.'

Mum always said the same thing. I was lucky to be

employed, times were tough, it was difficult to find something reliable these days. In her day she'd felt lucky to even have a job. And there hadn't been toothbrushes back then and she'd had to use a piece of wood with pig fat smeared on the end. They ate sugar sandwiches once a year at Christmas. That kind of thing. She was right but also had no idea how awful it was to work in marketing and fail at something that was so awful.

'*No I'm pregnant,*' I said.

'*Oh that's . . .*' there was a pause whilst Mum tried to possibly think up what it meant. '*Fabulous news. A little brother or sister for Bella. I'll tell your dad. That'll cheer him up. Well done darling. I hope,*' she stopped herself, '*it's all okay,*' she said eventually.

'*I haven't told Pete,*' I said.

'*Why the devil not?*' she asked. '*Doesn't he deserve to know?*'

'*It's only a few weeks. I don't want to jinx it.*'

There was a pause on the other end of the line.

'*It seems a little odd that you're telling me but not him.*'

'*I have a funny feeling that it might not happen Mum. And I don't want to put him through all that stuff again.*'

'*I think you're being silly. He has a right to know.*'

'*Maybe,*' I said.

I knew he'd be supportive eventually, but we were also going through this weird patch. Also Pete knew I'd struggled with Bella as a newborn (the relentlessness of it, the interrupted sleep, the advice that never worked, the anxiety) and it would potentially be worse this time as I was older and more tired. There were rumours that having another child was easier. That you were more relaxed, calmer, less neurotic. Again it wasn't clear if this was true or not. I got home and checked my emails. There was nothing too frightening in there. Sven was obviously happy with the questions I'd pulled together and Phoebe and Darren were off bothering someone else.

So I sat on the pregnancy information. I didn't tell Pete that night. I didn't tell Kath. Or anyone at work. I needed to style it out. The minute you told people you were having a baby, you became a human bean bag with Angel Delight for a brain. No one asked you to meetings anymore. You were left out of important communication. Women who had children were weak. Irrelevant and washed up. It didn't matter how many empowering, fist-pumping articles you read in women's magazines, the ugly truth was that pregnant women were pariahs.

Unless you were Phoebe and gave birth on the board-room floor with the minimum fuss. Ideally you came back to work the next day, never talked about your kids, pushed that prolapse straight back up your vagina, expressed milk, handed it to the nanny, and boarded a transatlantic flight to moderate twelve groups. Or you told everyone how tired you were but continued to tire everyone else out by your incessant, negative chat. Mothers at work who really made it were few and far between. They were either incredibly wealthy, had husbands who lactated milk or gave their children away.

Each morning that week I marched to work and chanted the self-same refrain.

I can do this.

I spent the rest of the week immersed in Project Ziggy and spent as much time as possible analysing the results of the digital work. I watched as women talked about their periods. Then complained about cramps, feeling bloated and manic mood swings. I thought about how unlucky we were to lose months, years of our lives dealing with this stuff. I worried that there was no product that was going to help women with their periods. What they really wanted during this time in the month was to stay in bed.

Simon and I started brainstorming our ideas on the future of sanitary towels. He was gaining confidence and I felt like he was very different to the boy I'd had coffee with a couple of months ago. It was as if the more confident he became, the more anxious I was. There was some sort of unhealthy, symbiotic relationship going on.

Would the pad be so light that you didn't feel it?

Would aspirational quotes on the packaging make women feel more positive and grateful for their periods?

We covered a wall of our meeting room with Post-it notes. Project Ziggy needed to be a trailblazing project that won repeat business for Mango-Lab. It would also be part of my re-brand *before* I told them I was expecting. And for a while, it looked like it was working . . . I was steadily re-branding myself just like Bryony had told me to. Phoebe actually smiled at me one morning (it was an awkward smile and slightly lopsided but a smile nonetheless). Perhaps my reputation was shifting. Just sitting in a room with Simon was making me more dynamic. His youthful enthusiasm worked well even though I DIDN'T like him as a person. We were becoming the Lennon and McCartney of the qualitative market research world.

'I'm enjoying working with you,' I said as we got into the lift one evening.

'We're freaking nailing it.'

'AWESOME!' I said, and I *sort* of meant it.

The thing is I KNEW about women and periods. It was an area I felt comfortable in. If I couldn't get this project right then I really was on the decline.

On Saturday Bella and I went to have lunch at Bryony's house. It was a beautiful detached Victorian number only a few streets away from ours, near to Acton Vale. She had lots of cool typeface posters in the kitchen (red shiny cabinets) and neon pillows on the grey, felt sofa. Ralph was having a lunchtime snooze upstairs but she showed me the other rooms in the house. Her hair was piled up on her head again and she had put on a bright, red lipstick and a denim shirt under her dungarees. I made a mental note to try this combination soon.

'It needed a lot of work when Mark and I moved in,' she said. 'But we've done it up bit by bit. Rescuing old stuff from skips and reclamation yards. Oh and gifts from my sister who works in a second hand furniture dealer.'

'What does Mark do?' I asked wondering how they could afford such a massive house in London.

'Oh he's trying to get his own craft beer event together in Old Street. He's got a couple of sponsors but the problem is everyone is into craft now so it's hard to be different and stand out. He used to work in PR but hated it.'

'But how do you survive?' I asked settling Bella on the sofa. CBeebies was on. This was a woman after my own heart. CBeebies was music to my ears.

'I sell old clothes on eBay. He sometimes does a bit of freelance consultancy here and there. I also got a bit of inheritance when my mum's sister died. She was pretty loaded. We can just about pay the mortgage and the bills but we're both doing things we love– well not quite but almost.'

The concept of NOT having a steady income, of piece-mealing each month together out of odds and sods was an alien one. I'd always relied on a steady income – enough to buy Oliver Bonas knick-knacks and the odd Boden jumper.

'Well I hope you like picky bits,' she said as we sat down at the kitchen table- there were dips, crudités, halloumi, pitta bread, tzatziki – all my favourite things.

'So what's your news?' she asked.

'I'm having a baby,' I said.

'WOW! CONGRATULATIONS!'

She leapt up and hugged me. It was lovely to have such a positive response. Mum's had felt more muted, like she wanted to flag up lots of challenges and warnings but was trying to hold back for now (they would all come though eventually).

'I'm terrified,' I said realizing this was the truth. *'I'm not sure I'd even have a job on my return. And I'm pretty old!'*

'God stop with the age thing again. Loads of women have kids later now. Sometimes I wish I'd waited a bit longer and got on with my business idea first.'

We ate lunch and took some snacks through to Bella who was watching another Peter Rabbit. Bryony didn't even mention not getting snacks on the sofa. I knew she was cool then.

'So let's say you leave Mango-Lab eventually,' she said. *'I mean it's obvious you hate it and it sounds pretty toxic.'*

I thought for a bit. This was the trouble. Too many

random ideas. No focus. No clear idea of what I might be able to do that was more fulfilling.

'I think it's too late,' I said. 'I mean if I was meant to do something else, how come I'm not doing it already?'

'Nonsense woman. There's plenty you could do. You just need to have a bit more self-belief- that place has ground you down- made you doubt yourself too much.'

'Do you think?'

'Yes and the reason I know is because I had exactly the same experience at my old agency. Too many cocks. Too many egos. Not enough listening.'

Again I wondered at Bryony's confidence. I was getting a girl crush on this woman. She saw obstacles and pushed them aside. She didn't opt for safety and security. She didn't let people treat her badly. Perhaps there were other ways of being successful that didn't require shoulder pads and power bob. Ralph started crying upstairs and she got up and returned two minutes later, cradling him in her arms.

Just seeing a baby made the pregnancy feel more real. Was I excited? I was starting to feel like maybe I was.

'I've got some photos to show you,' she said and reached into a folder on the kitchen table.

'These are the ones I took in the café.'

I stared down at the contact sheet. I saw a woman hugging a young girl. The woman had a slightly wonky eyebrow but was laughing. The girl had her arms wrapped around the mum's head. She had captured a moment of pure, unadulterated happiness. I wished that I'd appreciated it in that moment. That was the trick–to switch off all the mental load and just be. Why was it so hard?

'*Tell me which one you want printed and I'll do it for free,*' she said.

I pointed to the one where we were both laughing.

'*I hardly recognize myself,*' I said. '*I actually look joyful.*'

Bryony looked sad.

'*We need to do something about that,*' she said. '*You should be having more moments where you feel that way.*'

Ten

Pᴇᴛᴇ's ɪɴɪᴛɪᴀʟ ʀᴇᴀᴄᴛɪᴏɴ ᴛᴏ thᴇ baby news was shock.

'Is it even possible?' he asked. *'HOW?'*

'We had sex a few weeks ago, don't you remember?'

'But it took so long with Bella, I never thought it might happen again. I mean are you okay? Is everything okay?'

The acrimony and resentful of the past couple of weeks seemed to have faded somewhat now (though neither of us had talked about anything. We'd simply got tired of ignoring one another for so long).

'What do you think?' I asked sitting on his lap.

'Have you told Bella? Ouch you're crushing my leg.'

I stood up again.

'It's only a few weeks so we should probably wait.'

'Well I'm amazed. And happy. No honestly I am. I think I am anyway. Jesus I'm going to be a very old dad.'

'You already are an old dad.'

'That's true.'

The truth was I knew Pete loved his family and the security it offered. He'd been rebellious in his youth but now he was pretty traditional. He'd also not had an easy, upbringing – his mum had been domineering and had tried to control each and every aspect of his life. Did I have these tendencies too? Perhaps not as extreme but I had definitely tried to mould him into someone else. His parents had split up when he was a teenager and perhaps this made him crave stability even more than most. He was a reliable, lovely person. Perhaps my desire to make him more Ray Winstone was stupid. Who needed a raging, angry, man when you had children to bring up? It was about being realistic about what you wanted. It was impossible to have it all in one person.

At work, just when it felt like things were getting better, workload steadily increased. It felt like another test. I was busy already prepping Project Ziggy but now I was being inundated with emails first thing in the morning and last thing at night. Some were from Sven– asking about the groups, the insights, the earliest possible date we could deliver a debrief, and then others were from Phoebe. Sometimes Darren was sending me links to articles that he thought I should read. They were all twenty or thirty pages long. Many of them were on pet food. I worried that perhaps he was about to hand over his entire pet food empire (he had one regular client who commissioned about six projects a year).

I started getting the head detaching thing.

Waking up feeling like I'd forgotten something very important.

Waking up and thinking that maybe the house was on fire.

That I'd forgotten the portal password for the nursery again.

That I needed to buy new tights.

That we didn't have enough room for another child.

That any ideas I had of leaving Mango-Lab were naïve and stupid.

NEW PROTEIN DRINK BRIEF NEEDS IMMEDIATE ATTENTION.
EXCITING OPPORTUNITY TO PITCH FOR DENTAL FLOSS INNOVATION
PREP FOR SEMIOTIC BUSINESS DRIVE IN AUTOMATIVE CATEGORY MUST PROCEED TODAY.

When Phoebe didn't use capitals she <u>underlined key phrases</u> or she wrote them in red ink or VERY LARGE.

A typical email looked like this:

HEY REBECCA,
I NEED YOU TO READ THE BIRD SEED BRIEF
IMMEDIATELY. It's <u>VITAL THAT WE GET THIS</u>
<u>PROJECT IN THE BAG BEFORE THE END OF</u>
<u>MARCH.</u> GET ON IT FIRST THING.
PHOEBE

I'd left the gas on, my hairdryer had exploded, the cat had been hit by a car, Bella had had an accident, Pete had fainted into a saucepan of stewed cabbage . . . each day was the same level of anxiety. I typed emails on the train. I opened my laptop whilst standing and did some more. I sighed the moment the train lost Wi-Fi signal, and then went at it again as soon as it sprang back. I wasn't a good parent. I snapped at Bella and felt impatient for her to go to bed (even though I often hadn't seen her all day). I got bored of her long, imaginative stories and said things like – WRAP IT UP, MOVE ON! YOU'RE REPEATING YOURSELF, OKAY? I said these things in a screechy voice.

'Do you think I'm working hard?' I asked Simon as we stuck more Post-it notes onto our meeting room wall.

'You've written three proposals this week right?' he said.

'I know but the definition of HARD seems to be in flux. How many proposals do you write on average?'

'Twelve, maybe thirteen.'

'You've got to be kidding?'

'Darren says the ratio is that we win about one in fifteen proposals so you've got to do as many as possible to get business in. I stay late, I work on weekends. The usual stuff.'

'I'm working ALL THE TIME – is that normal?'

'It's perfectly normal.'

My heart sank. I was on a treadmill and someone was turning up the speed, a little faster, faster, then even faster still. I'd soon end up flying off and hitting a wall. I didn't have the stamina of someone like Simon or the youthful energy (or the dedication either).

'Right let's focus back on this for a while,' I said. 'So if we think about this towel of the future.. It's basically a giant pair of plastic pants. Isn't that just called an adult nappy?'

And still the texts came in.

Bella has eaten a good lunch of chick pea curry and rice. She also made a mobile out of Fuzzy Felt as part of our monthly 'underwater fishing,' theme.

Bella had a bit of a cold today so had a nap after lunch but is now in good health.

Bella ate turkey for the first time but didn't like it.
She had a vegetarian sausage instead.

Bella is in good health.

At least someone was.

I set my alarm for 5 a.m. so I could make a good run at it and then after Bella was in bed, I was hunched over my phone tapping away like a demonic monkey.

'Are you okay?' Pete asked. *'You seem to be on your laptop even more than usual.'*

'There's just this massive project on at the moment and I keep getting forwarded more proposals to write. The minute I finish one, Phoebe sends me another,' I said. answering an email about a Japanese client who'd demanded an IMMEDIATE cost for an automotive project.

'It's not healthy – you don't need stress at this point.'

'I BLOODY WELL KNOW I DON'T NEED IT,' I barked unhelpfully.

I stopped browsing the boutiques at lunchtime and ate my lunch (a white bread sandwich with something unidentifiable squished inside) at my desk. I didn't even look forward to lunch anymore! When I saw other mums on non-working days, I hid behind cars and got Bella to crouch down with me so I didn't have to make chit-chat. There was simply no time. I was either at work on my laptop or at home on my laptop.

I had worked hard like this before but now it felt different. I'd gone from apathy to panic in a matter of weeks. The pregnancy had something to do with it – it was hormonal – the fact that I was suddenly aware that I had limited time to get my head down and get as much done as possible (there'd be another maternity leave on the horizon if I survived that long). It was also that I'd now share responsibility for TWO children. Then on top of all that, I wanted to give Mango-Lab ONE MORE TRY. There was a loud voice saying – *show these bastards, show them what you're capable of. Maybe you ARE Phoebe. Maybe you are Sheryl Sandberg.*
SHOW THEM. SHOW THEM. THIS IS YOUR CHANCE

And so it went on. I was becoming one of those profiles you read about in magazines. The woman who gets up at five am so she can do a gym workout and bake cookies before she hits the office (well maybe not quite but almost).

'It's bedtime Bella,' I shouted down the stairs one evening.
'I'm busy on my laptop,' Bella shouted back.
Bella is in good health.

Her mum is not.
'How's work?' Kath texted.

'How are you?' Bryony texted.

There was enough time to type up one word.

FINE.

I didn't dare call my parents. I didn't have time. Either Dad was better and getting used to dry shampoo or he'd become a hobbit. There was nothing I could do about it anyway.

✦

'You were supposed to come in yesterday at midday and read a book to the children,' the nursery manager said one morning.

'Where did it say that?' I said a screeching tone to my voice which seemed to be becoming more common.

I was already sweating under my anorak and tapping away on my phone. There was a potential project for a carrot juice client, but the proposal needed to be done BEFORE the end of the day. I also had a few alterations to make to the discussion guides for Project Ziggy (Sven had sent another list of amends at midnight).

'Well it was all on the portal and you were booked in for yesterday.'

'But I don't remember doing that.'

'You didn't. If parents don't book themselves then we do it for them. You should have received a notification when you logged in.'

'But I haven't got the password anymore.'

'I'll create you a new one. I think this is the third time though so please keep it somewhere safe.'

Bella started crying as I walked towards the door.

'NOT TODAY DARLING NOT TODAY!' I shouted cheerily.

My brain was exploding.

My head was permanently detached from my body now.

✳

On my non-work days Bella would beg to be taken to the local park but I refused. The park took up too much time and had poor Wifi. Instead I put the TV on tried to choose something vaguely educational to assuage the guilt a little. Whilst Bella watched TV, looking pale and like she needed fresh air, I hunched over my laptop, like a primitive cave woman skinning an animal, trying to answer a query from a client who wanted a last minute cost adjustment for some groups happening in Mexico. I had no one to ask for help and besides it now felt like everyone was overstretched. A week before and another cardboard box of belongings had been handed over and a young research executive had walked out crying. They were getting rid of the pretty ones which worried me somewhat.

I started wearing my old power blazer. I felt like I needed props to make me look the part. I forgot about Bryony and the re-branding idea or the fact that I COULD actually leave and do something else. Instead I tried to join the Sandberg gang. Perhaps I needed more Botox. A facelift. One of those where they took a piece of string and then hoiked your neck so you looked nineteen and slightly manic like the joker in Batman. Morning sickness had set in. I always carried a packet of mints in my pocket to help me navigate the long journey to work. I texted Kath one morning- she now knew I was pregnant and was biting her tongue- trying not to tell me it was the worse thing that could happen right now.

My bosses are trying to kill me, I texted.
Don't be silly, she texted back, *you're paranoid*.

She is drowning me with work. I am literally DROWNING.
Turn your phone off. Don't look at it after five thirty.
If I do that I have a million emails the following morning.
LEAVE. Get a job as a teaching assistant- the pay is piss poor though.
SHOW THEM. SHOW THOSE BASTARDS.

Perhaps I'd have been okay if Phoebe and Darren were the only ones I had to contend with but there was Sven, the German sanitary product boss, too. Sven channeled ALL his energy into work. He probably had a more brutal routine than Phoebe and liked to send emails very late at night and then send a follow up if you didn't reply within ten minutes. He ate, slept and dreamt feminine hygiene products (which seemed weird). We now had ten different updates to the discussion guide. He was worried about lots of things. He was worried that women would feel too inhibited to talk (he had a point). He was worried that the venue wasn't right. He was also worried that we wouldn't emerge with any new thinking. He wanted this project to be GROUNDBREAKING. I peppered all my emails with the same key words . . . innovation, dynamism, energy, positive equity, new opportunities. I was in a computer game – somewhere on level eighteen, and the baddie was about to come down on me like a pile of bricks.

'Your blood pressure is higher than it should be,' the midwife said. *'Are you under a lot of stress at the moment?'.*

She helped me off the examination table.

AM I UNDER MUCH STRESS? LOOK AT THESE EYE BAGS! LOOK AT THE WAY I STOOP! AND SIGH! STOOP AND SIGH! There was a sign in the toilet that said you should put a red dot on your urine sample if you were suffering from domestic abuse. Would someone help me if I was being deluged with work? Being mentally abused by my boss? How did you get help for that?

'Didn't your partner want to be with you today for the scan?'

'He did yes but he's really busy. He has a lot of work on.'

Pete was working to devise some new menus for a demanding client. He too was being deluged with emails and texts. Between us we'd become glued to our screens and unable to extricate ourselves.

'Right let's have a good look,' she said, pulling my jumper up and rubbing gel on my tummy.

Suddenly I was holding my breath. There would be something wrong. The bleeding would start. I closed my eyes. There was silence whilst the nurse, rubbed my tummy.

'Lovely. Just lovely,' she said eventually. *'There's a tiny foot. Can you see that?'*

'What?'

'Open your eyes. Your baby is looking perfect.'

I stared at the black and white fuzzy screen. The last time I'd seen a scan like this had been with Bella. Bella who'd been nine pounds, five ounces. Bella who'd been a tricky infant but never suffered with colds or coughs or colic. This wasn't a ghost – this baby was real.

'And the heartbeat's okay?'

'It's exactly what we like to see at twelve weeks.'

It was really happening.

It was a moment but the moment was too fleeting. The things that were really important were being subsumed by work and life admin. My phone was vibrating in my pocket as I ran to the train station. The baby was fine. The baby was fine but Bella needed new socks. The cat needed flea medication. The downstairs drain was blocked. There were emails to answer. Proposals to write.

I was going to show them all.

Eleven

'*H*ELLO SVEN,' I SAID. '*So good to hear from you.*'
'*Hello, nice to hear from you too finally.*'
The only way I could manage the head-detaching sensation now was to hold onto something solid. I clutched one side of the desk. I was worried Sven would ask about the findings from the digital diaries. The learnings lacked clarity. We had a room full of post-it notes and scribbles. Strategy was all about confidence. Simon had taken it away and made it his own. We just had a lot of women who basically just kept going on about how tired they were.

'*I want to touch base with you,*' Sven said. '*I have some concerns. I read your topline last night. I need more DEPTH. This is why we hired Mango – you specialise in unearthing new strategy.*'

'I think we're getting lots of exciting insights,' I said, watching as my knuckles turned white.

Simon was the one who could talk shop right now. He was dynamic and not pregnant.

'Can you summarise the key themes with greater clarity please?'

'Well,' I paused and tried to remember what we'd written together in the email. It seemed as if my brain was struggling to recollect anything. Simon was walking across the office with a cup of tea in one hand. I gestured for him to come over and thrust the phone into his hand. *It's Sven*, I mouthed.

'Hello Sven, It's Simon. Mango Head of Cultural Insights and Semiotics. I am excited about what we've got coming out. Like Rebecca has said already. It's really very interesting.'

I tried not laugh. Had he really said MANGO HEAD? Was this his job title? The laugh came and when it did, it forced a terrible noise out of my mouth. I couldn't stop. MANGO HEAD! It was funny. It was the funniest thing. I put my hand over my mouth to try, and hold the sound in. Simon was talking very loudly. When had Simon been promoted? I realized I wasn't laughing anymore. I was just sitting with my hand over my mouth and breathing – PANTING almost.

'The cultural context of menstruation is a fascinating one,' Simon continued. *'Women have been faced with persecution when it comes to their monthly menses and now*

we are entering a new phase where menses' – DID HE USE THE WORD MENSES?! – *'is something to cele-brate because it is a vibrant assertion of female power in a patriarchal society. It has become more of a ritual, something to savour and indulge in even.'*

I was sure that everything Simon was saying right now was wrong but it didn't matter. He had been promoted and was now more senior than me. Me, who had worked in this company for years. Me, who had given them everything. I was providing a platform for this twat to be promoted. He was *playing the game* rather well. He was Phoebe's lap dog. A sap. He was why I would always fail no matter how hard I tried. He'd been a tiny embryo, and I'd been moderating and debriefing and schlepping about Europe like an inter-national shower curtain saleswoman. I got up from my desk and went into the toilets. I burst into tears. I was at that point now.

No amount of affirmations or meditation or fucking motivating Instagram quotes would pick me up. The receptionist knocked on the cubicle door and said another client was trying to get hold of me to talk about a proposal I'd sent two days earlier. I had no recollection which proposal this was because I'd written FIFTEEN in the past two weeks. When the coast seemed clear, I went back to my desk and Simon had gone. He'd left me a Post-it note which said 'SVEN OKAY. SEEMS

HAPPY.' I picked up my laptop, put it in my bag and went home. I needed to see Bella, Pete, the cat, to have some sort of semblance of normal life.

Dear God,

I realise that you think I only get in touch with you when I need something from you and yes that probably is quite true. I guess when everything is okay then there's less interest in you overall and that makes you sick. I would get pissed off too. And I know I got in touch with you when Bella was born and I was so tired and felt like I couldn't survive.

And then I got in touch with you when I thought Pete and I were on the rocks, and then of course I wanted you to know I AM grateful to be pregnant. I mean we both know I'm really OLD! I'm grateful because I know I can make a go of it this time. I promise not to lose my temper quite so much and not to drink any red wine until the new baby is at least six months old.

But that's not why I'm talking to you right now. It's work. I feel like I'm really going hard but it's never good enough. What am I supposed to do? Can you get them to cut me a little slack?

Love Rebecca xx

P.S. Phoebe is a wicked person and I wish you'd throw some shade her way. Also, if you have time can you knock Darren off his bicycle? Nothing too serious but perhaps a broken rib or two?

I'd forgotten that it was Bella's swimming class that evening (my least favourite activity). For some reason the temperature was always boiling, there were none of the associated benefits of swimming – not for us parents. We sweated in our clothes, with our hair frizzy and damp whilst the children floated about giggling and enjoyed all the stress-relieving hormones pumping through their tiny bodies.

'It's just struck me that Bella is small for her age, isn't she?' said Claudia, another mum – a mum that I only saw at swimming club – as her large, brutish son languished on his back, kicking slowly.

'She's standard size,' I said looking down at my phone.

I hadn't heard back from Sven or an update from Simon. I felt like the project was slipping through my fingers. I usually didn't mind a bit of healthy mum competition. If you were in the right kind of mood, it could be fun. All you had to do was emphasise your child's strengths and subtly (or not so subtly) take a poke at your adversary's child. Today I couldn't be arsed. There is only so much strife that one woman can handle and so I imagined Claudia's hair being even frizzier than it was now, and her nose more bulbous, and the pores on her nose full of bacteria, then her husband's tiny penis (Or perhaps he had halitosis, and was one of those men who grunted when they entered you, and then rolled off. Perhaps he had pimples on his back. Perhaps he wore her underwear on his head). All these thoughts helped me feel better.

'*How's work going?*' Claudia asked waving at the swimming instructor who was quite fit and looked a little like Jared Leto. '*I admire you going to work and leaving Bella all day long. It's a long time to leave a small child at nursery.*'

'*It's hard,*' I replied. '*But I'm a feminist and want her to grow up with a good role model.*'

'*Oh I want that too but I think it's important that you show them what's important in life and money isn't that important is it? I mean what they really want is their mum at home. That's what I think anyway.*'

Ooof that one hurt. So I visualized her smelly husband giving a monkey a hand job. Her husband crying because of his small willy. Her husband gargling with her gin and tonic and spitting it into a glass before he served it to her.

'*I could never miss that precious time,*' she said. '*And I'm so glad that Jude learnt to swim when he was born. A water birth gives them an innate confidence in the water. They're forever playing catch up otherwise.*'

Her husband farting into his hand and smelling it. Her husband picking athlete's foot gunk out of his toes and wiping it on her pyjamas.

In the car I put the radio on and it was Stevie Wonder so I turned it right up. Bella was giggling in the back, high on swimming and a chocolate biscuit I'd handed her to eat in her car seat.

It was a relief when you stopped and realised nothing mattered if you didn't want it to matter. Women all over the world were shoving cotton sausages up their vaginas to stop themselves from bleeding. AWESOME had become a cool word to show enthusiasm even if you were middle-aged. Bella was a poor swimmer and small to boot. She spent too much time on the iPad, because I had no idea what the right length of time was. I was not a good role model because I permanently eye-balled my phone.

Soon I would give birth and there would just be a ragged, injured, old, vagina left behind. I wasn't sure I'd even survive the birth at my age. I'd found it tough enough with Bella and despite second babies being easier (or this is what people said), I was older; my body had declined and my head was a mess.

'*Can you hear me?*' Pete asked that night as we sat on the sofa.

He was waving his hands in my face. I was so tired. I wasn't listening. I hadn't spoken to my parents in two weeks or more. Bryony had texted several times to arrange a meet up but I'd batted her away with excuses about work.

'A chicken tikka masala please,' I said.

We were ordering a takeaway. Pete had also made me a hot water bottle because I'd told him I'd got back ache (true).

'Are you okay?'

'Mmmm.'

Tonight he wanted to talk, and I didn't. Then tomorrow I would want to talk and he wouldn't. I couldn't focus on the TV or follow the plot. I was sick of all the hours I spent staring at other people. I would go to bed early tonight and things would seem better in the morning. At least the morning sickness had passed. It had been nowhere near as bad as last time.

'I'm worried,' Pete said, becoming more animated. 'You're usually bugging me about not talking enough and then the last few days you've been very quiet.'

'I'd like a Thai green curry alright?' I said.

'I wasn't talking about the takeaway. Why are you being so quiet?'

'I can't win can I?' I said getting up off the sofa. 'You ignore me ninety percent of the time, and then when I do the same back to you, you have a go.'

'I haven't been ignoring you.'

'Did you know I had Botox a few weeks ago?' I asked.

'*You didn't?*' he said in a horrified tone.

'*I did. And you haven't even NOTICED.*'

He studied my face.

'*I can't believe you would be so stupid,*' he said. '*Why would you mess with your face like that? What if something went wrong?*'

'*You have no idea what it's like to be a woman my age,*' I said.

I was punishing him but wasn't sure quite what for. He was trying to be communicative but I was pushing him away.

I sat in bed feeling mean. The lights were out and the house was quiet. My tummy was rumbling and I needed something to eat. I needed to share more with Pete but resented the fact that he never noticed. Then when he noticed it, I got even more fed up because I wanted to keep stuff inside. He couldn't win.

Twelve

Hi Rebecca,
After the conversation with YOUR EXCELLENT
BOSS and colleague Simon I am feeling reassured.
Nevertheless, I am worried that you seem to be
unable to discuss the findings with me ON THE
PHONE. I have given you my mobile, work phone,
Skype, email and the conference call details so I
think you know how to contact me. I hope the
groups go well. I am excited but also NERVOUS.
I hope you feel the same.
Regards,
Sven

Hi Rebecca,
I WANTED you to know that we lost a major client

because of your errors on one of the proposals yesterday. The advertising agency have said they won't work with us again. The FROZEN SWEET POTATO innovation was a massive opportunity. I thought you were picking up recently. I saw some positive signs. I was obviously wrong about that. Phoebe

Hey Dude,
Have you read those articles I sent over about pet food? We've been thinking you'd be a great addition to the account. You'd work with me, moderate lots and lots of groups (the client is detail obsessed so most studies are really LARGE) and we'd get to brainstorm cool thinking together. Have a think and see how you feel. Dog food can be super interesting. I certainly love it (but don't eat it obviously – ha ha!)

Darren ☺

This was a relentless assault course. Still the voice inside told me I had something to prove. It was now or never. I had one last chance to make an impact here at Mango Ltd, to re-brand myself and move away from the *unknown, suspicious German household cleaner* that Phoebe had cruelly summoned up, and into a more established brand territory. It was impossible to be excellent when you hated your job. There were serious things to worry about like climate change, and dictators, and terrorism, and poverty, but worrying about sanitary towels, and frozen sweet potatoes was silly. We could send someone to the moon and make a baby in a laboratory, but we were noodling about with diagrams to try and describe the strategic relationship between an orange-flavoured soft drink versus a cherry one.

> Hey Rebecca,
> It's Mum. Are you okay? I have left several messages for you on your voicemail or have you got a new number? Dad is coming in the house more now and has even accompanied me to one of my Spanish classes (I only started last week but it's good that he wants to get out don't you think?) How's the pregnancy going?
>
> Mum xx

Sometimes I forgot I was even pregnant. I looked down and saw the round tummy (still not big enough for others to tell immediately and no one had noticed or said anything at work). I needed to tell someone at some point. I needed to start thinking about things like maternity leave. Then again I knew that it would be career suicide. Could I have a baby and conceal it in my laptop bag? Continue moderating and doing groups and travelling and answering emails and just feed on my way into work and way home again? Is this what women did to get ahead? The head detaching thing had been a sign. My head was leaving the building and leaving all these numpties behind. There were people dying. Life went by in a flash. Soon the paper flying out of the printer would be shredded and eaten by worms. Packaging would ride on the backs of Humpback whales. We were busy but with what? For a giant tampon that smelt of bananas?! For a wipe that knocked out our baby so it slept for eight hours straight? For an edible cat litter? For what?

Were these true moments of happiness?

No.

In the taxi on the way to the focus groups, I played the same game I always played. It was called 'Can I Be You So I Can Escape From My Life Right Now?' I stared out the window, and as each person went past, I tried to figure out if they were on their way to something better than I was or worse. I was willing to swap places with ANYONE. This woman looked stressed, she was chewing a hangnail, but she was on her way home to have a lovely ready meal. So I'd swap places with her. This man on a ludicrous micro-scooter flying towards the tube, a forty-something teenage baby-man – I would swap places with him too. And this man eating a packet of cheese and onion crisps with a giant beer belly and an Ed Sheeran T-shirt, yes I would be him too. I hated the thought of the groups, the thought of an evening dedicated to sitting with a bunch of strangers trying to *work* the room.

There was the future of sanitary protection to be discussed. I thought about the writers, sitting down at their desks with their laptops at the ready, their creativity about to spill out onto the page, and the actors doing their vocal warm ups in the dressing room, and the policemen figuring out a really tricky case and the surgeon about to launch into a six hour stint of brain surgery. Here I was.

The future of sanitary protection rested on my shoulders.

When we arrived, the freezing air conditioning hit me first, draining all the moisture from my eyeballs, and making them itchy. This would be my home for the foreseeable future. It was four thirty and we were due to finish at eleven thirty. We'd then have more groups to finish up over the coming days.

My phone vibrated and there was a message from nursery.

Can you log into portal and book your appointment to come into nursery and read to the children? it read.

I typed my response- *Yes will do this tomorrow as am currently at work and busy. Thanks!*

If you do not log in today we will book the appointment ourselves. So please make it a priority – came the response.

Was the nursery manager out to get me? Or was the nursery manager actually Phoebe? Were these even from a person? Or was this all part of a broader plot to send me bonkers?

✵

There were two rooms – one for the clients to sit in that looked like an office from the 1980s, grey carpet, grey walls, and for some reason a trouser press and exercise bicycle in one corner (perhaps for clients who needed to squeeze in some exercise whilst they were watching). Then through the one-way mirror (so the clients could watch but the respondents wouldn't see them), a room with eight uncomfortable looking, hard plastic chairs. Again the theme was grey, but there was a flipchart on a stand to write notes as the group progressed and a small nod to humanity in the shape of a watercolour of a kitten playing with a ball of yellow wool.

I looked in the fridge to see if there was anything that would give me a boost. I was very hungry, the sort of hunger that only pregnant women feel. The need to eat something carby and enormous. There was no food. The food would be served when the clients were watching the groups and I'd have to satisfy myself with dry sandwiches put out for the group to eat. I wondered if maybe Simon would order me something I could eat in the taxi later but that would probably be too late and I'd get chronic indigestion and be unable to sleep (this was another unwelcome symptom of pregnancy-insomnia- it was already rearing its ugly head). I chugged down a Diet Coke. I then got my guide out, gave the incentives to the receptionist to hand out to the respondents and looked out the window. I always had the same thoughts just before a round of groups started. WHY WAS I HERE? HOW HAD I ENDED UP ON THIS ROAD? WHY WAS I INCAPABLE OF DOING SOMETHING ELSE? The tea dress I was wearing made my rounded tummy more obvious. It was funny that no one at work had noticed but generally people were self-absorbed (plus I'd always been on the larger side so it wasn't that unusual to see me sporting a big tum).

This was the calm before the storm.

Being a moderator was a bit like doing stand-up but you experienced a bad crowd much more regularly. It also wasn't fun. And it didn't bring you fame or profile. It was something that in ten years would be replaced by a robot. In fact it was probably something Darren was working on already (a robot with white teeth who just repeated the words *AWESOME DUDE* and held up one board after the other).

Can you please log into the portal or we will book your appointment to read to the children?

I looked down at my phone and tried to remember the password. The nursery manager would be furious if I'd forgotten it again. I texted Bryony. She would know what to do and she never seemed to struggle with tech in the same way as I did sometimes.

Do you think you could possibly go on this portal and request a new password and log in for me?

I typed.

It would take her two minutes. And she could pretend she was me and then I'd get a nasty message from the manager but I could just about deal with that right now.

Of course!

I loved her in that moment. I loved her more than anyone else in the world.

How's baby?

I'm hungry and there's no food as usual.

Grab some nuts from the client room. There's always salted peanuts somewhere. Or crisps. Go on the hunt for crisps WOMAN.

Bryony had no doubt watched lots of groups in her old advertising role.

I found some nuts. The appointment flashed up on my phone. I noted the date and made a mental note to make a REAL EFFORT and read something entertaining. Maybe I'd make some cakes beforehand and take them in with me. Nut-free, gluten-free cakes. All would be forgiven. I would be redeemed and a fabulous parent once more.

Half an hour later and there were fourteen clients sitting behind the mirror – all of them speaking a mix of German, French and English. They all sounded tired. It was six pm, and they'd had early starts, sat on planes eating synthetic rolls with ham that was eighty percent water, and were now locked in a dark room with overpowering aircon that was either on full blast, making the room like an ice rink or was off and sweltering like a budget, basement gym. They would spend their evening listening to women talk about their menstrual cycles. It wasn't the Oscars. Nonetheless Sven had also dressed up and had high-waisted leather trousers with a belt with the Ferrari logo on it. He was an imposing figure and he looked like he polished his face for several hours- his aftershave was something expensive and incredibly pungent. His team were a beige mixture of dough-faced, unhappy interns, and sharp-suited, grumpy men. Simon had arrived a little after me, and was sitting close to the mirror with his laptop light shining on his face, giving him an eerie rather than reassuring glow. He'd made an effort and the baseball cap was gone, and he was wearing a white shirt under his jumper. I still felt resentful about his big promotion and he seemed to be lording it about a fair bit. He clearly saw his role as client- hot-shot and I was the elderly minion that did all the drudge work.

'Shall we go through the guide Rebecca?' he said following me into my home for the next few hours.

I checked there were pens, and water and that my chair had a cushion on it so I could have a semblance of comfort. At the same time I was throwing nuts down my throat- aware that I'd not see any food for quite some time now. There were five concept territories to explore. Each was written on a piece of A5 cardboard, accompanied by a set of images of women dancing about in yoga pants.

I am always unhappy when I get my period but when I get my CosyFresh © out and cuddle up on the sofa all is right with the world.

I am worried about the political turmoil in the world but when I get my CosyFresh © out I feel like I'm safe and nothing bad will ever happen.

I feel ugly but then when I get my CosyFresh © out, I feel beautiful.

I feel dirty when I have my period but if I have CosyFresh ©, I feel clean and ready to face the world.

I love my CosyFresh © because it makes me feel energetic and ready to go to the gym (even though I have terrible cramps).

Simon turned the button down so the clients wouldn't hear us.

'*So the idea is that these could be for any kind of product?*' I said. '*So the idea has to work for a tampon or a towel or any other product idea they create in the future?*'

'*Yes Sven says he wants it to stretch so it'll cover their portfolio right now – which is mainly towels and a few tampons but will also give them 'wriggle-space' for the future.*'

'*I'm not sure about the name.*'

'*We suggested the name.*'

'*Did WE?*' I said, I couldn't remember as there had been so many calls and emails and back and forth, I must have tuned out that particular detail. '*But when you say CosyFresh, I just think of a nice, comfy towel,*' I said, gesturing at the boards around us.

'*Well you probably should have brought that up earlier,*' Simon replied and walked out.

'*Can you order me some food please?*' I shouted after him. '*Anything cheesy or with carbs.*'

The door to the client room had already slammed shut. I didn't like being locked in the room all night and not being privy to the conversations going on. It gave Simon the upper hand. It meant that he'd learn all the important details and be better able to write up the debrief. Perhaps this had been his plan all along.

You go girl!

A text from Bryony. I smiled. It was good to have someone on your team looking out for you. She knew how much these groups meant, how important this project was. I was glad we were starting to forge a proper friendship. Kath was brilliant but had never had a clear idea of what I did (why would you?). Bryony knew how tense clients could be, how their entire existence rode on the success of one project.

I could hear them ordering takeaway, opening the fridge to get drinks, settling down to watch the groups. They'd no doubt seen hundreds of groups like these. I felt like I was about to kick off a performance as a stand-up comedian but without any fun or laughter. I sat on the high-backed chair and read through the guide. It was fourteen pages long and had lots of comments in the margin where Sven had made last minute changes this morning. The guide was the thing that everyone got hot and bothered about, but then forgot once the groups kicked off. It was impossible to ask every single question, so instead I underlined key words. *Feelings. Moods. Associations. Periods.* I drew a smiley face in the margin. and the times that each group was due to start and finish. I'd done this for years because I had a fear that my mind would go blank once the women came into the room (this had never happened and the adrenalin usually carried you through). These were the small things that made the mundane tolerable. My tummy was rumbling, but it was too late to eat a sandwich, or perhaps I could eat one very quickly. *'You will not have to do this shit baby,'* I whispered to the bump as I stuffed a cheese sandwich in my mouth. *'I will make sure you never go into market research.'*

I felt like I was losing the drive that had powered me over the past couple of weeks. I was overcome with tiredness. Perhaps I'd show them one day, prove to them I was capable but now I just wanted to lie on the floor and sleep.

I hid the concepts under the table, put lip balm on, and took a deep breath. Heading into the world of women and periods now. The clients were talking behind the mirror. They would be discussing their flights, the hotel, the comfort levels of their beds, the quality of room service, what review they'd leave on TripAdvisor – anything but the project itself. I thought about Bella and what she'd be up to right now (it was five and so she'd still be at nursery, she'd probably be tired and cranky and eager for Pete to pick her up).

'Good evening ladies and thank you for coming to the group.'

'It's only five o' clock so it's hardly evening,' one woman replied.

The women glared at me with thinly disguised apathy.

I explained they were being filmed, that there were clients behind the mirror, that I wanted them to be honest and open. I introduced myself.

Whilst I was doing this, they grabbed sandwiches, talked about their journeys, the fact that the viewing facility was impossible to find on the map they'd been given, how they'd been promised taxi fare home, but it wasn't in the envelope they'd been handed before coming in. I made lots of reassuring noises and tried to chivvy them along. I enquired about their health, their children, their jobs, their lives. I realized that only one of them would possibly be helpful, and the rest would spend their time saying negative, stuff and/or excusing themselves to go to the toilet.

After we'd got all the initial chat out the way, we talked about adverts they liked (none.) The products they used when they had their periods (the cheapest bought on promotion), and then we moved onto the more 'interesting' stuff. We brainstormed the idea of 'Being a woman', and they shouted a list of words that I scribbled down on the flipchart. The flipchart was useful as you had more dominance over the group, and they usually stopped talking about the biscuits, how they couldn't resist eating more, how they were dieting but never lost weight, whether the panel on *The X Factor* were good this year or not etc.

Motherwhelmed

Being a woman today is . . .

Good

Bad

Difficult

Tiring

Sad

Happy

Positive

Negative

Fun

Not fun

Boring

I tried to do some *laddering* which basically meant saying the words – *why, why, why, why,* until everyone wanted to top themselves. Then one disagreeable woman, with a scrunchie, and bright orange lipstick started to get grumpy.

'*I don't agree with anything you're saying. I don't think you can generalize. It's different for everyone.*'

I nodded and did a sort of pleading expression with

my eyes. *Please work with me, I'm having a hard time, and you've been given sixty quid, okay?*

'Okay, let's move on. What are the five things that come into your mind when I say PERIODS?' I said.

'Cramps.'

'Pain.'

'Blood.'

'Death.'

'I'm not up the duff.'

The woman who'd said this cast her eyes at my rounded tummy. I smiled. I was over three months, and had seen a grainy image of the baby on a scan. Had she spotted my secret? She said nothing more.

'Okay, so let's think about a new sanitary protection brand – what could they talk about?'

'What do you mean TALK?' the unhelpful woman said.

'I don't want something TALKING down there,' another chimed in.

'Unless it's Benedict Cumberbatch,' another said laughing.

I needed to get the concepts out before the group deteriorated even more. It was becoming a free for all.

'Let's probe a bit more around feelings,' I said brightly. *'So, if we talk about cramps, what feelings do cramps evoke?'*

'*They hurt,*' one woman said as she bit into a tuna sandwich.

I grabbed a sandwich and stuffed it in my mouth whole. I was ravenous. The women looked at me in silence.

'*Can I go to the toilet please?*'

I ignored the toilet comment. It was so annoying that someone wanted the toilet just when the group was talking sense.

'*What about this word here? Death?*'

A woman with a pink shawl and massive overbite, was trying to be constructive – '*I don't know why I said death. Blood I guess. It's the end of life.*'

'*Or the start,*' another chipped in.

I had been standing by the flipchart for a while now but was worried that if I sat down, I wouldn't have the energy to get up. There was silence and another woman asked if she could go to the loo. Were they all menstruating? (the one with the shawl looked much older than the rest. I'd need to look at the printed profiles afterwards, as this was supposed to be a group of thirty – thirty-five year olds). Hopefully Sven wouldn't notice.

I thought about the book I would read to Bella's nursery class. We had a really cool kids book which was all about the life of Frida Kahlo.

I was certain that Frida would have never put up with this kind of shit.

I then thought about what I might eat when I got in tonight. Toast? Cheese on toast?

Then I thought about how people often told you the strangest things in groups; intimate things, secrets, fears and worries, and anxieties.

'The puppy on the toilet roll reminds me of my father. He died at Christmas,' a woman had once told me in a group.

'I hate my life and wish I could go back and change everything,' another had said (this had been for a group exploring different textures of duvet fillings).

Others had talked about loved ones dying, of being lonely, of feeling sad about their bodies, their husbands, their children, their jobs. So many unhappy lives. It was like that Beatles song- *all the lonely people, where do they all come from?* It was like group therapy. I was unearthing these feelings but was only interested in things that were helpful to the client.

We bought things because in that moment they spoke to us and made us feel better. It wasn't a rational thing. We saw something, and it reminded us of the way our mum used to stroke our forehead at night, or the colour made us feel safe, or we projected into the future, and imagined marrying George Clooney because we were wearing a new, *max-lengthening* mascara.

It was manipulative and dark.

Something was building inside – it wasn't nausea, more like exasperation, and not just for this moment right here, but for all the moments I'd spent locked in rooms when I could have been writing a novel or climbing mountains or volunteering to help people? SO MUCH WASTED TIME! I wanted to be more like Bryony; flexible, able to embrace new challenges, less fearful, less insecure.

'*Let's talk about the product,*' I said as they were now rapidly moving onto *how the fillings in the sandwiches weren't very tasty* and . . . *Was this one fish? Or liver paste?*

My tummy rumbled. I reached for another sandwich. The bread had no moisture, and it was a battle to swallow.

'*It would be white,*' pink shawl lady said (I was supposed to memorise their names but I usually used physical characteristics to navigate my way through).

'*It would be soft,*' scrunchie hair added.

'*It would be like a towel.*'

'*Or it could be like a tampon?*'

'*Okay a towel or a tampon shape, good. What else?*' I asked, still trying to swallow the golf ball of sticky dough in my throat.

'*It would be sticky so it didn't fall out of your pants.*'

'*Okay, it won't fall out of our pants,*' I mumbled.

'*A tampon shouldn't be sticky.*'

There was a knock and Simon stood at the door looking sheepish.

'*Sven has a question. He wants more depth. More probing,*' he said.

I nodded. The feeling inside was building – I was either about to break down or do something else, something more terrifying.

'*He's a bit agitated.*'

He gestured with his hands, bringing to life the level of agitation which was roughly *brick-sized*. The women were discussing George Clooney's wife, and whether she'd had her twins through IVF, how these Hollywood women could do whatever they wanted when it came to reproduction and it wasn't fair, and he was a bachelor at heart. So many times I'd stood at the door, and heard these demands from clients. Not enough. Too much. Keep up. Move on. Show the ideas. Leave the ideas to the end. You've not covered any of the areas we discussed or you've covered them all and we need MORE MORE MORE.

'*I'm pregnant,*' I blurted out.

'*That's terrible news. What will Phoebe and Darren say?*' Simon whispered.

'*No. I'm happy I'm pregnant,*' I hissed. '*Sorry, I shouldn't be talking to you about this. It's just that this whole discussion feels like it's going nowhere and I'm still hungry and want to lie on the floor and sleep.*'

'That's not a good idea.'

'Could you moderate the next group?'

'I don't moderate. I only do semiotics and analysis,' he said shaking his head.

'I'm just super tired and not sure I can do another two of these?'

'You're a great moderator and you're in the target market,' he replied remaining steadfast. 'And besides I prefer to watch so I can keep the macro trends top of mind.'

'And you get to sit on your arse,' I said. 'And eat takeaway'

Simon shrugged. I could smell a waft of chicken korma and closed my eyes. My head was pounding now . . . the sandwich had barely touched the sides.

The women were growing restless. They were talking about the difficulty of finding interesting vegetarian fillings for sandwiches. There was a stale smell in the air.

I launched into the concepts. I bought as much enthusiasm as I could to the discussion.

I read out the concepts.

'I feel ugly but then when I get my CosyFresh out, I feel beautiful,' I said. 'Do we feel ugly when we get our period? Can a tampon or a towel make us more beautiful?'

'No,' said unhelpful but perceptive pink-shawl lady.

'I asked you to be constructive right?'

'*But it's a stupid thing to say.*'

'*Patronising twaddle,*' another chimed in.

'*Okay,*' I said brightly. '*It's making us feel uncomfortable but maybe that's because it's a new idea?.*'

'*I don't like the name.*'

'*It doesn't have to be that name. Okay and these images. Do we like any of these?*' I said, pointing at the pictures of women leaping about like joyous lemmings in tiny white pants.

'*Why is Fearne Cotton in this photo? Is she going to be on the advert?*"

They talked about Fearne for a couple of minutes, and I went to fetch the next concept. I could just about make out Simon's ghostly reflection in the mirror. He didn't look happy. What was Sven saying?

Each idea was met with silence. It was every moderator's nightmare. The moment when you are talking to yourself and getting no response. I re-read each line with a slightly different voice, hoping this would give the impression more people were talking .

'*Is a towel going to get rid of global warming?*' one chipped in.

'*Is it going to get rid of the plastic in the sea?*' pink shawl said.

'*Do they think we're all morons?*'

'*I don't like this bit where they say having your period makes you ugly. Are these guys misogynists?*'

'*Well remember it doesn't have to be a towel. It could be anything at all,*' I said.

'*It sounds like it's going to be bulky.*'

'*Yes, really big!*' said another (her first contribution so far).

There was another bang on the door.

'*Sven wants you to go through the concepts again. He doesn't feel you got enough depth,*' Simon said.

'*But we only have three minutes left.*'

I went back in. Why wasn't I sunning myself whilst a minion massaged my back? Why didn't I have a husband who drove a helicopter to work, and showered me with money? BEING A FEMINIST WAS FUCKING EXHAUSTING! For so long I'd been NICE. I'd nodded, accepted and been a proper submissive, and now I was old and angry.

I'm gonna take this itty bitty world by storm.

And I'm just getting warm.

'*Okay, ladies,*' I said sweeping around the room,

I was *leaning in.*

'*These ideas are AWFUL,*' I said. '*They're unimaginative and regressive and say nothing new.*'

The women nodded in unison. A gangster rap kind of approach might shake things up.

'*So tell me in all honesty, how do you feel? Let me guess, you feel sad, yes? But can't quite put a finger on what it is that's causing this feeling,*' I tapped on the flipchart with my marker pen and wrote the words down like a religious chant, a mantra in fact. *TIRED. WASHED UP. WHY?* The women stirred in their seats. It wasn't every day that you saw a middle-aged moderator losing her marbles. They leant forward.

'*I'm so tired,*' pink shawl said shaking her head.

Another woman nodded. '*My mother was never this tired. She never had so much pressure.*'

I nodded and scribbled – *MY MUM JUST GOT ON WITH IT.*

'*So why do we feel lost and tired?*' I asked.

'*We are unhappy,*' two said at the same time.

'*What will make us better?*' I asked rubbing my tummy, feeling the new life growing, acknowledging that it WAS going to happen, that I was going to be a new mum again, and it would be fine, and unhappiness was everywhere anyway. There was no point trying to erase it.

'*What will make us better?*' I repeated.

Simon was at the door. His cheeks were red. I could tell Sven was probably even more agitated by now.

'*I am old and pregnant and I've done this job for TOO MANY YEARS,*' I said. '*I sit in a cold, sterile room with dried out sandwiches and a fluorescent light over my head, and I ask people questions they have no interest in answering. Then I buy myself stuff to make up for it. Do you do that too?*'

'YES, ALL THE TIME,' pink shawl said standing up. 'I am searching for something and whenever I see a product I think THAT'S the thing that'll sort me out. Then I buy it. When you buy stuff it basically makes you more miserable.'

'It's our expectations,' said another. 'We want to be great mothers and be successful at work and be sexy partners and we can't HAVE IT ALL,' her voice wobbled a bit at the end.

'We're trapped.'

'But who trapped us?' I asked.

'We did. Society did. Advertising. You did.'

I'd written the names of each woman down on my notepad. I read each name aloud: 'Mary, Suzie, Donna, Frankie, Fatima, Judith, Rachel and Harriet, I'm sorry because you're right, I'm the person who's been contributing to these feelings of inadequacy.'

'I haven't had a period for months,' pink shawl said. 'I thought I should tell you just in case you get in trouble.'

I nodded.

'Don't worry, Mary. Don't worry.'

The group finished, the women filed out. I sat for a moment, preparing myself for the clients to go mad and demand my head on a stick. I didn't care. This baby would be coming. I had a wonderful daughter. Pete was my soulmate, even if we got on each other's nerves. I was making new friends. I would leave market research and find another career. It could happen. Bryony had showed me it could. I went into the room, Simon followed behind, saying nothing.

'THAT WAS TERRIFIC, REBECCA!' Sven said, rising to meet me.

The other clients clapped, and one of them raised his coffee cup as if he was about to make a toast.

'Can we re-work the guide so we can start with this NEW set of questions?' Sven said. *'Such rich learnings! I had no idea women were so fatigued. I can see this new proposition very clearly in my mind. It needs to address these untapped needs!'*

'A brand that makes women less fatigued?' his assistant said.

'Yes,' Sven continued. *'I love this idea of offering comfort and support– A towel that taps into all the demands of modern life.'*

'I'm glad you're happy,' I said.

'Oh, and good news on your baby. Very surprising news, Rebecca!' Sven said.

But I'd done it. Somehow, I'd moderated the group and this demanding client was happy. I'd pulled it off. My hip-hop philosophy of projecting confidence at all times, being honest and authentic, being myself, had worked.

I would hopefully be home before midnight. There were only two more groups this evening. I was exhausted but also a bit exhilarated. I pictured that I'd turned a corner and invented a new style of moderating which was honest and authentic. I started making notes in the guide whilst Simon entertained the clients with stories about Japanese drinking culture.

Thirteen

'COME IN AND SIT *down*,' Phoebe said.

I'd had the initial elation after the groups, and then felt so tired that I'd fallen asleep in the Uber on the way home. Mum had sent a few texts about Dad which were ambiguous to say the least – I'd made a mental note to get in touch but there was just too much going on right now. I'd then received four emails from Phoebe about my *'revised new business generation targets'*. Phoebe was online and working even at eleven thirty at night.

EXCITING *LEAD IN THE CHEESY SAVOURY SNACK CATEGORY*
NEW SUNGLASSES RETAILER LAUNCHING MUM BAG

FOUR GROUPS AND **TEN** DEPTHS IN GLASGOW-
CAN YOU <u>COVER</u> THIS?

For some reason Phoebe didn't look happy. I'd made an effort style-wise, and was wearing a skirt with black tights, and these tights had no ladders. It was my attempt at looking professional. She looked drained and hadn't got her usual slick bob in place (she'd skipped the blow dry). I also noticed a few grey hairs poking through her parting (which was odd as Phoebe had her roots done every three weeks whilst she was dictating a global debrief via Skype). Some of her red lipstick had rubbed off on her teeth. The burst of colour against her white complexion made her look like a vampire.

'Is there anything you need to tell me?' she said.

I felt my stomach lurch. Had Simon told her my news already? Wasn't that my business?

'I was going to tell you that I was pregnant,' I said feeling worried about what was coming next.

Phoebe tried to smile but the muscles either side of her mouth weren't cooperating.

'Well I guess is explains your lacklustre performance over the past few weeks?' she said.

'Lacklustre? I won PROJECT ZIGGY didn't I?'

'I think talking to Simon that it's obvious that he played a pivotal role in that win. Without his slides and his input I doubt we'd have got it.'

281

'Did he also tell you Sven was over the moon with my moderating and said it was the best groups he'd seen in years?'

'Sven is very eccentric and whimsical. It sounded like it was pretty unruly and unorthodox.'

I looked at the floor.

'But then again you've always been a good moderator. We've never questioned your moderating skills. Problem is, it's not enough. Anyway, you've told me your news. I'll get in touch with HR. I take it you're planning a full year off again?'

'What's the alternative?'

'Well you must do what you want of course Rebecca but a year is a long time in a company like Mango-Lab.'

She sounded more than a little threatening.

'But my job will still be here right?'

'Of course. We'd be breaking the law otherwise. Oh is it that the time? I've got a 9.45 with Shanghai. Speak again soon.'

She picked up her landline and started cheerily saying hello to the clients.

Was she expecting me to give birth in the office? And then resume normal service? I thought about how she'd taken the minimum amount of time, and how she rarely spoke about her kids (unless there was a big company drinks and then she'd get a bit misty-eyed). It was hard to find an accessible bonding territory. She didn't read magazines. She didn't like fashion (or didn't look like she did). She hated reality TV. Her hobbies were all competitive – things like tennis or triathlons. She didn't like music. Or boozing. Or cake. Yes women were feminists now but what did you talk about if all those things were outlawed. There was no photo of her family on her desk. I knew there were three of them but not much more than that (her screensaver was a photo of another mountain she'd climbed for charity or some such.)

Phoebe opened the door and called me back inside.

'Listen, congratulations on the baby but I should flag up that I really want to avoid having one of those difficult appraisals again – it'll be a while now till mat leave so let's see you really going for it. I was tremendously energized by pregnancy and hopefully you will be too right?'

I stood by her chair.

'Bloody conference call was cancelled. Can you ask that intern, what's her name? Gloria? If she can re-schedule with the client. The whole day will be out of whack now.'

I nodded but didn't move. I could also see her point of view when it came to mums in the office. Why have someone like me when you could have Simon who worked all hours of the day and weekends and had no morals or ethics? He embraced opportunities to travel to far-flung places. He happily dobbed in his colleague if it meant a promotion. I wanted to see Bella for at least an hour a day. I wanted to give her a bath. I wanted to stroke her head as she fell asleep. I wanted to feel her squeeze my head until my head hurt.

Did that make me weak?

Phoebe rubbed her temples. I felt a tiny bit of empathy, but remembered that she'd never shown me any kindness. I only really came onto her radar when she wanted to tell me off and make me feel crap. Wasn't there a new female, empowering, collaborative, way of leading nowadays? Hadn't I read in 'Red' magazine that women were better in companies, rallying teams, inspiring people . . . because they weren't afraid to show empathy? Bryony would be one of these women when she was older. Perhaps in a different world I could have been one too. The truth was Phoebe had chosen a masculine management style (this was possibly the only one available to a woman coming into the workforce in the early nineties). You barked orders and dismissed tears as 'silly nonsense'.

'Listen Rebecca,' Phoebe said, looking up. *'Simon also told me that you tried to kiss him. I think that's quite worrying don't you? I won't mention it to HR but let's be clear, we don't' accept any form of sexual harassment in this office.'*

Simon! He'd even told her about my stupid lunge on the dancefloor. I felt myself sink into the carpet.

'Simon is a very talented semiotician,' Phoebe continued. 'One of our *'ones to watch'.'*

I nodded. Simon was also a twat and a turncoat.

'So don't waste his time asking him to moderate groups. He is part of this project to provide strategic insight. You can moderate. That's your responsibility okay?'

I nodded again. With each sentence she uttered I felt myself sinking lower and lower. It was the opposite of a team-building mission, it was all about getting me to roll over and surrender, possibly to resign. Me with my weak, feminine, floppy values. Me with my lack of strategic insight. Me.

'I sometimes think taking all that time off is a bad idea. We need to stay at work or we lose our ambition, our determination, our drive. Time off makes you weak, in the end.'

I left her office and all the positivity about the previous night's groups had gone. Instead I felt hurt and angry. I'd put up with being routinely lectured by a twenty-something about topics such as 'The Cultural Significance of the Grunge movement,' and 'Why the Summer of Love was bad for the Advertising industry.' I'd come to the breakfast meetings (where I'd usually had to leave Bella with a neighbour because the nursery hadn't opened yet), I'd been forced to listen to Miles Davis for an hour whilst an arrogant imbecile in tight trousers, and a bouffant lectured me on the influence of trumpets in contemporary fizzy pop advertising.

Dear Bouffant,
I like Miles Davis as much as the next person. I lived
through grunge. I didn't just stick a T-shirt on with
my super-tight jeans that make me look like a mime
artist. You are a silly man, very silly and I don't care
what university you went to but you'd never be able
to pull a girl in a bar. They'd laugh at you. I'm laughing
at you right now.
Rebecca x

The air conditioning was too high, we had to wear blankets to stay warm and were expected to write twelve proposals a week. We were like battery chickens – the only difference was that we were thrown an exotic breakfast every week and given a trolley of beers on Friday.

I was the old, knackered chicken ready for the stock pot.

Mum had left a voicemail. I sat at my desk and listened.

Dad wouldn't get out of bed.

He was playing Mahler very loud on his iPod (he was the only one I knew who still owned one).

He had only eaten soup for three days.

I rang her back and told her I'd come over this evening.

I'd had a bad feeling about all this.

Motherwhelmed

How did your groups go?

It was a text from Bryony.

Really good but they're still not happy.

What reasons are they giving?

Not good enough. Not strategic enough. I don't know. Just feeling demotivated. And now my Dad's sunken into a bad depression

Keep going love. You're doing so well. Remember to start hatching your escape plan. What do you really want to do? Good luck with Dad x

That evening I drove to the house. Puddles followed me up the stairs. His legs kept shaking.

'*Puddles can you see if you can cheer him up?*' I said picking him up and carrying him under my arm.

The room was pitch dark. Dad was lying face down on top of the covers. His hair fanned out around in him. His headphones lying nearby. He groaned.

'*Why can't people JUST leave me alone?*'

'*We're worried about you,*' I said perching on the bed and releasing Puddles so he jumped onto the bed, and tried to lick the side of Dad's face.

'I've got a mild dose of flu that's all,' he said sitting up.

The covers were printed on the side of his face and he had purple rings under his eyes. For the first time I saw how old and vulnerable he really was. I felt consumed with guilt. I was so fixated on myself all the time. I never seemed to be capable of thinking of anyone else. Pete, Dad, Bella, Mum . . . there was no room left in my head for them.

'Remember how the doctor said it was important that you keep busy. That you have a good routine?'

'I like doing the trains, listening to Radio Four and drinking the odd can of cider.'

'Okay but why haven't you been up and about these past few days.'

He stroked Puddles who responded by trembling violently and then presenting his tummy.

'What do you want to do Dad?'

'Do you know what I really want to do?' he said eventually. *'I want to be back at the university. I want to be invited to conferences. Instead I'm a grown man playing with sodding trains!'*

It seemed ironic that both Dad and I were in a similar situation. We were looking for a different way to live. We knew there was something else we should be doing to make ourselves happier. We knew our current lifestyle wasn't *serving* us (the yoga teacher had used this phrase once and it had stuck in my head- the idea that certain things didn't 'serve' you long term).

'Why don't you do what Mum does and enrol in a couple of courses? Or write? Or arrange a meet up with a couple of your old colleagues?'

Dad shrugged.

'Listen if you promise to sort your life out, then I promise I'll sort out mine. We can chivvy one another along okay?'

'Okay,' he said. *'Oh and good news on the baby. You did want another baby right?'*

'Yes,' I said and realized I really meant it.

Fourteen

'*T*HIS MORNING WE HAVE *a really exciting breakfast session and we'll be discussing Johnny Cash and his influence on pet ownership in the United States,*' said Darren.

He hadn't changed out of his cycling gear and I found the outline of his penis distracting. I didn't fancy him one iota but I couldn't help wondering what he might be like in bed. Did he leave his Fitbit on so he could record how many calories he'd burnt? Did he like to listen to motivational speeches so he was truly multi-tasking (sex on it's own was a waste of time and energy right?)

Did he ever lie back on his pillow afterwards and think – WHO AM I?

Darren was working at such an intensity that his hair

had gone practically white in six months. He was pitching. Winning business. Travelling to far flung markets and introducing people to the joys of expensive dog food. He had kicked off his career in the eighties and still thought it was funny to use sexual innuendo. He complained that women were too sensitive these days and when a woman was in a mood he blamed it on her period. He had once pointed that my lunch (two rather tired asparagus spears) looked like penises.

He was a tired old sexist creep and soon he'd be irrelevant.

For a moment I thought back to Phoebe's dishevelled appearance. Perhaps things weren't going as swimmingly as I thought. My own future looked very uncertain.

I was pregnant. A big pile of *lack*. They'd have to be cautious. Having said that they had lots of lawyers. I'd seen them get shot of people before. Usually old timers. Old chickens with no juice. One minute they'd be giving a talk in front of the office, and the next, they'd disappeared, their polaroid photo removed from the 'Company Squad Excellence Chart'.

Darren had an orange cube which contained a microphone, and he randomly threw it into the crowd so that people could be quizzed on key points during his talk. It meant any moment you might be called upon to do some public speaking. Darren hurled the cube into the crowd and a boy with glasses caught it and looked like he wished he hadn't.

'Why do you think there was an increase in dog food sales just after Johnny's death, Charlie mate?'

The poor boy looked nervous and mumbled something.

'CAN'T HEAR YOU MATE!' Darren shouted. *'SPEAK UP MATE.'*

A few people in the audience started chanting – *SPEAK UP. SPEAK UP.*

The boy shook his head. Darren looked on in frustration. He had no patience with LOSERS who didn't TALK. He hadn't read the book about how introverts were often very clever, far cleverer than their noisy, obnoxious counterparts.

'Okay Gemma you have a go,. You know what I'm talking about DUDE.'

Darren even called the sixty-five-year-old cleaning lady DUDE. The cube was now flying towards a new researcher who had been promoted three times in the last eighteen months. Gemma now suffered from chronic alopecia, and her finger tips were red raw where she'd chewed her nails off.

'Maybe the crisis in masculinity resulted in a rise in dog ownership which then impacted on pet food sales?' she said.

'Interesting DUDE but NOT RIGHT.'

My asparagus had looked nothing like a penis. Darren

wasn't a dude. I was Rebecca. I was a forty-two year old woman with lots of talent. I could do anything, be anyone, achieve anything. I grabbed the orange box and held it in front of my face.

'Right Rebecca! What do you think then?' Darren said nervously.

'Name me two Johnny Cash albums Darren,' I found myself saying. 'Do you even know any of his music?'

'Of course I do!'

'Do you know that Johnny Cash had more talent in his pinky finger than you do in your entire body?'

'That's not very fair is it?' he said.

A few people chuckled. Where was Simon? Simon and Darren. Darren and Simon. They were as bad as each other. Darren was always making me feel bad about my age despite the fact he was older than I was. He made references to old dance music hits and then said – Oh Rebecca will know that one. Or he pointed out some fashion item and reminded everyone – Oh I bet Rebecca loved that style back in the day. And Simon – well Simon was just a twat.

His annoying baseball cap had been right.

Darren had written a very boring presentation but had made it look relevant by adding in a few popular culture references. He didn't care who Johnny Cash was. He just thought he sounded cool and made his slides look more aspirational. Pete always went mad at people wearing Ramones T-shirts for the same reason – they didn't know anything about the band but it gave them credibility. You had to *earn* the right to reference these people; you had to know the score. You couldn't just use popular culture references willy nilly.

'*What's your favourite Johnny Cash song?*' I asked, my voice shaking now.

What point I was trying to make here – that Darren was stupid? Mango-Lab was stupid? People were watching us now. It was interesting to see two geriatrics colleagues having a face off.

I was now representing every mum who had taken maternity leave – only to discover that she'd been downgraded to loser-town on her return – every woman in her forties who was invisible because she had a few lines on her face and the occasional attack of the grumps.

'*TELL ME ABOUT JOHNNY CASH!*' I screamed into the cube and it released a terrifying burst of feedback so that the people around me clutched their ears and grimaced.

'*Can someone please take the cube away from Rebecca,*' Phoebe said as she appeared like a ghoul from the kitchen area and moved towards me. '*Rebecca, can you please come to my office?*'

I thought about all those late-night emails, the lack of empathy, and then I thought about how I'd wasted my time feeling sad about my lack of strategic prowess, and the meetings where I'd sat back and listened whilst people (men usually) went on and on for hours, and I thought about all those willies I'd drawn in the columns of my notebook, and the smiley faces to get me through. I thought about how no one asked me ONE QUESTION about my daughter, how I had to practically deny she existed, that Phoebe possibly didn't even know her name. The stupid meetings that were always labelled with a new title, but were essentially the same thing over and over. The hours I'd missed with Bella. The time that would have been better spent trying to find something I was really good at. I was a mediocre market researcher. I always would be.

'*Can we all congratulate Simon on his promotion?*' I shouted as I turned my back to face the audience, some of who were gazing back into their laps at their phones again. It was amazing what people were prepared to ignore these days. Simon wasn't here but I wondered whether everyone else knew. The truth was they probably didn't care.

'*My office,*' Phoebe whispered and I realized she was standing next to me.

She'd grown wheels on the bottom of her shoes and had glided towards me.

'*Can we have a round of applause for him. HE'S THE MANGO HEAD OF SOMETHING CLEVER . . . have you heard?'* I repeated again and then caught his eye as he was sitting right at the back.

I'd been working EVERY SINGLE HOUR OF THE DAY and it still clearly wasn't enough. I hadn't been promoted in four years.

'Stop it,' Phoebe hissed.

A few people clapped. Darren was still holding onto the cube like it was a giant teddy bear. I'd wanted to be triumphant, glorious, to set the office ablaze like a 90s hip-hop queen, but instead there was just this awkward silence, and nobody seemed to care. For many years, I'd fantasised about resigning, what it would feel like, the kind of emails I'd send to all my enemies. I would be leaving because of a book deal, opening my own shop, following my dreams, and detaching myself from this world of drones. The problem was I was no closer to discovering my true passion. Perhaps that didn't matter. Perhaps just giving this *drudge* the elbow was the key thing for now.

'That's enough,' Darren shouted cheerily as if he'd just woken up and realized what was actually going on. *'In twenty minutes we have an African Themed Lunch Treat. We'll also reschedule this session for next week!'*

'Is it the weird meat on sticks?' I said but nobody heard. It was a shame. It was actually quite funny.

The chairs were being shuffled about, and Phoebe was pulling me across the office, and then pushing me towards hers. *I'm gonna take this itty, bitty world by storm, and I'm just getting warm.* There was no fanfare. No LL Cool J to send me off. No drama. No shouts of – LET HER BE! SHE'S RIGHT! THIS PLACE SUCKS! WE HATE THE MEAT ON STICKS TOO! Nobody was interested because there was a free lunch, and it offered up a promising alternative to the canteen or Leon. Food was the way they controlled this army. A trolley of beers. Some bowls of popcorn. A trolley that brought round sweets every now and then. It was a winning strategy.

'*This is unacceptable behaviour,*' Phoebe said as we sat down in her office, the seat still felt warm from my last visit. '*Tell me, what do you actually hope to achieve?*'

I looked down at my phone. Was it Mum? Bad news about Dad? No it was a nursery text. The robot nursery phantom.

I couldn't look at it now.

I realized I was crying. I was sick of never being good enough.

'*I can't have you in the office when you're tired and hormonal like this,*' Phoebe said, dismissing the fact that this had been going on for YEARS, and was nothing to do with pregnancy. '*Do you actually think my job is easy Rebecca? Do you think there aren't some days when I simply just can't face all this SHIT?*'

She pressed a button on her landline phone.

'*Can you delay my lunch meeting by fifteen?*' she shouted. '*Oh and can you send the nanny a bunch of flowers? I forgot it was her birthday this week. Peonies. Nice ones. Spend at least forty quid.*'

If I had a PA and a nanny then perhaps I'd be Phoebe. If I could have someone who could remember the passwords, the appointments, the cat worming tablets, the playdates, the birthdays, check all my emails and only send me the relevant ones, book out my appointments, type up my charts, field enquiries from Sven, tell Simon I was too important to bothered right now. Maybe then I'd have a chance.

'*Phoebe – do you know that ALL this time . . . well you've never said a kind thing to me? You've emailed me on a Sunday at four in the afternoon. Berated me on one of our team away days and constantly made me feel like a flop.*'

Phoebe studied the ceiling as if it might offer up an answer. There was silence for a moment or two.

'*I said I was happy you'd won Project Ziggy,*' she said.

'*You gave Simon all the credit.*'

'*But he deserved it. Look I'm sorry that you're pregnant. It must be a a dreadful shock. What more do you want . . . blood? I am not your mum, I'm your boss. I have a HUGE RESPONSIBILITY.*'

I wanted to sit on top of Phoebe and use my knees to work pain into her upper arms. I wanted her to struggle, BEG FOR MERCY and say . . . *'YES, OKAY REBECCA YOU CAN FINALLY DO SOMETHING BETTER THAN ME.'*

What could I do better than Phoebe? Was there anything?

I cried on the train on the way home. I cried as I looked at my work pass, and the grim, rigid smile. I had worked at Mango-Lab too long. I hadn't noticed because I'd been too tied up with the future of sanitary towels, and new formats for rim block innovation, and why fish fingers weren't as popular as they could be, and why Johnny Cash and dog food were inexorably linked in ways that I still couldn't understand.

I read the text from the nursery. I had missed my appointment again. The children had been waiting and I'd failed to turn up to read them a story. Bella would be desperately sad and disappointed. I couldn't blame Phoebe. I'd written the date down but then forgotten it again.

Fifteen

FOR AS LONG AS I could remember I'd fantasised about never going back to that office.

HR said they were happier if I worked from home for the foreseeable future. So my fantasy was finally realized. The problem was I just felt more paranoid and isolated. I was fleeing but had nothing to flee to.

On the plus side it at least got rid of the commute. And actually seeing Phoebe, Darren and Simon in the flesh. I sat on my laptop at home. I wrote up all the notes for Project Ziggy. I realized that women were complex and difficult to understand. I learnt that periods were accepted as part of life and no products were really going to 'fix,' anything. I also learnt that the name – 'Cosy Fresh©,' was exceedingly patronising. I started to Google evening courses but couldn't land on anything that felt compelling enough. How was it that Bryony could be so certain that photography was the answer? Perhaps when you were in your twenties, you could afford to mess about trying to find your niche but what about when you were in your forties like me? I knew there was something out there that would *serve* me better (there was that yoga teacher in my ear again) but what was it?

I ordered new black-out blinds for Bella's bedroom as the baby would have to share with her after a few months. I fretted that she'd find it hard to adapt to having been an only child for so long. I wrote a couple of proposals. I tried to sound chirpy and enthusiastic in emails. Phoebe and Darren were oddly quiet. Simon didn't enquire how I was.

I went into Bella's nursery and FINALLY read to the children. I chose the Frida Kahlo that Bella and I loved and the kids seemed to like it. They were distracted because one of the kids kept getting out his chair and trying to wipe a bogey on whichever kid was closest.

I had coffee with Bryony (who was now well into launching her photography business and already had a couple of clients.) She presented me with a framed copy of the photo of Bella and I. I had hundreds of photos on my phone but this one was one that I'd look at for years to come. It captured a moment – the moments that as soon as I recognized were there, disappeared again. It captured love in its purest form.

'We'll find you something you enjoy,' she said as I told her that I had no clear direction, no sense of what would be good next.

'Writing?' she said.

'I'm not sure I have the patience.'

'Something with your hands?'

'I'm impatient and tend to botch things up.'

'Can you try and be a bit more positive about yourself?'

'Okay well I make a really good ratatouille but nobody seems to eat that anymore.'

'How about joining Pete and doing catering?'

'God that would never work. I mean we find it relatively hard to get along as it is.'

She poured more tea into the teapot.

'Do you notice how negative you are? Not just about yourself but about everything?'

'I'm afraid it's what happens when you get to your forties. You can't help but be more jaded.'

'But can't you see that it's the one thing that's holding you back?'

'Maybe not the one thing?' I said pointing at my growing belly.

She smiled. Ralph was napping across her lap. She always made motherhood look so effortless but I knew it was deceptive. It was easy to look at another woman and think she'd got it sussed. You weren't party to the tears at bedtime and the arguments with the partner and the struggles to remain calm and not lose it at any moment. Bryony had a point though about the negativity It explained why I was so bitter all the time and resentful of younger colleagues. The truth was there was a lot of envy there too- I wished I had that time again, that I'd made the decision to leave Mango-Lab a long time ago instead of just coasting along, my hair growing greyer, my skin saggier, my outlook bleaker.

'*I'm too bloody old to change.*'

'*I'm not going to get all Oprah on you but you're never too old. Do you think I'm confident that this photography business is going to work?.*'

'*You look like you are.*'

'*Well I'm not. I just know I can't go back to agency life again.*'

'*We're not the same though. I have been doing this stuff for far too long. I'm institutionalized.*'

Bryony glared at me as she put Ralph over her shoulder and rubbed her back. A new baby. A new career? I felt tired just thinking about it.

Meanwhile back at home, things improved with Pete. We started talking again. It felt a bit like we were prancing about on eggshells, careful not to put our foot in it or stray into unwelcome territory but it was better than it had been for a few months.

'*I thought you wanted to leave that place anyway,*' he said reaching over one evening and stroking my hand.

'*I do. I mean I should. It's kind of killing me.*'

'*Well I'll try and offer as much support as possible. I mean I'm not swimming in money but we'll survive.*'

I tried to think about myself as a brand.

I was Marks & Spencer constantly trying to get hip but always getting it slightly wrong.

I was Woolworths before it went bust . . . but the cool bit where they sold singles and sweets.

I wanted to be ASOS. Or maybe Whistles.

I was definitely more than the incomprehensible, out of fashion, German cleaning product Phoebe had described. She might never see that but never mind.

It seemed like I was continually reading profiles of women who were following their dreams, starting up their own businesses, managing children and successful careers and looking incredible. For some time there'd been a question around whether women could have it all. I realized I DIDN'T actually want it all. I wanted MORE that was all. More than I currently had, less circling round and round an ever, decreasing circle that was made up of home, work and buying Oliver Bonas candles.

Kath called to check in on me.

'How are you doing now you're at home all the time?'

'It's weird. I'm in limbo. I can't say I'm really enjoying it.'

'What are you going to do about work?'

'No idea.'

'This teaching assistant job is bloody hard. I can barely stand up at the end of the day.'

'Do you think it's the thing you really want to do with your life?'

'Christ no,' she exclaimed. *'But I get school holidays off and it brings a bit of cash in and it's better than getting lost in a world of bake sales.'*

Kath wasn't trying to have it all. Sometimes you just needed to prioritise. She had three kids and needed to see them and be there when they got home from school. What were my priorities? For too long they'd been the office and the people that inhabited that office. I'd been living a lie but the thing was I wasn't one of those women who suddenly upped to Bali and become a yoga instructor. I couldn't run off and *find myself*. As much as I loved the iconic book, *Eat, Pray, Love* by Elizabeth Gilbert, I knew it was impossible to roam around Italy eating pasta, and hanging out with Yogis if you had small children in tow. They still needed snacks and sun lotion and got whingey after too long in the sun. I couldn't do a massive walk along the Californian mountain ranges like Cheryl Strayed in *Wild*. I was scared of heights and didn't like TOO much time on my own.

If I left Mango-Lab then there'd be a massive change in lifestyle – no candles, bobble hats, expensive face cream, £8 a pop mashed avocado on toast, nice clothes, shoes, holidays, spontaneous trips to the cinema, and meals out. This is what Phoebe and Darren's lives revolved around. Their kids going to private schools, holidaying in exclusive places, membership of expensive gyms (in Darren's case spending upwards of six grand on one bicycle). Growing up I'd had none of these things. Dad had never made loads of money. Mum always had the pressure cooker on and we ate whatever was in it (sometimes the same thing for a couple of days). We rarely went on holiday unless it was to my uncle's caravan in Norfolk. The thing was it was easy to romanticize these times but I still remembered wanting stuff that other kids had. I'd been to a party once when I was about eight, and the other kids took the piss out of me because I was wearing cheap, jelly bean sandals instead of patent leather Clarke's shoes.

Despite everything being in flux right now there were a few things to be happy about . . .

The baby
Being alive

Not having to see work colleagues each day
Bella noticed a change in me too.

'Mummy you aren't like a monster,' she said when I went to get her from nursery.

'I'm still pretty much a monster,' I said snarling at her.

'Your eyes look pretty.'

I scooped her up and breathed in the salty, sweet smell of her hair- a day spent running in the nursery garden, playing with her friends, and eating cake because one of the kids had turned three. Could I construct a new life for myself that consisted just of these things?

How had I become so lost?

Sixteen

TWO WEEKS LATER, AND I was back in the office. I was giving it one more shot. The longer I'd stayed away, the more I'd felt that I could fake this whole shebang. I didn't need to be emotionally involved with the work. I didn't need to love my colleagues. Perhaps I didn't need to push myself quite so hard to try and prove I was worthy and a woman like Phoebe. Perhaps I could get back into the slow lane and just steadily beaver away with a steady income but no real glory. I could get my blanket and headphones on like everyone else did and shut myself away. I listened to podcasts about positive thinking. I did a quick meditation in the morning which encouraged me to repeat *I CAN DO THIS* over and over.

'*I thought you were thinking about leaving for good?*' Pete asked me on my first morning back.

'I am. I'm still thinking but I need to finish this sanitary towel thing up and then if I DO go I go on a high.'

'Is that really what you want as your legacy?'

'No of course not but there's unfinished business. I'm not quite ready. Besides we need as much wonga as we can get through the door right now,' I said patting my tummy.

I'd been lucky in that this time around I had zero morning sickness and the pregnancy (now sixteen weeks) was making me feel energized. I knew there'd be a phase soon when that'd change but for now I was feeling better than usual. When you're carrying a child inside you know there will always be some kind of future ahead.

Phoebe had calmed down and even smiled when she saw me back. My outburst at the meeting had seemingly been forgotten. Perhaps also the finances were looking more optimistic this week- certainly there seemed to be more projects. Sven had come back to Simon and commissioned three more projects (it irked me that the projects had come to him instead of me but then he'd had all the client chat and I'd ended up being more subservient). We'd written the presentation together and it was the day of the debrief. Sven had arrived with three colleagues. The dough-faced one and two men that were pretty faceless but took copious amounts of notes whenever Sven opened his mouth.

'So how is the lovely baby?' Sven asked when he walked in.

'All good thanks,' I replied. *'A few months to go.'*

'And how is world of menstruation? We are learning great things right?'

'Yes it's magical. I really think we've captured some insights.'

'Good – and Simon has done so well with writing up this presentation,' Sven said.

'Well he didn't do it entirely on his own but yes you're right. Simon you've been impressive.'

Simon smiled. The baseball cap had gone again. He was wearing a terrible pair of pink chinos and a yellow shirt. He was dressed like a man twice his age. His personality was slowly being dismantled and he was turning into a classic dork (but not in the trendy definition of the word).

We drank coffee, ate a couple of biscuits and then the presentation began in earnest. We talked about women and how stressful life was these days, how they were putting so much pressure on themselves to succeed, how periods were often a positive time in some ways as they forced women to *slow down*, acknowledging that they had a physical body, and weren't just eyes glaring into screens and fingers tapping into phones (all these slides were the ones I'd written). Then we came to the more strategic part of the debrief.

'*The format that has the most potential in these times of radical VUCA . . .*' I said confidently. '*Is the one that makes women feel safe. Like a cocoon of luxury.*'

I never used the term VUCA but Simon had insisted that it was very NOW and we needed to be more culturally relevant. VUCA stood for Volatility, Uncertainty, Complexity and Ambiguity. It was actually quite apt for where my life sat right now.

'*Yes it's all about retreating from the world and making a sanctuary,*' Simon said.

'*And this sanctuary concept idea does it link to a new product?*' Sven asked.

I took a sip of water. I hadn't looked through ALL the slides. I'd trusted Simon to take the lead (because he'd taken most of the glory so far, and that was the deal).

'*The positioning idea means you could link it to either a pad or a tampon – it gives you lots of flex for the future,*' Simon said.

'*But a tampon is not about retreat? It's about activity, facing the world, optimism,*' one of Sven's minions said.

She had a point. The idea sounded okay for a nice, comfy towel but didn't quite work with the imagery around tampons which were traditionally all about being out and about and jumping out of airplanes wearing white hot pants. Simon clicked backwards to a graph where we'd mapped our new positioning.

'This is all about a future where tampons are both comforting and active,' he said.

'Can they be both?' Sven asked, his face creased with concern.

I could feel the vibe in the room wasn't brilliant. My years of experience had taught me that debriefs quickly went downhill if you didn't sound entirely convincing. Simon's demeanour had changed and he seemed much younger, more boyish than he had when first entering the room.

'Maybe Rebecca can offer up her perspective on this,' he said meanly, trying to throw me under the bus.

'Oh no, you wrote all these summary slides, Simon, you're much better at talking them through.'

He mouthed the words – HELP ME – but I ignored him. He wanted the glory, so he got the glory (and the not-so-glory when things went batshit).

Sven sat forward in his plastic seat, he looked like a lanky vulture about to tear Simon apart. 'I thought we agreed that we want concrete recommendations on product. Not just some wishy washy.'

'Too vague?' Simon said pointing at a chart that was made up of lots of complex circles but was pretty much impenetrable. In the old days I would have gone through the deck with a nit comb, checking to see it all made sense. This time I'd given Simon much more responsi-

bility. He was more senior right? I was just the moderator right? I wasn't strategic enough!

'Rebecca these insights about women are very interesting,'
Sven said looking at me. *'I feel like we are getting somewhere, a territory that isn't clichéd, is more nuanced and
interesting BUT Simon these recommendations don't seem
to link to these insights at all.'*

'It feels like two different debriefs,' the minion said.
'The first bit said one thing and then this bit doesn't fit in.'

She was right. Whatever anyone said about me, whatever critique they hurled in my direction, I understood
people. Spending hours in badly-lit rooms across the
country and all hours of the day and night with different
configurations of people- men, women, parents, single-
tons, drinkers, health-nuts, depressed, optimists, old,
young . . . had made me extra-perceptive, more empa-
thetic and very tuned into people . . . probably more
than the average person. Simon was looking exposed
– he had lots of posh graphics but when you interro-
gated it all, the arguments didn't stand up. He also had
zero understanding of regular people. Mango-Lab
thought that they could succeed hiring these mega-
brains, these young whizzes who knew loads of words
but couldn't make the connection with how they applied
to real lives. You needed empathy or you were basically
Phoebe. Or Darren. And a bunch of people wrapped

in blankets because the company was too tight to switch the heating on.

'*But that's the beauty of this new territory,*' Simon repeated sadly. '*It fits for both products.*'

'*I don't think you even have an idea of what we're talking about,*' Sven said. '*I am not making a million Euro decision on the basis of your recommendations.*'

'*And that chart talks about pet food,*' the minion said pointing up at the slide.

'*No I don't think it does.*'

But it did. Simon had copied and pasted it from one of Darren's pet food presentations. The headline read '*Great opportunities in the dry cat food space.*'

It was a disaster. Sven was one of those clients that lived and breathed his brand. He thought about sanitary products when he was in bed. Whilst showering. When he made love to his wife. He required careful handling. He wanted to feel that others were equally as passionate about his product. Instead Simon had come across as ignorant and glib. Including a pet food slide in there just yammered the point home- Simon didn't really care about Sven's business. This was what happened when you tried to do too much. You dropped the ball. It was also what happened when you refused to acknowledge that your colleague had more experience than you did. He'd only sent the presentation over that morning so I'd had ten minutes to scroll through it before we kicked off. He'd been that confident in the content. He thought he didn't need me. Phoebe and Darren had convinced him of that too. I was interested to find out what would happen to those three additional projects Sven had commissioned. I was glad they weren't my responsibility now.

'*The product feels like a welcome retreat because it provides emotional need for women to escape,*' Simon said but he'd lost his nerve and Sven could tell.

I knew he wanted to go and grab Darren and bring him in but Darren would only make things worse. His over-friendly, fake demeanour wasn't right for this client. The thing is I was rather enjoying watching the whole thing flop. Nobody had thought to give me any responsibility. I'd been undermined at every turn. This wasn't my failure it was theirs. I was buggered if I was going to try and sort it all out. Sven sighed.

'*Simon, tell them again about VUCA. VUCA is an interesting concept. Don't you think?*' I said brightly, trying to lighten the atmosphere at least. There were only so many times you could use the term *VUCA* and get away with it. VUCA THIS AND VUCA THAT. We'd got lost on the way. Simon had disappeared up his own bottom.

'*This debrief is not acceptable,*' Sven said standing up towering above us like he was about to deliver a sermon. '*You guys go and re-write because I need something better than this. I have to say I'm disappointed. Rebecca, I sense that maybe you have worked hard on this but then been let down in some way?'*

Was I hearing him right?

'I have to take responsibility too,' I said. *'I can't blame it on baby brain. We're a team you know.'*

Sven tried to smile but I could tell he was too angry. A wasted journey. Wasted money. Losing face in front of colleagues.

I closed my eyes and tried to breathe.

They left and we stayed in the room. Simon had a red rash around his neck and looked like he was about to have a breakdown. I'd never seen him so uncomfortable (well there had been a company meeting once when he'd mispronounced the word 'hyperbole,' and Darren had publicly berated him but that had been yonks ago). Nobody had ever criticized him before and he was used to being showered with praise. I was the one that he'd thought would get it in the neck. His brain was ticking away and I could see he was trying to think of some way he could blame me but it was hard. He'd written most of the presentation himself and he'd shut me away. He'd wanted to be top dog and now he wasn't so sure.

'I'm working on a crisps project tomorrow with Darren, and so I think you'll have to sort this out Rebecca,' he said.

'I don't think so,' I replied. 'I've got anti-ageing eye cream groups this week (this was a lie). Besides, this is YOUR client, you wanted to head it up, you're more senior than me. How did that pet food slide get in there anyway?'

'I don't know. Why does it matter? It doesn't make a massive difference does it?'

'It makes us look stupid like we don't know what we're doing. I don't think you even bothered to read my context slides did you?'

'Of course but they were just loads of women's stuff. I know all that already. It's the recommendations that are more important for the client. The slides I WROTE.'

He was showing his true colours. He was worse than Darren because he was even more manipulative. Darren didn't take you out to a club and pretend to be your best mate.

'Well you've made a mess of this,' I said. 'So you're going to have to spend time sorting it out.'

'I've got plans for the weekend,' Simon said. 'I'm going to a music festival in Victoria Park.'

'Sven didn't spot it,' I said 'But one of your charts described the winning concept as – 'nutty and nutritious."

'I took that one out of a roasted peanut innovation work-shop.'

I looked at him in disbelief.

'Who cares?' he said his voice rising. 'Besides- who are YOU to judge?'

He was morphing into Darren in front of my eyes. Next his teeth would be fluorescent white, then he'd start stomping about in his tight, cycling shorts, swinging his tiny penis from side to side, then he'd be wearing one of those loathsome fitness monitors and boring on about his sleep patterns and how he'd biked twenty six miles in one morning. There was nothing I could do to save him. If he stuck around here then he'd end up a clone like all the others. Employees mirrored their bosses in order to succeed (which explained why I'd never quite fitted in). I had taken plenty of short cuts in my time, and perhaps everyone was right and I lacked strategic skills at times but I was always THOROUGH (and I never nicked slides from other presentations as I knew you could come a cropper when you were tired and didn't spot the anomalies).

'*Isn't it obvious?*' Simon continued, the rash now migrated so his entire face was bright red. '*Everyone here in the office thinks you're a joke.*'

I saw visions of Darren giving Simon a pep talk. Taking him to the pub and stuffing him silly with Korean buns. Buying him giant bottles of Kombucha or whatever the fermented shit was called. *Hey Simon you're awesome dude. Hey have a glass of this Kombucha. Hey that Rebecca is a loser.*

I took a deep breath. I had come back thinking I'd make a go of things but was already thinking it had

been a bad idea. I thought about how Bella was probably eating lunch now and I had no idea what that was
but in five minutes a message would ping up on my
phone and tell me and I'd have to be content with that.
And what about this baby? What kind of lesson was
I teaching them if all I was doing was staying in a
career that made me small, on the back foot and ultimately a laughing stock?

'*Your time will come,*' I said. '*You'll be hot for a few
months but if you continue making mistakes like these, you'll
unravel, they'll hire some other bigwig and you'll have to
moderate late at night in Slough, just like me.*'

'*But the difference is I'll move onto something else. I
won't just sit around like some sort of museum exhibit.*'

I shivered, stood up and left. Simon could sort his
own presentation out. I wouldn't be surprised if Sven
cancelled the others. He was too arrogant now to even
see the fact that I could help him dig himself out of
this hole.

He was one of *them*.

He was also right. I was a laughing stock.

A message from nursery when I got back to my desk.

*Bella tried some ravioli today with spinach. This
morning she collected twigs in the nursery garden
to make an autumnal scene.*

It sounded like she'd had a much more productive and positive morning than I had. I thought of her squeezing my head, the feeling of her breath, how I always tucked her hair behind her ear before she went into nursery. I thought about how she was changing so rapidly that I was having trouble keeping up. I thought about my tombstone and the engraving it would have on the front.

R.I.P. Rebecca Jones
She created an exciting new strategy for
sanitary towels and moderated more than
six thousand groups.
The market research world mourns her loss.

They always said that a good exercise when you lacked direction was to fast forward to your own funeral and then imagine what people would be saying about you.

What would people say about me?

That I was nice?

That I was a great moderator?

That I was a good mum?

I texted Bryony.

I think it's time to move on from this hell hole.

That time passed a LONG TIME AGO, she texted back. Plan your exit strategy.

She sent a GIF from *The Fresh Prince of Bel Air*. Will Smith was doing a celebratory, enthusiastic moonwalk. I had a moment of uplift, I looked around. No one acknowledged me, no one looked up from their screen. The cold air blasted in and the tinny speakers in the corner were playing Johnny Cash (was this a secret message from Darren, a message telling me I was wrong and he DID know all his songs after all?). No one would mourn me at Mango-Lab. I had no friends. It was every person for themselves. The Aesop was now Tesco. There were only budget biscuits in the kitchen cupboard and the pressure to churn out more and more work was growing by the day.

As I left that evening, I spotted Phoebe talking to Simon in her office. Simon's face still looked flush. He was gesticulating and Phoebe was looking at him with some sympathy.

I should have gone in there to explain my part in the Project Ziggy saga but I didn't care enough.

On the train home a email from Phoebe.

PROJECT ZIGGY: EMERGENCY SITUATION: ACTION REQUIRED

I ignored the message and looked out the window. It could wait. None of this was my fault. After dinner, after Bella was sound asleep, and Pete was peacefully scrolling his iPad, I went upstairs and fired up my laptop. There were fourteen emails now. I needed to try my best to put things right – even if it was just for my own sanity.

The long and the short of it was Phoebe was disappointed and alarmed at how the debrief had gone (no surprise). Sven was disappointed and alarmed (but still flagged up that he'd liked the insights at the start which were ALL my handiwork). Simon was strangely silent. Had he washed his hands of it all? Later the house was quiet as everyone slept and I sat in the front room, a pillow on my lap, my bump just starting to feel a tad uncomfortable if I sat down too long.

'*You won't have to put up with this shit,*' I whispered to the baby. '*I'll make sure you NEVER work in market research.*'

I felt a little spin inside. A flutter. The baby agreed. Was this the first time I'd sensed movement? And if so why wasn't I shaking Pete awake to tell him? Instead, I looked through the deck. I removed all references to nuts and pet food. I re-read my own slides (they made sense but there was no link to what came later). I went back through the notes that Simon had made weeks ago, right after the groups. My brain felt muddled.

Simon had had most of the key conversations with the client behind the mirror and none of those were captured anywhere. I didn't have a clear vision of what he'd promised Sven. This was an error on my part. I should have squeezed myself into those conversations. I'd had too much faith in Simon's ability to handle it all. Sven wanted more innovative product ideas but we hadn't heard anything interesting in the groups. Women didn't like towels or tampons much but they were used to using them and reluctant to try risky, new things. This wasn't ridiculous – it was more the fact that they didn't want to get blood all over their pants as they travelled to work. Tried and tested formats (with slight upgrades) were the way forward.

I went back to the screen and typed the words 'DISPOSABLE PANTS' and drew some arrows around them. I typed '*PAD THAT UNPACKS ITSELF FROM PACKET AND ATTACHES ITSELF TO PANTS*' and then deleted that too. '*A PAD THAT MAKES AN OLD WOMAN FEEL RELEVANT? A PAD THAT IS ANTI-AGEING AND GIVES CAREER ADVICE.*'

I typed one more idea at the bottom of the page . . .'A PAD THAT CURES A MID-LIFE CRISIS.'

I worked all Thursday night. I wasn't sure if I was going crazy or if the presentation was actually the work of a complete genius. I sent it to Sven, copying in Simon and Phoebe. I rang in sick the next morning.

I'd done all I could and couldn't face seeing any of them today. The next day Bella was booked on a farm trip with nursery so I dropped her off, said goodbye to Pete as he went to work and went out into the garden. It was overgrown with bushes and weeds and there was a stack next to the backdoor of old toys, a broken buggy (we'd need to either sort it out or get a new one) and three plastic paddling pools leftover from the summer that all had punctures. I knelt on a cushion, a cup of tea by my side and pulled up weeds. A PAD THAT GIVES A FEELING OF BEING OUTSIDE. That would be a good idea. I'd forgotten how good it felt not to be sitting inside, not to have grey carpet underfoot, not to only have lunch to look forward to. I worked steadily all morning, the flutterings in my tummy growing more intense as lunch approached. This had been the same with Bella – the baby was indicating that it needed carbs. I made myself a peanut butter sandwich (nuts were controversial for pregnant women but it was what I craved in this moment). I'd tidied half the garden and stacked the old paddling pools next to the recycling. The prep for the baby had begun. Next I'd talk to Pete about the buggy and whether we could fix it. I spent the next hour making a list of all the stuff we needed to do. It felt good. I had no idea what my next move would be but I knew there was practical stuff we needed to get on with for now.

Mum rang and we had a good half an hour catch up. Dad was making an effort to be more interested in her activities and was coming out of the shed at regular intervals. Again I saw the parallels with Pete and how he more often than not preferred his own company. At least after talking to her I felt less guilty. It was bad when people became 'things to do this week', but that was how it felt right now. There was work, there was family, there was the baby, there was also all the stuff that related to me like pelvic floor exercises and getting sleep and healthy nutrition (it seemed this time all that was kicked to the side and I was eating carbs, skipping sleep and my pelvic floor muscles were impossible to identify unless I was in the midst of a wee).

When Bella got back we sat watching TV and I jiggled her up and down on my knee.

'There was a pig and we gave it food,' she sang. 'But Mrs Green said I couldn't play outside because I didn't have any wellies.'

'You had wellies. They were in your bag.'

'She said they had to be black wellies, not ones with Elsa on.'

'What's wrong with Elsa for goodness sake?'

The nursery manager was another example of a woman who'd got it in for me. Perhaps she was related to Phoebe and they compared notes on how to bring me down?

'It was an ugly pig with bad teeth.'

I put on my most enthusiastic voice. Sometimes being a parent forced you to act as if everything was okay – this was a positive as it meant you didn't have much time to wallow. Kids noticed wallowing and it made them feel insecure. The more 'with it' you acted, the more you started to feel that way.

'Then the pig pooed on Mrs Green's foot.'

I laughed. Ha ha, there you go you witch woman, I thought. I looked Bella up and down. She was getting gangly. Her body morphing from toddler to girl. She would start school next year. The time was flying. It was a cliché but true.

'Shall we make some pancakes?' I said.

She jumped off and clapped her hands. I was rubbish at making them but we rarely ate them anyway. We just made interesting shapes and put them in the bin. It was lazy but better than watching YouTube all day.

Pete came in after we'd finished. He'd been upstairs trying to look at buggies online to see if we could find one second hand.

'Even a second hand one is about a hundred quid,' he said.

'Well let's leave it for now. Work is looking decidedly dodgy right now.'

I explained what had happened with Project Ziggy, how Simon had fucked much of it up, how I was taking the blame probably and had worked all night trying to sort it out.

'You let those creeps walk all over you,' he said. *'It drives me mental!'*

Bella went into the front room and I followed her in and switched the TV on so we could talk.

'I'm just trying to salvage a terrible situation. I don't want the client to be disappointed.'

'But they don't care about you. They let you take the fall. Has anyone checked in to see if you're okay? What do you actually owe them?'

He was right.

'Just tell them all to FUCK OFF.'

This was often Pete's business strategy. It worked if you were a bossy, authoritative *male* CEO but it would never work for me.

'That's not the right idea,' I said. *'I have to be cleverer than that.'*

'What and drive yourself mad in the process?'

'I'm not mad,' I said.

He was getting on my nerves now. It felt like even more critique which was the last thing I needed.

'I thought you were just going through some mid-life crisis bollocks– what with the Botox and the stupid nights out. All this weird out of character behaviour.'

I'd wanted him to look at me with fresh eyes. To realise that I was still the girl he'd met all those years ago. Yes I was older but I still liked to dance (even if I was shit at it) and I needed excitement and spontaneity. Those acting out nights had been all about trying to access that person again, to feel more alive, not like I was on a steady, downward decline. Instead he'd dismissed it as mid-life issues. Pete didn't really see me in the same way as I didn't really see him either. This was the challenge of long-term relationships. You took one another for granted. We were excellent co-parents (maybe not excellent but fairly good) but we never really noticed one another anymore. I didn't know how to express this without it coming across as more criticism. We would then continue to argue. He would say that I was too demanding, and never happy (he had a point) and I'd say that he was a zombie that rarely expressed his feelings (unfair but partly true).

'Just leave Mango for God-sake,' he said. *'You can't blame everything on me,'* he said.

He disappeared upstairs. I had no idea what was going on in Pete's mind anymore. We were very different. He was quiet and loved his own company. I was someone who needed to have people around me or I felt like I was going mad. Did I know anything aside from the fact that he worked in catering, and liked watching TV? What else did I know?

He was great with Bella

He loved old war documentaries on the History channel

He was addicted to buying navy hood tops

What client was he working with right now? How did he feel about the fact that we only had sex once every three months, maybe less? Did he feel tired and drained like me? Did he love me? Did he worry about where our lives were headed? Did he worry about ageing?

We didn't talk about this stuff. Perhaps we had in the beginning, in the getting to know you stage. Now it was just about recycling days, unloading the dishwasher, washing to be done, what we'd eat for dinner, what was on the TV that night.

Was THIS true for everyone else?

It wasn't that I expected we'd talk about literature and sex and society every night but there was an absence of anything meaningful. I was sure that he felt this too. I'd seen it in his eyes now and then. He was bored but towing the line. Treading water. Waiting for things to improve by themselves (which things never did, you had to take action, even if it just meant not watching TV for one night of the week).

It was too much to think about now anyway. My job was on the line. I needed to sort this terrible debrief and see if I could save the day. There was a baby on the way. I made a mental note to have a conversation with Pete about all this stuff in two years' time (once the sleep deprivation had passed and we were both feeling human again).

I went back to my laptop. I went back to it like millions of other hapless workers. I went back to see what news it would bring me on a Friday night, whether this news would be good or bad.

I typed up a message to Phoebe and copied Simon in.

Hey Phoebe,
I'm amending the charts for Project Ziggy and things are looking more positive. I'll send the new version to Sven and the team as soon as I can.

Simon- let me know if you want to input and we can brainstorm over the weekend?

Rebecca ☺

I knew Simon wouldn't respond. He was probably trying to save his own scalp (his hair was already receding like Darren's).

'*What kind of sanitary towel would you like to see in the future?*' I asked myself.

Thoughts of Pete flooded my brain.

I'd been too focused on the qualities Pete *didn't* have. I'd looked around and thought everyone else had a chatty partner, a partner who listened with enormous empathy and never moved their eyes from your face. A partner who read aloud from self-help books at bedtime, who massaged your feet, who made love each time as if you were the ONLY person who mattered. Everywhere you looked there was sex but it was novelty sex, one-night stand sex, topsy-turvy stand on your head sex. What about someone who made you a cup of tea? What about recording your favourite show because you hadn't had time? What about emptying the dishwasher? What about holding hands in bed?

That was love too.

I sat upstairs on the laptop with Pete downstairs watching TV. He came up, got undressed and climbed into bed without saying anything. Within five minutes he was asleep (this was the thing, he could sleep whatever was going on around him. It amazed me that he had this capability).

I woke at four and came downstairs and warmed up some milk, and made myself some toast. The pregnancy insomnia was kicking off in earnest now. The cruel fact that I'd not sleep again right until the baby was born and would then rarely sleep again. Eventually I got back into bed, turned my phone on so I could shine it onto my book shelf, and maybe find some words that calmed my frazzled brain. All these books were written by people who had this life sussed out . . . *Feel the Feelings And Walk On Through, Emotional Resilience: How to Become a Stronger Person Each Day, How to Not Care What Others Think About You.*

'*Live in the moment, live in the moment,*' I whispered to myself.

'*Can you turn your bloody phone off?*' Pete hissed. '*It's shining in my eyes.*'

'*Do you hate me?*' I said but he couldn't hear me because he had his ear plugs in.

Are you happy?

Do you find me attractive?

Am I repugnant?

Do you remember how you looked at me the first night we met?

The night we didn't stop snogging?

Do you ever miss that time?

The next morning we continued shuffling around. Everything sounded very loud. The cup being put down on the table. The spoon against the cereal bowl. The dishes being stacked. The kettle. I checked my phone but there were no emails from Phoebe. Bella was getting more excited about the baby now but had unrealistic expectations in terms of what it would be capable of. She thought the baby was going to be a girl. She wanted to call her Matilda after the Roald Dahl story (we'd watched the film version with Danny De Vito about fifteen times). *Matilda would like playing Playdoh, and*

*would also love Sylvanian Families. She would also enjoy
pretending to be hairdressers. She would watch CBeebies.*

'I'm going to push it in my dolly buggy.'

'I'll take it to the park so you can have a rest, Mummy.'

'It can sleep in my bed at night and I'll give it a bottle.'

'Mummy you are really fat like a pig.'

'That's not a very nice thing to say,' I said.

I was actually far less fat than I'd been with Bella.
With Bella I'd been ultra-cautious and had taken taxis
and buses everywhere. Now life was pretty much the
same but I just felt more tired and was starting to
waddle a tad.

'Like the pig at the farm you are. Mrs Green is round.
And Mrs Pearl. They are round people.'

'They're not having babies. That's what happens when
you're having a baby.'

'They're just greedy.'

'People are different shapes and that's okay.'

'Some people are pigs.'

She snorted loudly as I set her back down on the
pavement.

Pete went for a walk. It was Sunday. I'd finished as
much as I could on the presentation and would send
it later.

I sat with her in the garden for a little bit – there
was just a tiny bit of spring sunshine poking through
the clouds. I closed my eyes and tried to absorb the

rays. I couldn't even remember the last time I'd sat and done nothing. Each moment was filled and there never seemed to be time to just stare. I needed to take what was happening in. This pregnancy was going to be okay. I could feel it. I would be a mum to two kids. I couldn't stop what was happening.

I sent the presentation Sunday night. It didn't pay to send things on a weekend afternoon or you risked answering emails all day.

Seventeen

'*T*HIS IS THE FINAL *STRAW*'

Phoebe was screeching down the phone. Apparently, Sven had called her first thing this morning. He was extremely unhappy. I was only sad that he hadn't called to talk to me first. Perhaps then I'd have had the opportunity to talk him round.

'A pad THAT STICKS TO YOUR PANTS? A pad THAT CURES MIDDLE AGE? What the hell? This isn't funny Rebecca. I have tried to talk sense into you SO MANY TIMES but it seems it's pointless.'

'But Sven said he liked the insights I wrote at the start.'

'Yes I'm sure he did but this is just the ramblings of a looney.'

'I did the best I could without Simon's input. Did you

know that he'd just copied and pasted old slides in there? Or then took himself off to a festival all weekend.'

'You're the one heading up this project, not him. The buck effectively stops with you.'

I was walking to the train and had just dropped Bella. There had been more crying, more wailing and I wasn't sure why I was dragging my pregnant, sad body into town yet another time.

'It's funny how he's more senior than me now but I'm the one that's in the wrong.'

'You're older.'

'Yes but he had all the client contact. He sat behind the mirror. He wrote the recommendations.'

'It's still your responsibility Rebecca. How many times have I told you to be more strategic? The problem is I've now realized that you'll never change. You're a great moderator. No scratch that, you're a great moderator, people like you but it's not enough.'

I wondered why Simon was so strangely out of the equation now. Had they told Sven that I was responsible for all that had gone wrong? That was the most likely option. If they did that they could keep those other projects potentially and I'd take all the blame. I was the mad, old, pregnant lady. The ditzy, daft, poop head. And the strange thing was, I felt calm. I had done what I could. Okay maybe those ideas I'd written over the weekend were a bit bonkers but hadn't they said they'd wanted – BLUE SKY THINKING? And if you really asked the average woman what she wanted- like what she really wanted then these were the things that needed to be addressed- ageing, tiredness, feeling drained- if a sanitary towel could promise those things that what a wonderful towel it would be!

'There is NOTHING in the client's portfolio that fits with this pie in the sky jbber-jabber. It's mortifying.'

I put my hand over my mouth to try and stop myself from making a noise.

'Well all I can say is I tried,' I managed to say. *'I thought the client wanted innovation. Personally I liked the idea of the mid-life crisis pad.'*

'I just feel sorry for Simon,' Phoebe said just before she hung up. *'He was supposed to be learning from you but instead he's left traumatized.'*

'You mean he was supposed to spy on me and report back,' I said.

'Goodbye Rebecca.'

And that was that.

I saw there was another update from nursery. I increasingly felt like they were timed to coincide with moments of extreme stress. This one was about old tins of food and how we needed to bring them in for the Harvest festival. I made a mental note but knew I'd forget – there was only so much one woman could take in.

Later HR got in touch. I'd got two previous warnings on file. I would get three months paid leave. I would have one day in the office to sort out all my years of stuff. Nobody was bothered with doing a hand over because I was irrelevant anyway.

I was surprised that there was no word from Simon. I thought perhaps he'd at least drop me an email to say something. It was just proof of how little he cared (and how ruthless he'd become).

I texted Bryony.

It's all over.

A slight delay and then . . .

WOW! You'll have to fill me in. How do you feel?

Funny.

Funny ha ha or funny sad?

Both.

I would wait till I told Pete and Mum wasn't a good person to talk to now either. She'd immediately flag up the potential challenges (and there were many- MONEY being the main one) and I needed a little time to just take it in. Kath would be more level-headed – she just wanted to see me happy.

I wanted to get Bella and take her home again but then wanted some headspace so walked around the local park. There were loads of mums pushing buggies. Soon I'd join this brigade of saggy-eyed troopers. I felt excited but also rather weary. I would be the oldest mum amongst them. I'd have to get more Botox or I'd be mistaken for the baby's Grandma. I wanted Mum. I wanted a cuddle. I wanted to be a child again and just lie under a duvet with a hot water bottle and some nursery rhymes playing softly in the background.

Nevertheless, I had a sense that whatever came next would be better.

Had I sabotaged my own career with those final few slides? Yes I had. It was just a shame that I'd never really get a sense of revenge. I was the one who looked like the failure and Mango-Lab could simply continue as they were.

A couple of days later and I was getting used to no longer commuting into the office. I didn't miss anything. I didn't miss the cold. Or the tinny headphones. I didn't miss Phoebe, Darren or Simon.

I met up with Bryony in the local café. It seemed that mums were now breeding with other mums because it was impossible to get through the door because there were ten buggies lined up back to back. The whole place smelt like dirty nappies, and strong caffeine. There was a high volume of urgent chat- the chat that had to come out when you were knackered and only had one hour of adult time to vent before you went back into your baby cave. Women were talking over one another. Others were wiping their eyes from laughter (laughter and tears sit very close together in those early days). I would be part of this crowd in a few months. But what else would I be doing? Was it even possible to carve out a career and raise a baby? I looked at Bryony. She hugged me and we sat down. She was doing it. She was forging a new direction. I doubted she was making much dosh but surely it was worth trying? I hadn't seen baby Ralph in a few weeks and he seemed enormous all of a sudden.

'Are you coming out the other side?' I said.

'Do you know what?' she said picking him up and jigging him on her knee. 'Yes I think we are. I finally feel a bit more normal now.' He had crystal clear green eyes. I loved that baby phase. Not the wrinkled up one. This one where they started to look like little people and you began to have a relationship that wasn't just based on feeds and fear.

'How will we survive financially?' I said.

'You'll shop in Lidl and do meal plans and cancel the Botox appointments. You can't have that shit in your face when you're pregnant anyway.'

'When you get to my age you'll do it too,' I said. *'It's only young women who throw their hands up in disgust. You look amazing even without any sleep.'*

She shrugged.

'It's horses for courses. I don't feel the need to conform to other peoples' expectations. It's like your job. You've finally realized that you were living someone else's' life.'

'That's true.'

'And you don't have to do it anymore.'

'I still don't have a clear idea of what I'll do instead.'

'Go with your gut.'

'Not that GUT STUFF again. Listen I'm older than you. I don't even know what my gut feels. I'm a mum. I like watching TV. I would love to be creative and have big ideas but I'm not like that.'

'We'll see. I don't see you like that.'

'How do you see me?'

She kissed the top of Ralph's head.

'I see you as brave and inspirational.'

'GET OUT OF HERE.'

Bryony laughed.

'You are!'

'You've been reading too much Oprah magazine.'

'Start believing it Rebecca. It's never too late.'

And I started to feel like Bryony was right. Sure life wasn't an episode of Oprah where everyone vented their feelings, unearthed their true calling, and then had a giant makeover but if you didn't believe that change was good then what was life about? I'd stood still for too long, I'd let people undermine me and make me feel worthless. I'd settled. Yes there'd be plenty of woes to come but they'd be woes hopefully brought about by my own choices and a radical change in direction.

'What do your parents think about all of this anyway?'

They'd been extremely scared when I'd told them (or Mum had anyway, Dad had been more encouraging). For them you stuck at the same job your entire life unless something truly drastic happened (like you got sucked into a concrete mixer and ended up in a wheel-chair).

'Don't you feel lucky?' I said looking at Bryony. 'Your generation have it so much easier than mine.'

Bryony snorted.

'Are we really going to go there again? Don't you read the news?'

'I know the stuff about jobs and property and all that jazz. I just mean that you expect more from life, that you move on before too much time has passed.'

'Yes well there is that but massive expectations bring their own problems right?'

I'd spent so much time feeling resentful of younger people but it was true – expecting too much was exhausting. Simon would crumble eventually. He might end up wasting less time than me but he'd net out at the same place eventually (or he'd get used to the money and would be unable to move on and then trapped which where Phoebe and Darren were right now).

Eighteen

MY LAST DAY IN the office arrived. I had to pinch myself. I had hardly anything in my locker but a couple of files with old notes. An old project about treats for dogs. A positioning for a new hand cream targeting seventy-year old skin. And then two packs of the prototype for the baby-soothing, 'Goodnight Bum,' baby wipe. I would try them out and see if they worked but felt just as cynical as all the other mums had been.

Still I had an idea of how your last day at work *should* be. How you should look your best (I didn't – I was huge and had developed rosacea on my cheeks so looked like I was blushing). How you should have an impressive new job you could talk about. How you should laugh a lot and make it look like you were moving onto better things. I tried to hang onto Bryony's positivity.

Start believing Rebecca.

In fact even Pete had been positive when we'd talked about our new future – *we will do what we have to* – he'd said. The thing he'd always encouraged me to do had finally happened and he couldn't do a U-turn now.

'*If we're lucky Simon might salvage our relationship with Sven,*' Phoebe said as we sat in our 'sign off,' meeting.

There was a woman from HR sitting in with us. I didn't know her name. They'd sacked the last one the week before. Again there seemed to be more redundancies. I knew Mango-Lab needed the work from Sven. They needed those projects. Where was Simon anyway? Had they killed him and buried him in the car park? Phoebe had wild hair, and dark circles under her eyes. I saw her stripped of her status and authority. She was just another tired woman trying her best. I almost felt sorry for her (almost not quite, she was still a terrible bitch).

I'd schlepped and grovelled with the best of them. I'd set my alarm at four thirty and got on a flight, sitting next to a business man who smelt of whiskey and BO. I'd dashed around a foreign city looking for a certain brand of packet soup because we needed it for groups that evening or the whole project would crash to the ground. I'd written many, many debriefs. Whilst other people were writing their novels or painting masterpieces, I'd been hunched over a computer, grimly tapping away. It wasn't that I hadn't tried. It was just that my heart had never been in it and this wasn't the kind of job that you could fake – or you could fake it, I'd done this for many years but then you could only get so far before someone realised. I'd talked with authority about every product under the sun but a sanitary towel had pushed me over the edge. I would never be CEO. Or have a power-bob and be on the cover of *Time*. I'd never holiday in the Maldives. Or have a nanny that did all my childcare. We would be lucky if we holidayed again. Despite all this, I felt lighter than I had in many, many years.

A text from nursery:

Bella ate pitta bread stuffed with cod fritters. She played in the sandpit and then told everyone her mummy is having a baby.

'*We're getting shot of this place,*' I whispered.
The baby kicked.
'*No more air-con and dreary meetings.*'
It kicked again.
'*Soon.*' I said.
I looked at my emails.
One was labelled:

CANCELLING ALL FUTURE PROJECTS. WE HAVE

Motherwhelmed

A NEW AGENCY.
Dear Simon, Rebecca and team,

We have taken the decision to remove all our business and future projects from Mango-Lab. Project Ziggy has been a disaster (but there were actually some great insights in there – I think Rebecca was responsible for these). I got the impression the past few weeks that the team weren't collaborating as they should.

Why did Rebecca send the deck and not Simon? You said he was heading up the strategic thinking? And why weren't the two working together to produce the final edit?

Phoebe – I know we spoke already but it is a base line requirement from our agencies that the teams work well together. We rely on them to get the quality we need. I got the impression that you were blaming one person throughout this process. That did not feel fair or reflect the groups.

We're prepared to pay some of the fee for this final project but will require you to figure out a discount. The other projects we will take to 'Dance-Monkey Insights,' – they have a different way of working and suspect we will have more success.

Sven

I sat at my desk re-reading the email several times. I saw Simon come out of the lift, walk through the corridor and head straight to Phoebe's office. I saw Darren follow close behind. Simon was alive and they hadn't killed him off. The email made me feel conflicted – on the one hand I was happy that Sven could see they'd framed me for all that had gone wrong on the project, but on the other hand I felt sad that I'd been unable to fix everything. The San-Pro account was worth a lot of money. Each project probably over 300K (as they'd been global and not UK like Project Ziggy). The fact that Sven was taking this project to 'Dance Monkey' would drive Phoebe wild. It had been founded by an ex-Mango-Lab employee. A lovely girl called Rachel who had seemed quite normal but had left five years ago (probably when I should have gone if not long before).

None of this was my problem.

I saw a future life where I stayed, tried to win more all this work back again, tried to fix it all, staggering home hunched over my phone, grey hair, nails chewed to the quick, a screen permanently projected onto my eyes. I'd hold up one board after another and repeat the words . . . *you like? You like? You like?* Then they'd push me off in a wheelchair, and I'd have to go to a retirement village to live out the rest of my days. There was a home for retired market researchers. It was a sad place. Relatives came to view you through a one-way mirror. You ate stale sandwiches for lunch. You kept saying the same things.

You like?

You like?

You like?

I WAS *LEANING IN*. I was sacking off Sandberg and crew.

It seemed like a positive sign that the song that came into my headphones in that moment was LL Cool J and 'Mama Said Knock You Out'. He was giving me some backbone – the resilience to leave this place without making a fool of myself. To stay strong.

'Phoebe wants to see you,' Simon said standing above me, his face pale.

'Long time no see,' I said.

'They've just fired me.'

'Can they do that?'

'They said it was gross malpractice or something. I had a couple of warnings in the past. I'm going to talk to a lawyer but I don't love this place. I've been thinking for some time that I needed set up my own agency. I mean how hard can it be?'

'You think you could manage that?'

I thought about the cut and paste slides and the fact that he was so quickly angered when clients demanding more stuff. He would have a very steep learning curve ahead.

'Why on EARTH not?' he said.

'Yes why not I suppose.'

Simon had treated me badly but he'd got his come-uppance. Hopefully he'd use this experience to learn more empathy. Perhaps he'd realise that you could learn from other people instead of stab them in the back. He went back to his desk, packed up his stuff and went without waving goodbye. I thought about our nights out drinking, the dancing, the way he'd won my trust. I hoped the agency he started wasn't a success. Then I realized I had other fish to fry. I wrote my emails. The fantasy ones that had sat in my head for too long. I wasn't prepared to go in and see Phoebe and have a list of my weaknesses read out yet again.

Darren never worried about whether people liked him. If he did then he'd have a nervous breakdown because everyone hated him. It was irrelevant. He ploughed right through people like a combine harvester- he chopped their heads off and ate them for breakfast. Phoebe was a frightening hybrid of Alan Sugar with a dash of the Wicked Witch of the West. She was what happened when you left your feelings at the door, when you drowned out your thoughts with strategy. YES, I ADMIRED HER but in the same way I admired a lion eating a live buffalo.

'*I hope you learn how to be more human,*' I said just before Simon walked away.

'*What?*'

'*Be a human okay?*'

He seemed to have heard but I wasn't sure.

The beats grew more intense, and I felt my stomach somersault with each word. This was better than just slumping off into the shadows. This was better than a lame drink in the pub and a half-hearted congratulations that you'd reached twenty-five years. It was better than an Amazon voucher and a card signed by people you didn't know.

Dear Sven,

I'm sorry to hear about the business. I understand though and hope you feel I did the best I could. I have never been particularly good at 'blue sky thinking' and think I'm probably in the wrong industry. Good luck with the new projects. I think there might be something in the idea of a 'mid-life' towel though.

As a woman in her forties, it's certainly a life stage that I find tricky to navigate.

Thanks,
Rebecca

Dear Darren,
No man over the age of forty should use the word
DUDE.

Your penis is very small so my advice would be to
change into trousers before you come to work in
the mornings.

Cheers!
Rebecca

I took a sip of water. LL ringing in my ears. Like a call to victory.

Dear Phoebe,

I won't come into your office because I've spent
too much time being told I'm not good enough.

For a long time I believed this was true.

Just for reference here's a short list of my skills
– I don't think you've ever seen much positive in
terms of my character.

- *I know all the words to 'Mama Said Knock You*
  Out'.

- I can swim underwater for a length (or could about ten years ago but haven't tried for a while)

- I understand people and I always make an effort to understand where they're coming from

- I think women should have at least a few months off after they've given birth – it's not a competition to see who comes back to the office first

- I don't feel ashamed that I've never been a CEO

- I don't like power-bob hair or Sheryl Sandberg. In fact, I think Sheryl is old hat and there's surely a new style of aspirational female leader in town?

- I don't want to be remembered for writing a great debrief either

Rebecca

I waited a couple of minutes. I wondered whether to leave my laptop on the desk but the problem was I needed to take loads of stuff off it first. In an ideal world, I would have hurled it across the room screaming, but instead I popped it into its case, and put it in my rucksack. It was silent. Phoebe was probably reading her email and thinking what a waste of space I was. Whatever. There were just a couple of people wearing blankets, tapping away. I wanted to shake them out of their stupor but perhaps they were happy.

I'd tapped away just the same for years.

Then Phoebe strode towards me with her hair swooshing from side to side. She looked like she was going slap me in my chops.

'I will personally blame you if Mango-Lab goes down,' she said quietly leaning over my desk so I could smell 'Boss Woman' or whatever scent it was that had the perfect mix of sweet with a sour, aggressive after-tang. *'This has all been your doing.'*

Darren came out of his office. I noticed he wasn't wearing his cycling shorts.

I looked round the office. *Goodbye watercooler. Goodbye poster telling me to put stuff in the recycling bin. Goodbye offices with old people inside possibly asleep. Goodbye reception with artful objects. Goodbye photo of Phoebe receiving an award on behalf of the company at the 'International Paper Products Awareness conference.' Goodbye bean bags that nobody sat on because you ended up too close to the carpet that smelt like death. Goodbye windows that never opened. Goodbye.*

I could only hear a few key words as there was a slight buzzing in my ears . . . *hygiene, new territories, pads versus tampons, new insights on women, disappointed, thought you were bigger than this, massive account, financial data, serious rewards, team player, childish, let-down, not strategic enough, long term poor decision making*. I looked down at the face I'd drawn on the sheet of paper. It was a smiley face. I realized all this time I'd been trying to find the little girl that loved drawing. I'd been trying to find happiness. That little girl was sitting inside this pregnant forty-two year old.

And she was laughing like a drain.

The thing is once you'd removed the competition, the horror, the fact that life was getting worse, the ageing, the daily fear and anxiety that something bad was going to happen, the desire and daily pressure to achieve, be more, have more, be better, have a kitchen extension, a loft with an en-suite, longer legs, thicker hair, smoother skin, no noticeable signs of ageing, babies, more babies, career, a career you could actually brag to other people about, seniority, flexibility, more time with your family, less time and more time for yourself, friendship, a sexually exciting relationship with your other half, a big income, feeling relevant and in the cut and thrust and not on the downward trajectory . . . well, when you removed all of that and just allowed yourself to be nothing . . . well, that was rather liberating. I felt like my head was finally back on my shoulders again.

'*Shall I walk you out?*' Darren said.

Phoebe was struck dumb, not moving – someone had taken her batteries out. Perhaps it was Sven's bad news. Or it was not knowing how to punish a person who didn't care.

'*No thanks,*' I said getting my bag.

There was a very faint twitch in her left eye.

'*I CAN ACTUALLY do MORE than a length,*' she said as I walked past, Darren holding my arm.

'*I didn't appreciate what you said about my penis,*' Darren said in my ear. '*You know how cold it gets in the office so I think it was just a massive misrepresentation.*'

'*Not a massive one.*'

'*Now you're being childish,*' he said sullenly.

'*I COULD HAVE HEADED UP THAT SAN PRO ACCOUNT,*' I said as the doors closed. '*I could have fixed it all.*'

The doors shut. For better or for worse my career at Mango-Lab was over. So was Simon's. I suspected there were troubles on the horizon. I didn't care anymore. I'd said my piece. I'd expressed myself.

I was light as a bird.

Nineteen

WALBERSWICK WAS BEAUTIFUL, a long, gorgeous pebble beach, faded wooden beach huts and a couple of cosy (and pricey) pubs. It was also full of posh people driving around in Land Rovers. Everything was expensive. We couldn't really afford a break but we all needed one. Pete had been working extra shifts and his new client was even more demanding than the last one. He often left for work before Bella and I were up in the morning and came home looking pale and drained. So we'd booked a week away last minute. We were staying in a cottage behind the village green. It was like an episode of *Inspector Morse*, like stepping back in time. People on bicycles, crab-baiting, cream teas. I didn't care if we never went abroad again— this suited me perfectly. I'd forgotten how it felt to be outside for long periods of time. It was a cliché but sitting in an office all day made you go mad after a while. You got things out of proportion. You developed a routine where all you did was sit over your laptop and then get up every couple of hours to visit the toilet or fetch a cup of tea.

One morning I sat in one of the cafés. Pete had taken Bella down to see if there was any crab-baiting happening, it wasn't the right time of year quite but people usually hung about and gave it a go anyway. There were a bunch of wealthy mums at another table (wearing Joules/ Barbour/Boden) and they were complaining about how hard their lives were. They had missed Pilates two weeks in a row. Having their own jewellery business and bringing up two kids was a challenge. How the local clinic was now charging over four hundred pounds for Botox – that kind of thing. There were times when I wished I was a 'kept woman' and then I realized that it was better to have a level of independence. Mum had brought me up this way – *'If anything ever goes wrong, you can look after yourself,'* she used to tell me. For the foreseeable future Pete would have to support the family but then I'd quickly need to get back into the cut and thrust of things. I could not afford to do Pilates and have a 'hobby- business' (one that didn't generate much income but gave you something to brag to other mums about). I stroked my belly.

'*Bet you're glad we're not in the office anymore,*' I whispered.

It did a karate kick and then went back to sleep. It was definitely more active than Bella had ever been. It had a particular pattern. If I had a drink hot or cold then it leapt about like a salmon. If I lay on my side in the evenings it went mad and it felt like it was trying to get out through my belly button. I felt guilty that I wasn't lavishing much attention on this pregnancy. It was six months now and I sometimes forgot the baby was there.

'*I'm sorry. I'll try and make a bit more effort,*' I said patting it again. '*But first I must try and come up with a plan.*'

I'd got a brand-new notebook which had 'MAKE THIS DAY COUNT' scrawled on the front. It signalled a new direction, a fresh start, a load of exciting possibilities. On the first page, I'd outlined a few different scenarios.

What next?

Barista – too old but nice as don't have to think too much or be strategic

Open my own café – looks perfect on social media but could be very boring and can't cook. Also, customers would get on my nerves as always asking for stuff

Start my own research agency – NO I hate doing this and would have to do even more of it and would be moderating in my seventies

Yoga teacher – can barely touch toes and still feel intimidated by the whole concept

An app that makes millions? What though?

Be a stay at home mum – not an option as need CASH and would go insane eventually like Catherine Deneuve in Repulsion

I scratched these out. I felt like I was sixteen again and trying to weigh up different options. This was the problem – I'd never had a clear idea of what I wanted to become. I'd set off and been chiefly motivated by money (and the idea of being able to sit down as my previous jobs in retail had involved being on my feet). The next generation were different in that they had more direction, more verve, more flexibility – if something didn't work, they tried something else. Or maybe this was just my romantic vision of young people.

The other option was moving to the countryside and making cheese like a retired rock star. If you couldn't keep up in London that this was what you did (or if you simply wanted more space). Could I hang out with a bunch of Land Rover mums like these? (but Pete and I could never afford to live in Walberswick). I'd looked in property magazines and it was clear that countryside living was not cheap. It seemed that you needed an aga – this was compulsory. And a Barbour jacket. Ideally a few muddy dogs (one needed to be a whippet in a tweed waistcoat). You also needed to be hardy and not too sentimental. I'd once stood in a field with Dad, and watched a farmer throw piglets into the back of a truck. They flew fifteen feet in the air and squealed like mad. Dad told me they were collecting them so the farmer could count them but he was lying. I didn't like wearing those puffa gilet things like they did on *Countryfile*. I wasn't keen on posh people, because I'd been to a crap secondary school. I didn't know any kids called *Tarquin or Figgy or Wigbert*. I didn't 'summer' in the South of France or own a second home. My granny (long dead now) had loved pound shops and cheap toothbrushes (despite having dentures she'd once bought fifteen in one go because they were 5p each).

I didn't use Waitrose washing up liquid. What were the advantages of country living?

Fresh air. The great outdoors. Hens. Pigs. Pubs. Flat caps and baskets of wild flowers. Long petticoats. Running through fields with long hair and violins playing in the background. Homemade bread . . . Rain. Damp. Gossip.

Isolation. Being trapped inside for long periods of time staring at pigs and hens outside and feeling guilty. No option to ever return to London as priced out forever. More isolation. Growing old with one bar on the electric heater, and nothing but a packet of tomatoes and half a bottle of salad cream for tea. The post office closes and you rely on a grumpy lady to come in once a week to massage your feet. When you die no one comes to your funeral as they all live in London and can't be arsed.

Before we'd come away Bryony had come over for lunch. I'd felt nervous about what to cook because I kind of wanted to impress her. In the end I chose a vegetarian recipe and spent about forty quid on ingredients. I also spent a long time cleaning the house. I wanted her to be impressed at how tidy it was but the cat was sick down the back of the sofa just before she walked in the door. I quickly mopped it up with a sponge and she didn't seem to notice.

'This is bloody delicious,' she said as we sat eating my fancy concoction.

Ralph was asleep on the sofa next to Bella who was sticking Troll stickers into a book (and one or two were finding their way onto Ralph). I loved seeing them together- soon this would be our family unit. I hoped Bella would acclimatize quickly.

'How's the photography going?' I asked. 'I saw you've got loads of new followers on Instagram.'

'It's gone a bit bonkers. One of those influencer mums tagged me, and then invited me to take some photos. The next thing I knew I had fifty mums emailing me wanting to book sessions. I think there's a bit of a backlash against all this perfect stuff. They want something real that shows family life as it is.'

I thought about the photo she'd taken in the café of Bella and I. She'd managed to capture a moment that was realistic but also tender. She had a knack for being able to spot these moments (because nobody wants a visual of their kid screaming with a bubble of snot out of their nose – that's too much REALITY thanks).

'And so what are you planning on next?' she asked spooning another forkful of pasta into her mouth.

I'd bought truffle oil which was something we never ate but I thought she'd appreciate. It was about seven quid. I left it out on the side so she could spray more of it about if she fancied it.

'The more I think about it, the less clear it is. I don't want to do anymore focus groups. And I don't want the boss from The Devil Wears Prada.'

'Oh I love her! God we must do a film afternoon one day and watch it again.'

I thought about Phoebe. The longer I spent away from her, the more empathy I felt. She was passionate about marketing. It'd frustrated her that I was so laissez faire, that I didn't worry incessantly about getting things right (or hadn't towards the end). I wished I'd said something more meaningful on that last day.

She was a woman, a mum, a business leader. She deserved admiration? Then a film reel kicked off in my brain with all the different occasions she'd been mean to me. The time she'd scrawled notes all over my presentation (back in the day before you just presented it from your laptop) or the time she said it was uncouth for a woman to drink pints (that had been back in the days of the ladettes when it was all many women drank). Or the time I'd tried to speak up in a board meeting and she'd just talked right over me. I'd always got the impression that there wasn't enough room at the top table for someone like me. That I had to conform to her way of being or give up.

I will personally blame you if Mango-Lab goes down.
She had been a cartoon villain.

'*Well it's exciting. Now at least you can start on a new journey. And please don't tell me – it's too late again!*'

'*It's going to be a challenge with a new baby,*' I said.

'*Listen I'm cynical about all that affirmation stuff, much like the next woman but you have to change the stories you tell yourself. So you screwed up and stayed in a horrible job too long. You're shot of it now. You still have a chance. Try and stay positive.*'

'*How do you do it?*' I said standing up and scraping my plate over the bin.

'I survive on four hours sleep a night and I often need four coffees each day to keep me going.'

'Yes but you have such clarity. I sometimes think you're older than me. I feel naïve!'

'I hope you're not fishing for compliments again,' Bryony said going into the front room to check on the children. *'I don't mind being your cheerleader now and then but I think you secretly know just how great you are.'*

She came back carrying Ralph whose tiny face was now covered in stickers.

'Bella can you come and apologise?' I said. *'And have a bit of pasta?'*

She came out looking sheepish.

'I was just decorating him. And he'd been good because he didn't do a poo in his nappy.'

It came back to those moments again. I was happy to have someone like Bryony who represented opportunities and new directions. I'd been in the café over an hour and the posh mums had gone. A sparrow landed on the chair next to the table.

In a few weeks I would be mum to a newborn.

In the afternoon we went to the beach and Pete returned with a picnic from the local café.

'What's in this sandwich?' I said holding it up.

'Prawns.'

'Am I allowed prawns?'

He tried to look it up on his phone but there was no reception.

'I think it's okay.'

'The waves are enormous Daddy. Can we swim?' Bella asked waving her arms about excitedly.

'It's a bit cold for swimming darling,' I said.

'I WANT TO SWIM!'

'I'll take her in for a bit. You finish your lunch.'

Pete shoved his sandwich into his mouth and together they ran down to the sea. Bella pulled on his arm the whole time. She wanted to go deeper. She didn't want to paddle. She wanted to go right in up to her waist. I watched them. Everything about this moment was perfect but still my brain tried to latch onto something bad. I still had that feeling that I needed to go back into the office, that I'd forgotten an email, that the stimulus for the groups had got lost somewhere.

Slowly with each passing day, it became easier to forget The Future Strategy for Sanitary Protection in the UK. To forget Phoebe, Darren, Simon and all those other chumps. They'd find out soon that it wasn't strategy that made your heart sing. I spent the days sitting on a blanket, watching Bella and Pete playing in the waves, as Pete tried to roll up his jeans another two inches, then the waves soaking him up to the knee, then Bella flicking water into his face, then him lifting her up so she dangled over a wave and he threatened to throw her in head first, her laughing and shouting with joy.

This thing here. This was okay. It was more than okay.

Perhaps I could devote myself to parenting, and not lose my marbles. Parenting was most definitely a job – especially if you strived for perfection. There were millions of things you could feel guilty about. Small things – like giving your kid a sweet, or making chicken nuggets for the third night in a row. Medium things – like being irritable and shouting, when they're testing your patience. Then big things, and the big things were the ones you tried not to think about. I'd once smacked Bella and had cried for days afterwards – it was something I tried not to think about as it had only ever happened once (and was certainly not something I ever mentioned to other mums). I thought I'd damaged her in a fundamental way, that she'd be scarred for life. I knew that motherhood was often about losing control and trying to manage those feelings so you didn't strike out. It was tough and would only be tougher with two. Then the other big thing was the fact that motherhood could be quite boring. Bryony had realized that early on. It had taken

Kath longer. Mum had just accepted it as most of her generation had.

Yes there were mums who rose at 5.30 to make spelt pancakes, ironed sheets and pants (there were women who did this REALLY!), and drove around in a whirlwind of children's activities – gymnastics, ballet, swimming, macramé for tots, French lessons and karate. The kind who enjoyed mess, doing craft, and didn't spot a Tiny Tears staring gormlessly up from the kitchen floor, and get the urge to toss it out the window, or pop it in the microwave until it's face melted. And then in the evening, in her cashmere PJs, kids squeaky clean and happy, she'd serve slow cooked organic stew through teeth clamped together so tight, her dentist would have to remove her molars because they'd cracked. *I have totally got this* she would whisper but she'd still be drawing those imaginary penises. In her *mind*.

Bella had clean hair and clothes – she seemed happy. I could rustle up a decent meal.

There were many things I hated about being a modern woman – shaving legs and armpits, keeping a sort of respectable bikini line, trying to stay youthful but not being seen to resort to extreme measures like Botox and then not being too fat or thin, and the need to have a career you felt fulfilled and passionate about, and then the drive to be a perfect parent.

Motherwhelmed

The thing I hated most was the relentlessness of it all.

It was a miracle that women didn't just lie down and refuse to get up ever again.

Twenty

T HE LAMB WAS WRAPPED lovingly in foil with anchovy, lemon, and garlic smeared all over the shop. Pete was sitting in the front room on his iPad scrolling through jeans on eBay.

'*Why do you need another pair of jeans?*' I asked popping my head into the front room.

'*I just like looking at them. It's soothing. Look I don't tell you off for spending hours on ASOS?*' Pete said then paused. '*Sorry let's not argue.*'

Today I was checking my phone a lot (in the absence of work emails things felt weirdly quiet – I even felt some pangs of withdrawal). I realized the potatoes had disintegrated into porridge.

'*Can you mash the spuds up?*' I shouted from the kitchen.

Pete came over and looked in the pan.

'Is it really so hard to cook things properly?'

'Maybe if you weren't on your iPad you'd have helped?'

'Of course it's not like I cook ALL THE TIME IS IT?'

Bella wandered into the kitchen.

'I have bad legs,' she said. *'They hurt from too much jumping.'*

'Are you jumping on the sofa yet again?' I said.

'No but I took my socks off and they smell like bum holes.' She shrugged.

'Can we not say that please? It's pretty revolting.'

'Bum holes. Bum holes,' she chanted.

Sitting down at the table, I cut the lamb – it was delicious. I rarely cooked anything edible but this time it was a success. It was pink inside and perfect. Pete sat down and helped Bella onto a chair. We ate in silence apart from the odd interruption from Bella. *This meat is SO chewy. I don't like peas. Peas are rabbit poos. Rabbit poos come out of a bum. Can we have a rabbit? Can our rabbit wear a nappy? Does a rabbit have a bum hole?* We took it in turns to field these questions.

'There's a new BBC drama thing with that woman out of Downton Abbey,*'* Pete said helping himself to seconds.

'Brilliant – sounds good,.' I said.

'I want to watch it too,' Bella shouted.

'It's too late for you. Can you eat some veg as well?' I said pointing.

I stroked my tummy. The kicks were more obvious now. The baby was especially active whenever I ate food, as if it was encouraging me to eat more. I was getting the breathless feeling as it expanded and pressed against my lungs. Pete reached over and put his hand on my tummy.

'Has it been moving a lot?'

I nodded. He patted my tummy softly again. He was making an effort. I reminded myself that I wasn't perfect in any shape or form. I'd spent the past few months focused purely on work, Bella and own mid-life crisis.

Pete had become an afterthought. I needed to give our relationship more attention.

Later when Bella was in bed I went upstairs and sat on the edge of the bath. I looked in the mirror and raised my eyebrows. The Botox was wearing off it seemed but at least I looked more cheery than I felt. I thought about Pete and felt a pang of guilt. It was true that he'd been bottom of the priorities for far too long. I imagined going it alone and raising our family without him. The sleepless nights, the walks in the park that went on until your legs felt like they were falling off, and the conversations where you pretended to be okay but secretly wanted to cry your eyes out. I knew I couldn't do it without Pete.

I also knew I loved him and wouldn't be happy with anyone else. It wasn't just convenience or having another person about the place (but on a practical level that was a big deal when you had kids). He made me feel safe. His quietness could even be a blessing when everyone else on the planet was desperate to vent. The next few months would be difficult. When Bella had been born, I'd been a dreadful harridan. Then things had got better. I'd stopped seeing Pete as the source of all my tiredness (this was the cruel thing about having a newborn- you never blamed the baby and so your partner usually hoovered up much of your resentment). After a while, when we were sleeping more, we'd started to see the traits in one another that we loved. We would recover like we had countless times before.

And would I ever discover the one thing I was meant to do? Did anyone? I had a horrible premonition of my future – mooning about, worrying about money, and getting anxious because a mum had blanked me in the playground. I needed something to occupy my brain. Perhaps I was better off writing charts on pet-food strategy. I knelt by the bath and put my face up against the mat. It smelt of mildew. There were simply too many things to think about. After a couple of minutes, Pete came in. He pulled me to my feet and shuffled me to bed, pulling the duvet up so it was around my neck.

'Try and get some rest,' he said. *'Do you want me to make you a hot water bottle?'*

'*I don't know what's going to happen next,*' I whispered fearfully.

'*Stop overthinking. It's going to be okay.*'

He planted a kiss on my forehead and stroked my shoulder.

'*We are always okay aren't we?*' I said.

'*We're more than okay.*'

Pete was right. I could even visualize us back in Walberswick in a couple of years time. The kids would be paddling. We'd be staring at them both, knackered but happy.

That night I dreamt of Phoebe. We'd never had the showdown I'd hoped for. Some kind of epic hip-hop battle where we finally decided who was the winner. There'd been no sense of closure. In the dream we were two boxers in a ring. There was a baying crowd (made up of Mango-Lab employees), and the stadium was full of smoke and the stench of stale lager. Darren, the referee, kept jumping from side to side in his cycling gear, flashing his white teeth (it actually wasn't that dissimilar this dream to a team-building day we'd had in St Albans several years ago). I stepped into the ring to face Phoebe. I clenched my fists.

'*You're pathetic,*' Phoebe spat under her breath as she circled around, the relentless marathon and HIIT training had paid off. '*You and your year-long maternity leave. And the part-time hours. I bet you never downloaded the productivity app did you? What time are you in bed? Nine?'*

'You're not human,' I said. *'How come you never cry in the toilets like everyone else?'*

'ROUND ONE,' Darren shouted. *'TIME TO GO DUDES!'*

I grabbed Phoebe's hair, and pulled her to the ground. I got my foot and pressed it into the side of her face. I felt strong and resilient. It was liberating to see her subservient for once. Perhaps she was human? I'd never seen an ounce of vulnerability in her before.

'It's impossible to hurt me! I'm indestructible,' she screamed twisting her head round and looking up at me.

'I don't need market research in my life,' I shouted back at her. *'Do you hear me? I'm never moderating another group as long as a live!'*

'What are you going to do then? Knit baby hats? Make cupcakes? Sell Aloe Vera cream at the local market?' she said pushing herself up and against my chest.

I felt temporarily winded and fell back against the ropes. Her hair was sticking up on one side and mascara was running, chased by tears of fury.

'At least I'm trying to find happiness,' I said. *'I'm not going to rot in an office all my life.'*

Phoebe's face came close enough that I could smell her breath; mint Tic Tacs masking strong expresso. Her skin was perfect but there were a couple of stray fair hairs poking out of her chin.

'I'm happy in the office!' she said pulling off her glove and stabbing a finger into my chest. *'I love market research! I love strategy. It's my life!'*

I managed to push her off and got down onto the floor and collapsed. I'd forgotten I was pregnant. At least there'd been no blows to the abdomen. Phoebe ran her fingers through her hair and took a deep breath.

'The daft thing is I actually respect you,' she said after a while. *'I never thought I'd say it but we're not that different from one another.'*

'We're plenty different,' I said looking up at her. *'I can't think of one way that we're similar.'*

'You're stubborn and pig-headed and . . . I can be a bit like that too.'

'I draw penises in the margins of my notebook when we're sat in meetings.'

'Well that's a silly thing to do.'

'And I just want to find happiness and feel proud of myself. Is that so wrong?'

'We have different definitions of happiness,' she said getting up. *'Mine is work and I'm not sure what yours is.'*

'How's it going DUDES?' Darren said skipping about like a jack-rabbit.

'Oh shut up will you?' Phoebe said.

He sauntered off, his shoulders hunched over.

'Don't you realise how BAD you make people feel Phoebe? Not everyone can be such a high achiever. You set the bar much too high.'

'Well I'm sorry if I made you feel bad,' she said walking away. 'There I said it.'

She turned back again to where I was still slumped against the ropes.

'And sorry that I criticized you but I thought it would . . .' she hesitated for a moment, '. . . Make you stronger. You see I just don't believe in all this positive reinforcement crap. Us Gen X women are hardier than that right?'

'But you NEVER ONCE said anything nice.'

She screwed up her face, thinking hard.

'I must have said one thing.'

'I was actually quite a confident person when I joined Mango-Lab but I lost that as time went on.'

'You were never really meant to work in market research,' she said. 'I tried to tell you but you never got the hint.'

It was true. I had to take responsibility for the fact that I'd stuck around far too long.

'And now that I think about it,' Phoebe said, 'The charts you wrote for Project Ziggy were good. I just said they were rubbish because I was angry.'

We both stared at one another for a moment.

'Do you want to fight more to get this closure thing? It's just a dream so you can basically do what you want.'

'No I shouldn't . . . I mean I'm six months pregnant.'

'Righto, well I need to do a debrief call with Brazil. With Sven cancelling all his future innovation projects, it's all hands to the pump.'

She climbed over the rope and strode back to the dressing room. The back of her gown had the word CHAMPION emblazoned across the back. The crowd were subdued and no one was cheering. It had been a complex fight and it wasn't entirely clear who had won.

So, I got the apology in my dream at least.

Twenty-one

THE PARK WAS DESERTED aside from the occasional jogger, and a young guy on a bench drinking an energy drink. I pushed the buggy into the wind and closed my itchy eyes. It was seven in the morning but I'd been up for two hours. I'd had two coffees and a chocolate croissant. I was already planning what I'd eat for lunch. It was uncanny how you could forget the newborn phase so easily. It was exhausting.

Our baby boy was called Alex.

For now I had to fight the mood swings and the desire to cry. One minute I was okay and the next sobbing. I worried that maybe it was the menopause announcing its arrival but no it was more likely those pregnancy hormones being replaced with a weird sense of emptiness.

'*Just keep your head down and barrel through it,*' Kath said on her first visit.

'*You're doing brilliantly,*' Bryony had said later the same day.

'*Can you believe you're a mum of two now?*' Mum said that weekend after I came out of hospital. '*I always wanted two but didn't manage in the end.*'

'*He looks a bit like me don't you think?*' Dad said. He looked ten years younger because he'd finally got his hair cut. '*I'd like to introduce him to my Italian class one day.*'

'*He smells of bum-hole,*' Bella said the day after he was born.

'*He's perfect,*' Pete kept saying over and over.

People often dwell on the negative when it comes to newborns but the truth was there was nothing better for keeping you *in the moment*. You had no choice. It was all about them and their needs. I tried to stay off social media because I knew it would just pile on more pressure. I watched TV in the middle of the night. I switched my phone off. I looked at Alex and rejoiced in how perfect he really was (I'd had a superstition that something would be wrong, that I was too old to have a healthy baby, that leaving work had been the first step in a chain of bad events). And what about the sanitary towels? I noticed that Sven's company had launched a new product. On the side it had a mighty promise – 'The Superwoman Towel for Tired Women Everywhere.' I liked to think that had been some of my influence. It was moving the whole thing into a more emotional territory.

I had no idea what was going on at Mango-Lab. Simon had started an agency and I'd seen the website. He'd called himself a 'Master Semiotician and Cultural Theorist.' The company name was 'Hula-Hoop.' He was wearing the silly baseball cap again. I hoped he was remembering to stay human.

Pete and I stopped watching hours of TV just for the sake of it. We went to bed at eight thirty or nine because we were both so tired. His work was taking off and he was juggling three big accounts now. It felt lucky that we had this sudden boost in finances. We made an effort with one another. We tried not to bicker. If we could get through the next year we'd be fine.

I noticed things in the world were shifting. Women were complaining about how impossible it was to combine children with careers. There was a younger generation of feminists who didn't find the old guard aspirational. They questioned whether materialism was worthwhile. It seemed there was an army of women drawing penises in the margin of their notebooks, trying to muster up the courage to speak, then crying in the toilets. These women appeared on daytime talk shows, they were writing books. They criticized bosses like Phoebe for not being more supportive. It was encouraging to see that the tide was turning – even if sometimes the messages felt trite – a bit like the tampon adverts where women leapt about being empowered and powerful all over the shop.

There were so many women out there, struggling to make things happen, struggling to build a life that felt rewarding and *right*. Women missing their kids, trying to juggle diaries, dropping the ball, those who boasted about their children's achievements, and those who's vaginas were broken by birth, beautiful women who peered into the mirror and cried at the wrinkles around their eyes, women who *had to exercise every day*, women who danced in the kitchen to classic, hip-hop tracks, women who fantasised about expressing their fury but just ended up flinging washing into the machine instead. Women who stared into their phones and slid through others' lives and judged themselves as failing. Then there were the women who died young without discovering who they really were, and also the women who grew to a ripe, old age and got up at five am to buy salad cream from the Co-op, and the women who stocked up on Christmas cards in January because they were *so much cheaper*, and those who watched reality TV to forget their lives for a bit, and the women who were at the very top of their companies and were incredibly strategic, and those who cried in the office

In this moment I was happy. In this one not so much. Oh, here was a sliver coming back again.

The sense that there were endless possibilities was good and bad – we could no longer sit in a long cardie, with a Yorkie dog, and eat shortbread. The onus was on staying relevant and youthful –

energetic and equipped with a plan. In this context, the mid-life crisis didn't exist. There wasn't a clear definition of what constituted old age until you got to eighty (then finally you had to fess up perhaps). These changes brought opportunities but they also brought vast amounts of tiredness.

Bryony and her endless optimism. Her ability to turn anything negative into something good with potential. Dad and the way he'd turned everything around when it was oftentimes easier to just give up. Mum and her insatiable desire to learn new stuff and to be social and meet new people. Bella saying she loved me *more than all fish in the sea*. The way she wrapped her arms around me at the end of the day and squeezed. Alex, his tiny hands balled into fists, in a constant state of readying himself. Pete's hand as it crept under the duvet to clasp mine.

Rebecca is learning how to live in the moment. Today she had a walk and saw a green parrot in the trees.

There was so much beauty once you learnt how to see it.

Acknowledgements . . .

This book has been a real labour or love and written in snatched moments. There are however key people who have helped. First off my agent Louise Buckley for believing in the book. Also Kate Bradley, my editor, who has been super-encouraging. I'd also like to thank all the women who've shared their work/motherhood/life stories. I'm sad that so many women struggle when it comes to the world of work and hope we can initiate change by sharing our stories. I'd like to thank all the people who didn't believe in me and have provided me with the determination to get it done.

Finally I'd like to thank Paul, Rae and Greta.

Read on for a Q & A
with Anniki . . .

Tell us about yourself.

I'm a 46 year-old mum of two. I used to work for a big corporate market research agency but now write and work part-time. I started writing as an escape from the job and it then turned into a real passion. I also co-founded a podcast called 'The Hotbed' and have a book called *More Orgasms Please* which is all about sex and relationships which came out in 2019. And like most women I'm frequently overwhelmed or 'motherwhelmed'!

What was the inspiration for Motherwhelmed?

I was inspired by my own experience of ageing, trying to be a good mum, stay relevant, be fashionable, stay on top of things; the relentless struggle to do everything and be everything to eveyone. I realised loads of other women have the same experience and feel that they're lacking, but in reality they're doing well and just need to lower their expectations and be kinder to themselves (and potentially tell annoying colleagues where to get off!)

It isn't just motherhood that is overwhelming Rebecca, but also her boss. Have you worked with women like that?

Oh yes, definitely. Rebecca is a combination of different women I've worked with. Unfortunately, some women lose their humanity a bit when they become more senior. They feel they must adopt a very narrow, rigid, masculine way of managing people and they lose their empathy skills and heart. I have also had to behave like this at times too, but I hated it - I felt like I was losing myself and my identity because I was trying to be a BUSINESS WOMAN. Things are changing now which is good.

How much of you is in Rebecca, the central character?

A lot! I worry a lot like she does. I get anxiety. I feel depressed. I basically feel like she's me but I'm probably a bit more robust than she is right now.

Q & A

Why do you think women still struggle so much with trying to juggle everything?

We set ourselves very high standards. We want to be great parents, we want to have interesting jobs, we want a relationship that is great, to have a good sex life, to have friends and a social life, to go on nice holidays, to be fashionable, to look okay and not like we've been dragged through a hedge backwards. It's only when you compromise some of this stuff that you can feel free. It's impossible to do it all unless you're very wealthy and have 24/7 childcare.

Have you always wanted to be a writer?

Yes - I love writing and my dream has been to earn a living from it.

Tell us about your podcast, how did that begin?

We started 'The Hotbed' because we wanted to share our experiences of being in long term relationships and how it impacts on sex. Small kids often mean that intimacy is no longer on the agenda. It's another pressure we put on ourselves. The podcast has had some great guests so far- Rose McGowan, Jess Phillips and many others. We talk about sex, body image, nostalgia, dating, relationships, kids - the whole caboodle.

Why do you think women still find it hard to be honest about how they feel?

I think we want to keep up an appearance. We don't want to appear weak or seem like we're not winning at life. Having said that the minute you show vulnerability is the minute others will share theirs too. Everyone is the same. We just want to be happy. We want to feel less stressed. We want to appreciate what we have but we're also in a constant pursuit of more. And tech doesn't always help either - we aren't always honest on social media. Even when we're being more honest, we might be showing off at the same time.

Have you found the secret to balance, and if so, can you share it?

There is no such thing! I know however that I use a meditation app when I feel anxious. I also seek out friends. And writing. I don't ever feel like I've got it all sussed though.

Q & A

What single thing would change your life for the better?

Money. My baby daughter sleeping. More sex. A live in Nanny. A swim each morning. Sorry that's five!

What are you writing next?

I'm writing a novel about a woman who is desperate to have a baby.